JACK TRACY
&
THE PRIORY OF CHAOS

2017 EDITION

Boyd Brent

Author Contact:
boyd.brent1@gmail.com

Dedicated to Jack Sharpe.

This one's for you Jack ...

Prologue

On a leafy suburban street on the outskirts of London, in a place known to all the world as Wimbledon, there lived a 12-year-old boy called Jack Tracy.

The years that had delivered Jack to the cusp of his teens could best be summed up in one word: uneventful. Their highlights, if you could even call them such, where as follows: Jack's realisation that he *finally* had teeth enough to tackle solid food without serious risk of choking. His ability to stand on two legs as opposed to crawling around his playpen like a tortoise. And last but by no means least, the feeling of extraordinary freedom that his first stabilised bike had given him as he pedalled furiously around his little garden in search of a gap in the fence. Why the need for a gap? Jack longed to escape to the world of adventure that he had reliably been informed was chronicled truthfully in the pages of his books. Unable to find a gap, and as the years rolled on, Jack had only managed to escape to the school run, where he'd been forced to rely upon his extraordinary imagination for the adventures he craved.

This explains why Jack spent much of his time, spare or otherwise, as his mother liked to put it, 'Away with the fairies'. An unfair comment as during his bouts of day dreaming, Jack had not encountered a single fairy. You see, whenever Jack got his glassy-eyed, far *far* away stare, he was engaged in derring-do. And the more derring the do the better. And, like most children, in his more reflective moments, Jack seriously doubted that he possessed the courage of his daydreams. He wished he did with all his heart because the one thing that Jack liked to imagine above all else was protecting the kind of heart against tyrants and bullies. And so it was, on a cold and windswept morning in February, soon after his twelfth birthday, that Jack Tracy was to discover if he truly possessed the courage of his daydreams …

ONE

Jack Tracy's neighbourhood, 7.30am

"I don't want to go to school, Mum! It's too dangerous."

"Oh, now you're just being ridiculous, Anthony."

Anthony peered through a gap in the drawn living room curtains. "I'm not! They've gone now ... I *think*, I can't see them but you *must* have seen them when you went outside just now."

Anthony's mother shook her head. "All I saw was old Mr Grimshaw cleaning his car."

"*What*? One of the gang was *standing* on his car when you went out there! You're not blind ... you must have seen him!"

"No Anthony, I didn't. Now stop this nonsense. Do you hear me? This is *Wimbledon*. And there are no gangs in Wimbledon. Okay? Good boy. I have to go to work and *you* have to go to school. It's called *getting on with life*. What have I always told you?"

"That mother always knows best," murmured Anthony uncertainly.

"That's right. That mother always knows best. Now fetch your school bag and *go* to school."

Many cars had driven past Anthony's assault on Barton Road. But while children in their back seats gasped and pointed – their parents looked at the same street corner, and saw only a little girl playing hopscotch. Some children going to school on foot hurried past Anthony's ordeal, while others did 180s and sought safer routes. There was one exception: a 12-year-old boy with a pale face and spiky auburn hair stood transfixed across the street – his mouth fallen open, his nut-brown eyes wide in bafflement. A police car turned into the street. *Yes,* thought Jack Tracy, t*he cavalry's here ...*

The police car pulled up. An officer climbed out of the driver's seat holding a letter. "Come on ... *do* something," muttered Jack. The policeman crossed the road to a letterbox, popped the letter inside, and strolled back to his car, whistling. As he climbed in and pulled the door closed, he noticed a boy staring at him.

"You'll catch flies in that mouth if you're not careful, son," said the officer.

Jack darted across the road and rapped on the car's window. The window whirred down. "Is there a problem, lad?"

"*What*? Are you joking? They're killing that guy!" said Jack, wincing at the sounds of Anthony's cries.

The policeman scratched the end of his nose and asked. "What guy?"

"That guy! There!" said Jack, pointing at the post box where the thugs now cheered every failed attempt to post Anthony's head. The policeman followed the tip of Jack's finger and saw only a little girl holding a letter – she smiled sweetly at him and posted it.

"I suppose you are aware that it's a criminal offence to wind up a police officer, son?" said the policeman, smiling at the girl.

Jack felt dizzy. "I can't believe this … maybe I'm dreaming?" Jack took a step back from the car and stumbled slightly. *If this kid* isn't *a glue sniffer then I'm a monkey's uncle,* thought the policeman.

The squad car's engine purred into life. "I suggest you wake up young man … or you'll be heading for a whole heap of trouble."

"Well, if you won't do anything about it … I'll have to try," murmured Jack. The policeman pointed to his own temple and made a circular motion with his finger. The window whirred up.

Jack's heart pounded as he squeezed a path through the jeering bodies. He emerged beside Anthony. Anthony gazed up from the pavement into Jack's sympathetic face. His bloody lips parted and he said, "P … please. I'm Anthony … help me."

Jack felt that age old hatred of injustice surge within him, and he clenched his fists and bellowed "**WHY!**" towards the heavens.

Unbeknown to Jack, his question had travelled as far as his extraordinary imagination – to a place beyond human perception; to where even light from the brightest stars failed to reach.

And it had been heard.

Back on Barton Road, silence descended like a hangman's noose. A thug scratched his chin, narrowed his eyes at Jack and said, "Before we kill you kid … why what?" Jack felt his anger slip away … replaced by a terror that wrapped itself around his gut … and squeezed. *I'm going to die now.*

The silence was shattered by a chirpy ring tone. A girl answered her phone. Her eyebrows furrowed, "Albion Street!" The gang scattered into the surrounding streets like rats.

Anthony gazed up at Jack like he was some kind of superhero. Jack looked over his own shoulder. "What? It wasn't me. They got a call."

TWO

Running the gauntlet

The following morning …

In the alley that ran down the side of his house, a boy climbed onto Jack's garden fence and tumbled into his backyard. The gang out front had left him little choice. The boy sat in the vegetable patch, thinking.

Mrs. Tracy heard a 'tap tap tap' on the back door. *Must be Henry.* "I wish he'd just use the front door like everyone else." Mrs. Tracy drew a deep breath and opened the door. Henry Roscoe gazed at her with an expression of wide-eyed innocence. "You're right to look concerned, Mrs. T. It's bad news, I'm afraid. It looks as though you've got a *serious* mole problem."

Mrs. Tracy's hand went to a cluster of moles on her neck. "… *What?*"

Henry spoke up as though talking to someone hard of hearing. "Serious – mole – problem."

"I'm not deaf."

"Oh, right." Henry craned his neck to see what Mrs. Tracy was covering with her hand. He said, "I recommend dousing the infected area with rat poison. Or you could just hire a farmer with a shotgun … they love blasting furry little moles. No need to *wince*, Mrs. T. It's quite painless."

The boy's gone mad.

"I mean … *anything* that could tear up your tomato patch like that," he went on, brushing some dirt from his backside, "should be shot as soon as possible."

"Oh. I *see.*"

Henry shook his head. "I'm just sorry I had to be the one to break the bad news."

Mrs. Tracy placed her hands on her hips. "Second time this week, isn't it?"

"I'm glad you appreciate my position, Mrs. T.," he said, squeezing past her. Mrs. Tracy returned to her kitchen and added 'tomatoes' to her shopping list.

"Still out there?" asked Henry, as he entered Jack's bedroom.

"They just left. They're *psychotic* … they just dragged a couple of guys away. In broad daylight! It's only a matter of time before they kill someone. Mum can't even see them. I don't think any adults can. They're untouchable." Jack turned and looked at his best friend. Henry was half a head taller than Jack and twice his width. Jack shoved his school tie into place. "Listen Henry, as soon as Samantha comes out, we'll join her okay? … Make sure she gets to school in one piece."

Henry stroked his chins. "Interesting plan, Jack … now if we can just find someone to make sure we do too …"

"You managed to avoid them. Well done."

Henry nodded. "Unfortunately, your mother's tomatoes paid the ultimate price."

"Hedgehog?"

"Mole. Keep up. Big blighter too," said Henry, noticing a button on his shirt had popped.

Samantha closed her front door and gazed up at the sky: the blackest clouds *ever* stretched as far as she could see. "Wasn't it supposed to be *sunny* today?" she said, heaving her school bag onto her shoulder and walking down her drive.

"Sam's on the move," said Jack.

The boys trampled down the stairs side by side. "Guys! Take it easy! You've had no breakfast, Jack," said Mrs. Tracy, poking her head out of the kitchen.

"It's okay, Mum. I'll get something from the shop."

"Make sure you do, Jack."

"I'll make sure he does," said Henry, giving Mrs. Tracy the thumbs up.

Samantha's shoulder drooped under the weight of her bag. It held not only her school books but two fat petitions against animal cruelty. She smiled as the front door opposite burst open and Jack and Henry got momentarily *wedged* in it. They spilled out onto the driveway and shoved one another as they crossed the street. "Hey, Sam. Have you got bricks in that bag or something," said Henry, panting.

"Certainly feels like it," she replied.

"No problem. We've got the bag covered …" said Henry, lifting it off her shoulder and handing it to Jack.

"Oh," said Samantha, "sure you don't mind?"

"I really don't," said Jack, only too pleased to take the weight off her slender shoulder. Samantha had dark wavy hair, clear pale skin and warm blue eyes.

She raised an eyebrow and said, "Thank God those cretins moved on. I told my mother about how they attacked that guy yesterday."

"And?" said Jack.

"And nothing. She accused me of exaggerating. God ... even by her standards the words 'head', 'bucket' and 'sand' have never been more appropriate."

Henry patted Jack's back. "Jack saved that guy's life."

"No, I didn't. They got a call. What's up with everyone? Even the policeman ignored what was happening."

Samantha shrugged. "I expect he had to fill in some forms back at the station."

Jack stopped in his tracks. "No, Sam. It was like he couldn't see it. It was happening right in front of him ... and he *couldn't* see it."

"I thought policemen were supposed to have 20/20 vision? Or is that fighter pilots?" mumbled Henry.

Samantha pulled a scary face. "All the adults have been placed under an enchantment and the world is being sucked into Hell, ha, ha, haaar."

Jack and Henry looked at her, horrified.

"*Metaphorically* speaking, guys. Lighten up."

They walked around a corner and spotted the gang standing under a tree. They were following the evasive manoeuvrings of a cat in its branches. A number of stones, empty bottles and bricks had been collected as missiles. "They're actually placing bets on who can knock it off that branch first," said Samantha, stepping towards them. Jack grabbed Samantha's arm. "Leave it, Sam. There's nothing we can do." Samantha grimaced as though she'd just heard the worst news *ever*.

The next moment, Jack heard himself say, "I suppose we could ... you know ... draw their fire or something. Give the cat a chance to get away."

"Are you nuts?" said Henry.

Must be, thought Jack.

"I always suspected you might be nuts and if you *insist* on this 'plan' then you'll just have confirmed my suspicions beyond any reasonable doubt and ..."

"Oh, stop babbling Henry! I think it's an excellent idea," said Samantha, her heart racing now. They were a stone's throw from the bus stop.

Jack went on, "If we time it just right, we could save the cat ...and maybe even ourselves." He looked for the number 23 coming along the high street.

"Oh, God ... there's a bus coming," said Henry, squinting into the distance. "Although ... let's not be hasty, it might be a Post Office van or ..."

"That's a bus and it's moving fast ... it's now or never." Before he could change his mind, he took a deep breath and yelled: "At least cats only catch rats! You cretins are evolving into them!"

9

The gang turned. A lanky thug pointed at Jack and said, "Isn't that the kid from yesterday? The one with a death wish?"

"Yes, it is. I say we grant him *and his mates* three death wishes," said another, taking aim with a broken bottle.

"Run!" croaked Jack. Jack and Samantha darted in the direction of the bus stop. Henry attempted to dart but could only manage an amble. Empty bottles and stones flew at them: the bottles smashing on the pavement, the stones zipping past with spiteful intent. Jack reached the bus stop first. The bus had just pulled up and opened its doors. An elderly man stepped down onto the pavement. A bottle shattered on the ground – and filled the turn-ups of his trousers with glass. The old man grinned and shook his leg as though he'd just remembered something funny. Jack didn't think his reaction at all funny. In fact, it chilled him to the bone.

Once Samantha was safely on board the bus, Jack began shouting words of encouragement at Henry. "Come on, Henry!" he yelled, followed by "WATCH OUT!" as a bottle skimmed Henry's head and exploded against a lamppost. Jack gave Henry a shove up onto the platform of the bus and climbed in behind him. The bus driver closed the doors behind them and drove off, oblivious to the commotion. The trio made their way past a number of anxious young faces and sat down at the rear of the bus. "Did you see that?" Jack panted. "That bottle landed *right* in front of the old guy and he didn't even flinch! He couldn't see it."

Several anxious looking children within earshot nodded. "The old-timer was probably just playing it cool?" said Henry, turning in his seat and gazing out the rear window.

"That old guy looked way past cool … the important thing is that he wasn't hurt," said Samantha, taking her bag from Jack and unfastening it. Jack noticed her hands trembling as she pulled out a petition and went on … "There will always be homicidal cretins roaming the streets unsupervised. But life goes on and many of our furry friends still face great perils. I've got something here I want you both to sign …"

"That's a surprise," said Henry. "What are we saving today?"

"The pole cat … also known as the foul mart due to its delicate odour."

"Pole cat?" said Jack, only too pleased to take his mind of what had just happened. "Isn't that like a badger?"

"Yes, that's right … only smaller and smellier."

"So what's wrong with it?"

"Nothing's *wrong* with it. The conservation programme was going great until some celebrity 'chef' discovered that it tasted 'simply fabulous' when served on a bed of indigenous vegetables."

"Really?" replied Henry, licking his lips. Samantha clenched her fists. Henry's expression became one of concern for the little stinker. He said,

"Perhaps you could raise awareness for its plight with a sponsored event?"

"What do you suggest?" she asked, relaxing a little.

"Oh, I don't know … how about a sponsored 'Hold-Your-Nose-a-Thon?" Henry pinched his nose and raised his elbow into the air. Samantha thumped him.

THREE

The Signpost

That night when Jack went to bed, he found it impossible to sleep. The events of the last few days kept replaying in his mind: Anthony's beating, the old man who'd seemed oblivious to what was happening, the bottle thrown with such spite it could easily have killed Henry. Weirdest of all, what *was* the deal with the adults? These were things they clearly couldn't see. *But that's impossible! It just doesn't make sense. Maybe it's a wind-up? Or some sick joke? Or a reality TV experiment!? I want to understand what's going on!* He clenched both fists and struck his bed in frustration. *I need to understand!* Behind his closed eyelids, three golden blocks materialised – letters and symbols had been painted on the blocks – which suddenly spun like tumblers in a fruit machine. One-by-one they slammed into place and spelt the word: **W-H-Y**

Huh!?

A blazing rectangle of light mushroomed behind the blocks. *Has mum switched on my light?* Jack attempted to open his eyes to investigate … but couldn't. *What the …!?* Jack felt himself being propelled through the blocks and into the light at hyper speed – his stomach felt as though it had remained far behind him – and his cheeks bristled like a fighter pilot experiencing G-Forces …

What the!

The question 'Why?' appeared again and flew at him as if shot from a crossbow. It was followed by similar worded missiles: Why Wickedness? Why Cruelty? Why Hatred? Why Murder? Why Wars? Why Injustice? Why Can't Adults See? The questions flew, buzzed, and dive-bombed him with increasing venom. *Kamikaze questions! If I'm asleep, then I must be having a nightmare! Wake up, Jack! Wake up!*

The blazing light went out and Jack found himself lying in a wood. "I'm obviously still dreaming," he muttered, sitting up. The stench of rotten tree bark triggered a grimace and pollen from the surrounding bluebells tickled his nostrils. "At least this dream's an improvement over those angry questions," he muttered, wriggling his nose. He looked up and shielded his eyes from shafts of sunlight that tore through the forest's

12

canopy. He lowered his gaze and spotted a signpost. Curiosity dragged him to his feet and he walked towards it. "Ouch!" He'd trodden on a pine needle. Jack realised his feet were bare and he was wearing the same t-shirt and boxer shorts he'd worn to bed. Mindful of the prickly pines, he carefully navigated a route to the wooden sign.

The signpost had two branches – the one that pointed to the right was blank. "That's useful," thought Jack, "a sign that points *nowhere*." The branch that pointed to the left did have something carved into it, but the letters had been obscured by red creepers. Jack tugged at them. They came away easily enough and left a crimson stain on his palm. He had uncovered two words: Cerca Trova. He'd never heard of such a place. He pondered what the words might mean. They sounded a bit like 'instant death' or maybe 'certain doom'. He shuddered and took a backward step. "Ouch! Not again!" A pine needle had buried itself in his heel. "This pain feels all too real for my liking!" He hopped over to a small mound and sat down clutching his foot. As he pulled out the needle, an electronic beeping echoed through the woods. The wind gusted, and a swarm of butterflies took flight from some grass around the signpost. Jack watched as they fluttered into the trees. *Isn't that a car alarm?*

Moments later, he was lying in his bed – the sound of a car alarm screeching through his open bedroom window. Dazed, he glanced at his wristwatch. It was 8.30am. He got up and stumbled across the landing into the bathroom. He squeezed some toothpaste onto his toothbrush and looked in the mirror. *That's odd*, he thought. One of his eyes had red stains around it. He noticed similar stains on his t-shirt. Then he remembered his dream. "The signpost … the red creepers … my *foot?*" He steadied himself on the sink and reached down to his heel. *It feels okay.* Then he looked at his fingers … "Is that *blood?*" Jack's gaze fell to the floor where red specks peppered the carpet. His heartbeat quickened as he followed the bloody trail back into his room. Jack stood beside his bed and felt a strong urge to look under his duvet. He gripped the duvet's edge – and tugged *hard*. The duvet flew away, and a swarm of butterflies took to the air. Jack staggered backwards and watched them flutter towards the light beyond his curtains. "Move … Jack … Move!" He darted across the room, drew back the curtains and flung the windows wide open. He shooed the butterflies out and *snapped* the curtains closed. A moment later, the sun peeked from behind a cloud and vaporised them.

Jack sat on his bed and tried to conjure an explanation for all this. He couldn't. And the more he tried the more his brain ached. Then he remembered the words that had been written on the signpost. Not wanting to stain his carpet further, he hopped over to the small desk in the corner of his room. "Pen, pen, pen … there's never a pen when you need one!"

Anxious to write down the words before he forgot them, he searched frantically through the drawers of his desk for anything he could use to write. He found a thick black marker and scrawled two words on a pad: **CERCA TROVA.**

It was Sunday morning. His mother was still in bed when he crept downstairs and switched on her computer. He was convinced that when he entered the two mysterious words into Google, he would discover that they were meaningless and that, in all probability, they didn't even exist. He typed the letters in carefully and clicked "search". The first ten entries in a list of several thousand appeared. They were Italian and meant: 'seek and you shall find.' "Seek and you shall find?" he mumbled. *Seek and you shall find what? Am I looking for something?* "Have I lost something?" Then he remembered the questions that had sped at him: Why Wickedness? Why Cruelty? Why Hatred? Why Murder? Why Wars? Why Can't Adults See? "Why, why, why," he muttered. *No. It couldn't be. Could it? Was the sign pointing to an answer to* those *questions?* "None of this makes any sense!" He had to tell someone. He switched on his mobile and sent a text message to Henry. 'Playing flds 30 min?' He received a reply almost instantly, 'Do my best.'

Henry was sitting on a park bench and finishing a packet of crisps. One look in the direction of his approaching friend told him that something was up. He licked the last grains of salt from his fingers and said, "What's Samantha done now?"

Jack flopped down onto the other end of the bench. "You're not going to believe this but … I think I had a dream last night."

"I do believe it," said Henry. "They're actually not that uncommon. I have them all the time."

"No. This one was different. It was …I don't know how to put it, Henry. It felt *real*." Jack told him every detail of the dream and the events that followed. After he'd finished, the pair sat in silence. Jack looked at his friend, desperate for a gem of reassurance.

Henry observed him, head to foot and back again. "You don't look any more mental than usual," he said.

"But it did happen! How can you explain the ivy stains and the bleeding foot and all those butterflies in my room?"

Henry shuddered. "You're actually starting to wig me out."

"I'm just telling you what happened."

"Well, suppose it did happen, just as you said? Then what?"

"Well, I obviously have to go back … to that signpost."

"*Obviously.*"

14

"It could be our only hope, Henry … of discovering what's up with everyone."

"That's a hell of a leap don't you think? I mean, seek and you shall find? It could be anything."

"It's something important. I know it," said Jack, a dogged expression on his face that Henry recognised only too well. "So, what's the plan," asked Henry, gazing into the empty crisp packet and hoping beyond all reason that he'd overlooked something edible.

"Tonight, I'll do all the same things. I'll ask the same questions … do everything the same, except one thing. I think you should stay over."

"OK, cool … any particular reason?"

"You can watch me. That place is obviously dangerous. If I can hurt my foot, I could probably break my neck, or …"

"Have your head bitten off by something hairy and scary in those woods?"

Jack grabbed his knees to his chest and began rocking as if caught in a sudden gale. Henry glanced sideways at him … *Now he definitely looks more mental than usual.* "Rocking? Always a good sign," he said. "Look, even if you do return to the same place, how will I know what's happening to you?"

"You'll stay awake and watch me … you know, for signs of distress."

"Cool. It's not like I haven't put in years of practice. And then what?"

"Then you wake me up, before it's too late."

"It seems to me it's already too late," said Henry, screwing up the crisp packet and tossing it over his shoulder.

FOUR

Cerca Trova

Henry asked his mother if he could spend the night at Jack's. "He's having a bit of a crisis and he needs my help," he said, feeling it best not to elaborate.

"It must be a hell of a crisis if he needs your help. I don't know it's always something with you kids. Don't forget to take your school bag for the morning. And don't eat Mrs. Tracy out of house and home!"

Henry entered Jack's bedroom. Jack was wearing the wet-weather gear his mother had bought him for a recent school trip to Wales. Jack smiled and beckoned his friend in. Then he reached down and tightened the laces on his hiking boots. "Right!" he said, standing up. "I'm ready for those pine needles, now. Bring on the pine needles!"

"You may also be ready for a psychiatric assessment. Are you expecting rain?" asked Henry, tugging on Jack's blue mac.

"Rain may be the least of my worries … which is why I need you to stay awake tonight."

"No problem."

Jack switched off his bedside lamp and lay down. "Oh, pass me that backpack, would you?" he said, pointing to a black bag on his desk. Henry picked it up and handed it to him. Jack had brought a small armchair from downstairs and placed it beside his bed for Henry. He'd also provided him with two candles, secured in a saucer on his bedside table. Henry slumped down into the armchair, and gripped its arms in the candlelight. Jack said, "Now, just do your best to stay awake and watch me for anything suspicious … or life threatening. Okay?"

Henry nodded.

"I think we're ready then," said Jack, clutching the backpack to his chest.

He closed his eyes and went back over his experience from the previous night. He began by asking the simplest question of all: *Why?* He thought about the cruelty of the gang. And again, asked, *Why?* Jack concentrated hard. *What makes people … monsters? Why can't the adults*

16

see *what their kids are doing? I don't get it. Any of it! I want to understand. I* need *to understand*! He clenched his fists and, once again, brought them down hard on his mattress.

Nothing happened.

Maybe Henry's right … maybe I have lost the plot.

He tried asking the same questions again, and focused on the frustration that comes from *desperately* trying to understand something you just can't. He thumped his bed again with more intent, more purpose and … *Yes!* … As though a dead heart had been jolted into life, the rectangle of light returned – *It's working!* – The rectangle transformed into a swirling tunnel – and the questions flew at him down it again … "Henry, I'm going back! … Stay awake –" These were the last words Jack uttered before the light engulfed him completely. A minute later, Henry sat slumped in his chair, fast asleep.

Jack felt a breeze exploring his face. He opened his eyes and gazed up into the trees that had replaced his bedroom ceiling, "All right! I've made it back!"

Jack stood before the sign. The words were still visible where he'd torn the ivy the previous night. *I did that,* he thought. "It's like returning home." He put his arms through the straps of his backpack, secured it to his back and set off in the direction of Cerca Trova.

A change had occurred, so subtle at first that he'd failed to notice it. A fog had begun to form … delicate wraiths of cloud that caressed the forest's floor. Several minutes later, when his view had become worryingly restricted, he finally clocked it. *I've only seen fog like this in old films.* He placed his backpack on the ground and crouched to retrieve a bottle of water. "It'll be fine. It's not like fog's dangerous," he said, standing and taking a swig. Then he glanced down. "What the!?" *Where's my backpack!* Jack dropped to his knees and reached into the fog – his anxious fingers foraging through stones and dead leaves. "It has GOT to be here somewhere!" He shuffled a couple of steps forward and saw the straps of his backpack. He reached out to grab them but they slid beyond his reach! Jack leapt to his feet. "Hel … hello. Is someone there? I'm Jack … this is *my* dream."

In response, something growled. A deep, confident growl that said, 'You're someplace you *really* don't want to be. The last place you're *ever* going to be.'

"Henry!" whispered Jack, "Wake me up." If Henry had been awake, he would have noticed that Jack's backpack had disappeared. Jack was now clutching nothing but his chest. The creature growled again, so close now Jack could smell its dog-like breath. *Why did I come back to this place? What was I thinking? Hold it together. Maybe, if I stand completely still,*

17

whatever it is will decide I'm not a threat and go away? Or maybe, I should try and scare it? It is my dream after all. In a blind panic, he cried, "Back off or I'll hurt you!" Far from backing off, a large hairy snout loomed from the fog ... followed by a pair of blood-red eyes. Jack's eyes opened wide. In contrast, the creature's narrowed – it tilted its head skyward and loosed a bone-rattling howl. Jack jumped. And then he ran. Desperate, loping strides from legs that felt weak and unresponsive. He thudded against a tree and, correcting himself, staggered in the direction he'd seen the path go before the fog set in. The ground suddenly opened beneath him and he plunged into nothingness. Moments later, he crashed onto his side and began rolling down a steep embankment. Jack cried out as sharp stones tore into his legs. If Henry had been awake, he would have seen rips and tears slicing through Jack's trousers. Jack rolled to a stop at the bottom of the hill. His legs throbbed and his world spun and he knew another sprint so soon would be impossible. He shut his eyes tight. He could hear small animals darting about in the bushes. "Please," he muttered, "just go away and don't eat me ..." Once or twice he heard water lapping softly against a riverbank. He opened his eyes and peered through the lifting fog towards a river ...

It was dusk. A veil of mist hung spirit-like over the water. It had grown considerably darker – the only light provided by a sky awash with brilliant stars. Jack looked directly overhead and couldn't believe his eyes *–two moons!* – hanging side-by-side in the heavens like enormous, all-seeing eyes. He swallowed hard and wondered what Henry and Samantha would make of them. "Oh yes, Henry," he muttered, rolling his eyes. "... he must've fallen asleep after all."

Jack had all but given up hope of finding Cerca Trova when he spotted something jutting from a clump of bushes up river. "Is that another signpost?"

The same two words had been hurriedly carved into this signpost: Cerca Trova. But it pointed to the *other* side of the river. Jack was a good swimmer but didn't fancy a swim in that water, not one bit. He knelt down and felt the water. A layer of green slime clung to his fingers like webbing. *That's gross ...*

A noise erupted behind him.

Jack glanced over his shoulder and leapt to his feet – several *massive* wolf-like creatures were sliding down the side of a steep hill – they clearly had one target in mind – *him*. Jack drew a deep breath and threw himself into the river. He disappeared below the surface and reappeared coughing and spluttering. Sensing a jaw snap close by, he swam from the edge – fretful, half-completed breast strokes that pulled him unevenly to the middle of the river. He turned to see if the creatures had followed him. The pack stood motionless along the banks of the river, drool dangling from their jaws onto the grassy verge. Jack thought it was probably his imagination, but they looked, well, sort of, *sorry* for him. "That can't be good." Then he saw something skirt along the top of the water. "Is that a *snake?*" It was a snake. An enormous black snake: its roving head the size of a truck's tyre. The snake opened its jaws to reveal two dagger-sized fangs. Jack screamed and spun about. In a flash, a prehistoric crocodile burst from the water and chomped the snake in two. Jack turned to see the crocodile drag the snake's head under the surface. Panicked and numb, he kicked for the shore.

Jack climbed out of the water and lay on his back, panting and shaking. "Wake up, wake up, wake up ..." he muttered. Once his breathing had calmed, Jack gathered his courage and sat up. He scrutinised the bank on the other side of the river. As far as he could tell, the wolf-like creatures had gone. *I hope you enjoyed the show ... miserable mutts.* Jack removed his boots and poured their watery contents onto the ground. A tiny fish fell out and began flapping about. He scooped it up in his hands and dropped it into the water. This small act of compassion made Jack feel like a giant. Trying desperately to hold onto this comforting feeling, he pulled his boots on and hurriedly tied the laces. "I'm completely soaked ... but I might as well just keep going ... and see how far I can get," he muttered, standing up.

Another signpost directed him onto a short path that led into a vast clearing. The view, lit by the two moons, unfolded for miles into the distance. It reminded him of those African savannahs he'd seen on wildlife documentaries ... *apart from those two moons.*

Twenty minutes and two signposts later, he came to a dramatic halt. He'd reached a chasm between two rock faces. The only way across was a narrow stone bridge. The 'bridge' was no more than 30 centimetres wide. *Very useful*, he thought, "For hobbits."

He walked to the edge of the chasm and peered over the side. A ravine lay hundreds of metres below, its bottom engulfed in mist and shadow. Fortunately, heights had never bothered him all that much. *I can't believe I'm even considering crossing this thing ...* He placed a foot on the end of the narrow bridge ... and applied more pressure. It didn't budge. "I must be insane," he muttered, as he walked out onto it. "Keep going ... just keep going and whatever you do ... *don't* look down."

He was making good progress towards the other side when he felt something flap against his boot. A bootlace had come untied. "Oh, *please!* Not now!" Jack looked up and focused on the trees on the other side of the ravine. "I'm almost there ... just keep going." He took another step and ... "Oh – Please – NO!" Jack had trodden on the end of the untied lace; and was stuck, one knee raised above the other, as though posed for a hiking photo. He began toppling sideways to his doom. Instinct kicked in. – *Go limp! Just go limp!* His bottom crashed onto the beam and he grabbed at the stone pathway and *just* managed to pull himself upright. He slid to the other side on his bottom and collapsed onto the grass verge. "That's it. I'm spent." *I'm just going to lie here until I wake up ... or get eaten.* Jack closed his eyes. *I wonder if it's possible to fall asleep when you're already sleeping?* His nose twitched. He sat up and sniffed the air. *Something smells good ... which is* seriously *out of character for this place.*

Jack negotiated his way through several bushes and came upon a small clearing. On a log beside a camp fire, a man sat with his back to him. A black stallion with a shield strapped to its side grazed close by. Jack moved closer and noticed a sword resting on the log beside the man. *I don't fancy being on the end of a swipe from that thing.* Jack was about to take a backward step when the man spoke. "Do not be afraid ... and welcome!"

FIVE

Perkin Beck

The man stood and turned to face him. "I'm a friend," he said. "Please, there is nothing to fear." He was dressed in the clothes of a medieval warrior – a brown leather shirt just visible beneath a vest of black mail. The iron vest was badly damaged. *This guy has obviously been in some serious fights,* thought Jack. The man smiled. "I'd all but given up hope. But you *are* here ... a child of Earth. I can scarce believe it."

"You were expecting me?" said Jack, stepping into the clearing. The stranger placed his thumbs inside his wide leather belt. "The Reader," he said, "she spoke of a human boy ... a boy who would find his way to the southern forests. I have spent many months placing signs in the surrounding woods in the vainest hope that ... are you injured?" he asked, noticing the tears in Jack's trousers.

"No. I'm okay, I think. My name's Jack ..."

"And I am Perkin. Come ..." he said, beckoning to Jack. "Sit by the fire and dry your clothes."

They sat beside the campfire on a tree root which rose and fell from the ground like the Loch Ness Monster. The warmth of the flames sent a wave of contentment through Jack's chilled body; it couldn't have been more welcome.

"Are you hungry or thirsty? I have plenty of food and drink," said Perkin, motioning to a pot nestled above the lapping flames.

Jack gazed at the sword resting on the tree root beside him. "I'm not hungry ..." he murmured.

"Would you like to hold it?" asked Perkin. "The sword is not as heavy as it looks."

"May I? It *looks* the business." Jack clasped the hilt with both hands and raised the blade up in front of him. Jack noticed a white rose carved into its ivory handle. "Did you pull it from a stone ...?"

"No," replied Perkin, smiling. "It was made a long time ago by the finest sword-smith in this realm."

"You mean this dream."

"You're not dreaming, Jack. Everything you see is real."

21

Jack's arms ached under the weight of the iron sword. He lowered its tip to the ground. "O… kay. Where am I?"

"You are in The Dark Matter."

"Dark Matter? You mean … that invisible stuff that's supposed to be everywhere?"

Perkin nodded, gravely. "Dark matter *is* everywhere … and it contains all within the universe that is hidden from humankind. But not at this moment … *everything* you see here is made from dark matter."

Jack thought for a moment. "I'm human," he said, "so why can I see it? And, in the unlikely event that I'm not having the weirdest dream ever, how did I get here?"

"I do not know how. Only why. And our time is limited," he said, his voice betraying urgency. "You could vanish from The Dark Matter at any moment. There is much to tell and a great deal more to do." He placed a gloved hand on Jack's damp shoulder. "But be warned, once the veil is lifted there can be no lowering it, no going back. Are you sufficiently braced, Jack?"

"For what?"

"The truth."

"About *what*?"

"About what has been placing hatred and violence into the hearts of the people of Earth since the dawn of time. And why adults have suddenly become oblivious to the terrible deeds their young are now committing in plain sight."

Jack raised his head and glanced sideways at Perkin. "If you know why … why the grown-ups can't see what these gangs are doing right under their noses, then please … tell me."

Perkin nodded. "Deep within the northern reaches of this forest there lies a fortress … it is known as The Priory of Chaos."

Jack swallowed hard and shuffled nervously on the tree root. "A Priory?" he said. "That doesn't sound so bad."

"Do not be deceived. It's the place where evil began, Jack."

"Began? *When*?"

"At the dawn of choice."

"Oh ... then."

"The Priory of Chaos is overseen by The Order of Dark Monks. Except for The First Evil, Dark Monks are the most feared beings within this realm."

"The *First* Evil?"

"The closest reference to The First Evil on Earth would, I suppose, be the Devil."

"Oh, right … large, reddish chap? Pointy horns? Partial to heat?" Jack was trying desperately to make light of this information.

"It is not by chance that your description has such merit, Jack. The First Evil has provided inspiration for many a legend back on Earth."

"If you're trying to freak me out, you're doing a great job. Anyway, what goes on at this ...Priory of Chaos?" asked Jack, his heart thumping in his chest.

"As you have already borne witness, The Priory has but a single purpose ... to implant evil into the hearts and minds of Earth's young."

"From this place? How's that possible?"

"They breed creatures that make it possible. These loathsome beasts are called Snatcher-Gar ... and they possess abilities unique to their kind."

"What kind of abilities?"

Perkin leaned forward and collected a fistful of earth. As he went on, he allowed the grains of dirt to fall slowly through the cracks between his fingers. "Where to begin?" He shook his head. "The creatures are hideous to gaze upon. Their physical forms were created by fusing the DNA of mammoth bats and goblins. The resulting anathema is the only being from The Dark Matter able to move between our two worlds without suffering disfigurement ... or death. Once they reach Earth, the winged beasts are invisible to all but animals and the very young. In later years, some toddlers who have glimpsed them grow to see them again in their dreams. This would explain the many likenesses of these creatures atop Earth's cathedrals."

"Are you talking about ... gargoyles?"

"Yes, Jack. The Snatcher-Gars are sent for children between the ages of nine and fourteen. They seek them in their beds and place them in a deep trance." Perkin paused and wiped the few remaining grains of earth from his hands.

"And then?" asked Jack, his mouth remaining open.

"They snatch the child's essence from its body." Perkin fell silent.

"Well? What do they do with it? What do they do with the essence?"

"They carry it here. For nine months of tutoring within the walls of the Priory. It is your essence that sits beside me now, Jack." Jack sat quietly, taking stock of what Perkin had told him. *I must be dreaming after all,* he thought. "Nine months? It's not possible ... they'd be missed!"

"They are never missed. The Dark Matter exists in a time frame nine months behind Earth's. This means souls can be snatched away and returned the same night, just moments later ... their parents none the wiser. After nine months at The Priory of Chaos the children are changed – experts in the arts of cruelty, deception and wickedness. They have no memory of their time at the Priory when they wake ... and any guiding conscience they once possessed is extinguished. Since the dawn of mankind, millions of children have been changed by the Priory in this way."

"But why? For what reason?"

"To tip the balance on Earth from light to dark. Once this is achieved, The First Evil will be able to pass from The Dark Matter to Earth. The remaining goodness in humanity will be routed and despair and wickedness will reign on Earth. The last time the Priory was this close to tipping the balance was during the early part of your 20th century. German children were the focus of their harvest then. Those children grew to swell the ranks of the Nazi army."

"But why am I here? Why are you telling me all this?"

"Once again, the Priory is attempting to purge humanity of its goodness. There is only one way to stop them, Jack … and only a human child who has resisted the initial trance of the Snatcher-Gar can achieve it … from within the walls of The Priory of Chaos."

Jack's mouth fell open. "I hope you don't me mean me," he murmured, "I not up to it."

Perkin stood up and took several steps before pausing with his back to Jack. He was about to play his trump card. "Believe me when I say that what I'm about to tell you … it gives me no pleasure."

"What is it?"

"You have a friend? … A girl who possesses a kind, unselfish heart?"

"Do you mean, Samantha?"

"I do not know her name but, if you're here, it can only mean one thing." Perkin turned to face him. "Your friend's essence has been removed this very night and taken to The Priory of Chaos. The Reader has foretold it."

"The Reader? Who is this reader you keep talking about? And how does she know about Samantha?" Jack's tone had turned from intrigued to angry.

Perkin said, "All you need know is that if Samantha has been taken to the Priory this night then, when next you see her, she will no longer be the girl you knew. But there is a way to return her true-self … and stop the Priory before it's too late."

Just then, Henry's voice could be heard all about them in the woods. "Jack? Jack? Wake up, Jack!" Jack's physical form began to fade. "A Snatcher-Gar!" cried Perkin. "It will be coming for you too soon …" Jack vanished and Perkin slumped to his knees. "You must prepare for its arrival … or else, all will be lost."

SIX

Samantha? Is that you?

Jack sat up with a start. "Samantha!" he cried.

"No. It's me, Henry. The guy who may have nodded off for five minutes. What happened to you?" he went on, poking at Jack's damp clothing.

"Me?" replied Jack, looking dazed. "It's not me we need to worry about. I think something's happened to Samantha!" He jumped out of bed, threw his curtains open and gazed at Samantha's house across the street. It looked normal enough. Henry stood beside him. "Samantha? What's Sam got to do with anything? What happened to you? I'm sorry for falling asleep, but ..."

"Don't worry about that now. It's probably for the best that you did. What time is it?" he asked, now scrutinising Samantha's bedroom window.

"... 8.00 am."

"Kids!" shouted Mrs. Tracy from the bottom of the stairs. "Get up! Breakfast's ready!"

"Hurry!" said Jack. "We mustn't miss Samantha. Maybe Perkin was wrong. He *must* be wrong. Perhaps he doesn't even exist!"

"Who's Perkin?"

"I'll tell you everything over breakfast," replied Jack, removing his damp sweatshirt and heading for the shower. Henry stood beside the bed. He stared down at a collection of leaves and dead insects on Jack's wet sheets. It occurred to him that his friend may be winding him up.

Henry picked up one of the leaves and looked closely at it. "It looks *prehistoric* ..." The scent of freshly cooked bacon reached Henry's nose. He dropped the leaf and went downstairs.

Five minutes later, Jack hurried into the kitchen. Henry was tucking into a plate of scrambled eggs and bacon. Jack sat down and grabbed a box of cereal. As he shovelled wheat, he told Henry about the wolf-like creatures, the giant water snake, the enormous crocodile, the crossing of the gorge and, finally, the conversation he'd had with Perkin about The Priory of Chaos and Samantha. Throughout this 3-minute-rapid-fire-monologue, Henry remained open mouthed and speechless. A neglected rasher of bacon lay on his otherwise spotless plate. He'd even ignored the milk that Jack had spat on his face. "Is that all?" said Henry, finally. "I was worried you might have been in danger."

"It's lucky you didn't wake me at the first sign of trouble … I'd never have met Perkin if you had."

"Yes, but you could have been killed. I'd have lost my appetite and then all this delicious bacon would have gone to waste."

"It's definitely going to your waist, Henry."

Mrs. Tracy entered the kitchen. "What are you two plotting now? … Oh, Henry … you're *such* a messy eater. Here, wipe the milk off your face with this." She handed Henry a paper towel and went to the kitchen sink to wash up. "If you want to catch Samantha, she's just walking down her driveway," she said, plunging a mug into the soapy water. The boys jumped up, grabbed their coats and bags off the pegs in the hallway and bolted out the front door. *How sweet*, thought Mrs. Tracy, *those boys are mad about that girl.*

By contrast, Samantha wasn't carrying anything. Apart from this oversight, she looked normal enough. "Where's your bag? Your petitions and stuff?" asked Jack, looking her up and down and trying not to be obvious about it.

"I thought I'd travel light today," she announced. "There's only so much saving of the world a young girl can do. And how are you two boys on this sunny morning? Been up to anything interesting?"

Henry was about to tell all when Jack grabbed his arm. "Oh … not much … the usual," replied Jack. "So how's the pole cat campaign coming along?"

"Oh, yeah," said Henry. "Any luck keeping the little guys from being cooked and added to a plate of steaming vegetables?"

Samantha rolled her eyes, "*Indigenous* vegetables, Jack. It's vital the vegetables are home grown. It's the only way to exploit the full flavour of the foul mart. Don't forget to go indigenous, guys! … otherwise your dinner party could end up being a complete disaster."

Jack looked at Henry as if to say, 'Is she joking?'

They turned a corner and the boys felt a sense of déjà vu. The gang were loitering in the same spot as the day before. Only now their numbers had swollen: thirty hooded, skulking youths had assembled to finish the business they called 'dead cat'. Once again, the none-too-bright moggy had been unable to resist the newly hatched temptations in a bird's nest. *I don't need this right now*, thought Jack. "You guys are nothing if not persistent!" said Samantha, striding confidently towards the gang. Jack and Henry froze in their tracks, mouths wide open, and watched the gang surround her. Samantha stood nose-to-nose with one of the shorter gang members.

"Give me that!" she barked, and grabbed the stone he was clutching. Then she turned and hurled the stone up into the tree's branches. What happened next impressed the gang and sickened Jack and Henry. The cat shrieked, crashed to the ground, and limped off amid a hail of missiles.

"Idiots!" shouted a female gang member. "I can't believe you all missed it! It was limping for goodness sake. Limping! Only this sister knows how to hit cat. Maybe she should give you lessons?"

"I'd be glad to boys," said Samantha, enjoying the attention of the male gang members.

"*Sam*?" said a dazed Henry. "What's wrong with you?"

"Nothing's wrong with me … the question is what's wrong with you, fat boy?" Jack walked towards her. "Samantha? Please … just come with us … you don't like these people … don't you remember?" Jack reached out a hand, but she slapped it away.

"Get away from me, loser!" The gang were about to set upon Jack. Henry hurried forward, grabbed Jack around his waist, and hoisted him up from the ground. As Henry backed away, Jack struggling in his grasp, the gang fell about laughing. Samantha stepped forward, her usually pretty face contorted with hatred. "That's it, Whale Boy! Get your idiotic side-kick out of my face. Otherwise we will *stamp* the life out of him!" The gang whooped and cheered and stamped as though marching on the spot. Samantha raised her voice above the increasing din: "It looks like we're gonna need a harpoon gun to take you down though!" Henry backed around the corner and out of sight, Jack continuing to struggle in his grasp. Henry lowered his friend to the ground and released him. Jack spun about to give Henry a piece of his mind, and froze. Tears were streaking down Henry's cheeks. This was the first time Jack had ever seen him cry. His best friend had always had to endure stick about his weight – but he managed to cope thanks to his wicked sense of humour. There were times when Henry's humour made him seem uncaring, but Jack knew it was just his way of dealing with painful stuff.

They sat on the curb, stared at the ground, and said nothing for almost a minute. Henry broke the silence. "Sam's the only girl who ever treated me like an equal, Jack. How could she say those things?"

"It wasn't her talking, Henry … something terrible has happened to her."

Henry wiped the tears from his face in disgust. "That place you went to … it was real, wasn't it?"

"It must have been. Perkin said there is much to do. I don't know what he meant by that … but he said there's a way to get Samantha back." Jack fell silent. Then he placed a hand on Henry's shoulder and said, "You know there's only one way to find out how."

"You're going back there?"

"Yes, Henry. Tonight."

SEVEN

Back?

Henry entered Jack's bedroom clutching a flask of inky black coffee. "You can call me Night Watchman, because that's what I intend to do, watch you all night," he said, sitting in the armchair, upright and alert.

Jack sat on his bed. "I'm hoping I won't be in as much danger this time. That, if I do return, it will be to the same spot I left … Perkin should be there waiting for me."

"Which is why I brought you this," said Henry, pulling a cricket bat from a holdall he'd placed beside the chair.

Jack took the bat from him. "Nice. What am I supposed to do with this? Join The Dark Matter's second X1?"

"Sarcastic comments are my domain. No, I thought that if Perkin turns out to be one of the bad guys after all, you could crane him with it."

"Crane him with it? He's a warrior … he has a sword and chain-mail armour and … I really can't see that craning him with a cricket bat is the way forward." Jack handed it back to Henry and lay down.

"So you're not taking *anything* defensive to The Dark Matter?"

"No. It's time to find out how to get Samantha back." Henry turned out the light and lit the shrunken candles. He sat down in his armchair, and stared at his friend.

An hour later, Henry whispered, "Are you still here?"

"Yes," replied Jack, shuffling impatiently. "What time is it?"

"… Midnight."

Half an hour later, Henry whispered the same question "… Still here?"

"Yes. Nothing's working tonight! I can't find the tunnel of light … and it's driving me nuts."

"You and me both."

Similar exchanges occurred between the two boys at regular intervals until 6am. That's when the situation reversed. "Henry?" asked Jack, "Are you awake?" Henry didn't reply.

It was no good. There would be no returning to The Dark Matter that night. Jack climbed out of bed quietly, so as not to disturb Henry, and opened the curtains a little. All looked well over at Samantha's house. It wasn't. As hard as he'd tried, he hadn't been able to conjure the tunnel of light. He just couldn't concentrate. One moment he'd been thinking about Samantha, beside himself with worry and wondering if he was up to the task of reuniting her with her conscience; and the next, imagining what The Priory of Chaos was *really* like. For instance: what did Dark Monks look like? Did the kids sit in regular classrooms or were their heads plugged into some kind of brainwashing thingamajig? He'd tried to fathom how the children could have no memory of spending nine months in such a terrible place. *It would have to be some trance to achieve that. Perhaps it's black magic?* He'd thought about the gang and wondered about their time at the Priory. And, with alarming frequency, the most unsettling question of all had gate-crashed his mind: *had The First Evil* really *been the inspiration for the Devil?*

He stood by his window and watched the sun rise over Samantha's house. A bright new day beckoned. But a dark new Samantha slumbered across the street.

Henry woke up the following morning to find Jack sitting at his desk and doodling. "You're back," muttered Henry, yawning. "And, with any luck, doodling me up some breakfast."

"I'm back all right ... just back from the toilet."

"No luck then?"

"No. What if I never make it back there, Henry? Samantha will be lost to us, forever."

Henry stretched and said, "It's just a temporary setback. You'll be back in Darkest Matters in no time."

"The Dark Matter," replied Jack. "I hope you're right, Henry ... for all our sakes."

Following breakfast, during which the boys remained silent, and Mrs. Tracy wondered if Henry's presence was becoming a permanent arrangement, they left for school. "Not waiting for Samantha today?" asked Mrs. Tracy.

"No, Mum ... it's best if we *all* give Sam a wide berth at the moment. Okay?"

Kids. So fickle these days, thought Mrs Tracy.

The first class of the morning was geography with Mrs. Kane. Neither boy was in the mood to discover more about the sand drifts of the southern Sahara. They were seated at the back of her classroom and relieved that Samantha was absent without leave.

After a few minutes, the sound of Mrs. Kane's soft voice began to exert a kind of magic over Jack. He struggled to keep his eyes open. *It's no use. I can't seem to stay awake. How rude of me,* he thought, as he gave in to a peculiar sensation of drifting away.

It was as though the tunnel of light had been delayed, held up in some cosmic tailback. And now here it was, asserting its otherworldly authority in Mrs. Kane's geography class.

Of all places ...

"Ouch!" Jack removed a stick from under his bottom and gazed at the forest about him. "Yes! I've returned to the Perkin's clearing!" He stood up and loosened his school tie. *It must be 90 degrees ...*

There was no sign of his warrior friend. Jack picked up the stick and walked over to the campfire. He prodded the blackened embers and discovered that some of them were still burning. "Perkin must have stayed here overnight."

In the classroom, Mrs. Kane had her back to the class as she wrote some bullet points about sand drifts on the blackboard. Henry leaned across to Jack's desk with the intention of asking him if he thought Samantha was playing hooky with the gang. He did a double take. His friend appeared to be fast asleep. *Has he gone to Darkest Matters?* Henry was overcome with indecision. After all, where should he look? At his friend who may need to be shaken back to consciousness for his protection? Or at Mrs. Kane, who might spot Jack and wake him before he'd learnt all he needed to help Samantha? If someone had been sitting behind Henry, they'd have thought his neck had gone into spasm. To make matters worse, a black butterfly suddenly appeared from nowhere. Henry watched it, open mouthed, as it fluttered down and landed on Jack's desk. *Things could be about to get very weird,* he thought.

Jack had just shooed a butterfly from his shoulder and was wondering what to do next when he heard a growl. He turned to see one of the massive wolf-like creatures, crouched low, its eyes narrowed, preparing to pounce. "Oh God! Please! No!" Jack shielded his face and screamed from the pit of his belly. Much to his surprise, the wolf screamed louder. Jack lowered his arms ... Perkin was turning his black charger around to face him. Sword in hand, he galloped back and, leaning off his saddle, sliced the beast's head clean off. Jack gazed down at the headless creature – and the forest began to spin about him. "Quickly!" said Perkin, "Give me your hand!" Jack reached up and Perkin lifted him onto his horse. "The rest of the pack will not be far," he said, kicking his heels and galloping off up a steep embankment.

Jack clung on for dear life as exhilaration, terror and curiosity pounced on him. Several bumpy and painful minutes later, Jack breathed a sigh of relief as Perkin pulled the horse's reins and it cantered to a stop. The horse panted and stamped his hooves as Perkin climbed off and helped Jack down. "We should be safe here for a while," he said.

"What was that thing?"

"One of the Priory's werewolves. It's been tracking you since you escaped from its pack. Thousands of them roam The Dark Matter, where the twin moons are always full."

"Werewolves ... you've *got* to be kidding?"

"That wretched creature was a man once. Or, should I say, a child ... one of the unfortunate ones, those children that are never returned to the families from which they are snatched."

"I thought it was only our essence that comes here, not our actual bodies."

"If the child's essence is not returned to its body after nine months, the body will dissolve into The Dark Matter and rejoin its essence. Once their body follows their essence here, there is no way back. The Dark Monks keep as many children as they need for slave labour or to patrol the forests as werewolves."

In the classroom, Henry's mind had been working flat-out. He had to prevent Jack being spotted and brought back too soon. He had a pair of shades in his pocket and hatched a plan. "These should buy him some time," he muttered, sliding the shades onto Jack's nose. By no means a perfect solution, it would at least stop Mrs. Kane thinking that Jack had taken a nap. *Not bad ... but he needs to look more ... studious.* Henry picked up a pen and rested it between Jack's fingers. *Voila!*

Mrs. Kane finished writing on the blackboard and turned to face the class. She immediately caught sight of Jack sitting at the back of the room wearing shades, a butterfly poised elegantly on his exercise book. Henry held his breath as she paused momentarily, looking at Jack and then at the butterfly. Thankfully, she seemed to shrug off the rude boy and his insect as though she couldn't quite believe it.

In the forest, Jack was attempting to settle his nerves by stroking Vargo's nose. "He's a great horse," he said.

"He's eight years old ... and a loyal and trusted companion. So, you've returned to The Dark Matter," he smiled.

"Yes. Everything you told me about Samantha ... it came true. She's become a monster. She even made Henry cry. Henry never cries."

"She'll make a lot of people cry before she's through."

"You said there was a way to get the old Samantha back?"

"I'm afraid it's not that simple, Jack."

"What? But you said ..."

"I know what I said. And you can save her ... but first you must save yourself."

"I'm in danger?"

"There's no easy way of telling you this but ... they're coming for you

32

... the Snatcher-Gars. They're going to take you to The Priory of Chaos. Unless you prepare for them, you will end up like Samantha, and the goodness within you will be lost."

The colour drained from Jack's cheeks.

"Fear not," Perkin went on, "there *is* a way to guard yourself against the brainwashing magic of the Snatcher-Gars and, should you succeed, you will be the first child to attend The Priory of Chaos whilst in possession of his own mind."

"Are you saying I *have* to go to that place?"

"The only means of waking Samantha from her hateful trance is located within the walls of the Priory." Perkin took several steps towards an increasingly agitated Vargo. "You have a simple choice, Jack. Either you are taken to the Priory and changed by them in the usual way ... in which case, both you and Samantha will be lost forever. Or, you can prepare for the Snatcher-Gar, become my apprentice and let me guide you on your quest."

"Quest?"

Perkin turned to face him. "Yes, Jack. To save your friend and prevent chaos engulfing Earth." Jack began to pace up and down. It felt as though it would take a monumental effort to hold it together *right now* ... let alone do what Perkin asked. Perkin watched Jack, knowing that the next words to leave his lips could determine humanity's fate.

Jack stopped pacing, folded his arms and said, "How? I mean ... *how* would I prepare for this ... Snatcher-Gar?"

Hiding his relief, Perkin said, "Firstly, you will need to collect tears from the eyes of someone who has been schooled at The Priory of Chaos."

"You mean, Samantha?"

"Her tears will fit the purpose. You will also need a lock of her hair."

"That sounds simple enough. But I have to make her *cry*?"

"Tears of joy or pain; either will do, but you must collect her tears. Just a tiny amount ... and add them to a phial of water with a single strand of her hair."

"And then what ..." Just then, Vargo reared up on his hind legs and released a warning cry.

"It's the pack ... they're closing in, Jack."

In the classroom, Mrs. Kane was finding it increasingly difficult to ignore the rude boy in shades. Not to mention his winged 'pet.' "Jack Tracy!" she finally snapped. Mrs. Kane's angry voice echoed through the woods, and sent Vargo into a blind panic. Perkin leapt into his saddle and attempted to calm him as Jack grabbed the saddle and clung on for dear life.

"Get the tears and the hair! Then return and I'll tell you what must be done with them!"

In the classroom, Mrs. Kane shouted: "Jack Tracy! I'm talking to you! Take off those sunglasses, right now!" Jack seemed to draw an endless breath as his essence returned to his body. He opened his eyes to discover he was still grasping Perkin's saddle! It was sitting on his desk for all the class to see (the butterfly flattened beneath it). Mrs. Kane blinked several times. "What's that on your desk, Jack?" she asked.

Jack removed his shades and gazed at the saddle, lost for words.

"It's a saddle, miss," said Henry, providing some.

"Yes. I can see it's a saddle, Henry. What's it doing on Jack's desk?"

"It's my saddle, miss," said Henry, "I've got a riding lesson after school today … I really love 'em. Horses." The rest of the class gawped at them both.

A little later, the strange looks were accompanied by a number of insulting remarks as the boys struggled onto the crowded bus with the saddle. Henry said, "I don't understand. Why can't we just dump this thing, again?"

"It's Perkin's saddle and he probably wants it back."

Henry shook his head, "If Mrs. T. finds a saddle in your room, she'll think you're seriously weird."

"That's the least of my worries." They sat down at the back of the bus and rested the heavy saddle between them on their knees. "I have GOT to go, Henry," said Jack, thumping the saddle.

"What are you saying? That you can't wait until you get home?"

"… To The Priory of Chaos."

"The place Samantha got her new and definitely not improved personality?"

"Yes. Perkin said that going there is the only way to help her."

"How does he know all this stuff? Who is he, anyway? You're not actually considering *going* to that place are you?"

"You think I want to go? Perkin said I have no choice. That one of those monsters will come for me no matter what I do. Either I go and end up like Samantha, or you can help me prepare for this Snatcher-Gar."

Jack told Henry about the tears and the lock of hair they needed to collect. "Apparently, they'll shield me from the Snatcher-Gar's trance."

"The hair shouldn't be a problem," mused Henry, who relished nothing more than hatching a plan. "I can distract Samantha while you move in with the scissors and give her the snip. She'll probably insult my figure again, so collecting my tears shouldn't be a problem … but Samantha's tears?"

"We'll just have to improvise, Henry," said Jack, his attention suddenly grabbed by something outside. He twisted in his seat and stared through the bus's back window. "Quick, Henry! We have to get off the bus!"

"What? Here? With this thing?" replied Henry, tapping the saddle.

"Yes! All three of us are leaving the bus … at this stop!" They struggled to their feet and made for the exit.

Jack and Henry stood on the edge of the curb. "Please tell me you haven't spotted a horse to go with this saddle," said Henry.

"No …I spotted the gang. They're over there down Turnstall Street."

"I'd have preferred it if you had spotted a horse."

"I saw Samantha, Henry … she's with them."

"You had to be blessed with 20/20 vision, didn't you?"

The boys needed a safe place to observe the gang. They made for a yellow builder's skip that seemed ideally placed. The gang was seated along a low wall next to a housing estate. Henry, who had carried the saddle from the bus stop, plonked it down behind the skip and sat on it, puffing. Jack crouched and peered around the skip. An elderly woman was pushing her shopping trolley along the road in front of the hooded teenagers. "How's it going, granny?" shouted one of the gang. The old woman took no notice. The boy leapt from the wall and approached her. "What's in the trolley then?" he said, shoving his arm inside her shopping basket and retrieving a packet of chocolate biscuits. The woman stood still and muttered to herself as if trying to remember something. The boy ripped open the packet and began tossing biscuits along the wall to the other gang members.

Samantha caught one and took a bite out of it. "Umm … tasty! What else has she got in there?"

The boy turned her tartan shopping trolley upside down, emptying its contents onto the pavement. "It's just a load of old zombie rubbish." Then he peered at the old woman's hair. "What's this rat's nest doing on your head?" he continued, producing a carving knife from his jacket. Oblivious, the old lady fluffed up her silver bouffant and grinned as though she had just received a compliment. The boy grabbed at tufts of her white hair and severed them with his blade while his cohorts whooped and cheered like a pack of demented jackals.

"What's the situation?" asked Henry, shuffling uneasily on the saddle. "They're giving people makeovers. An old lady … they're assaulting her! It's horrible …but, she doesn't seem to care. It's like she doesn't know what's happening."

"Senile?"

"I doubt it, Henry. She's just like all the others. The gang's even bigger now … there must be at least forty of them."

"Great … and the odds just keep getting better and better."

"All we can do is wait and hope Samantha separates from them."

"Even if she does, we don't have any scissors to cut her hair."

"These are desperate times … we'll just have to yank out a few strands."

"The old Samantha would have killed us for less. I don't even want to think about how her evil twin is going to react and, in the unlikely event that she bursts into tears, how are we going to collect them?" Just then, Jack spied a mother with her toddler across the road. The little girl was winding down from a tantrum, her face awash with tears. Her mother bent down and wiped the girl's indignant face with a hanky.

The scene had given Jack an idea. "Doesn't your mother usually put a tissue in your jacket pocket, Henry?"

"Yes, she does. Thanks for bringing that up." Henry reached into his trouser pocket and produced a crumpled tissue.

"Is it clean?" said Jack.

Henry thought for a moment. "I don't believe I've cleared a blockage all day."

"If you have to blow your nose, don't use that tissue. We can use it to soak up Sam's tears."

"Okay," said Henry, sensing the day shaping up to be one of the weirdest of his life.

An hour later, the gang appeared to be going through some kind of parting ritual: this involved hearty whooping, palm slapping and improvised body popping. Jack felt a surge of adrenalin as he watched Samantha separate from the pack and make her way towards the bus stop. The other gang members scurried off and dissolved into the environment like rats.

"She's heading for the bus stop … this is it," said Jack. Samantha crossed the road and walked past them, checking her mobile for messages. "We're on …" said Jack, striding out across the road. Henry lifted the saddle and followed. "Samantha … hey!" said Jack.

Samantha swung round with clenched fists. "What do you two losers want? And what's Fat Boy doing with a saddle? I hope he doesn't expect a ride home?"

Henry was no longer affected by her insults; he knew it wasn't Samantha talking. "I wouldn't ride you if …"

"Why have you started wearing a hoodie, Sam?" interrupted Jack, moving close enough to reach her hair.

"What's it got to do with you?"

"I'm sorry," said Jack.

"I agree with you," she replied, "you are so VERY sorry."

"I mean, I'm sorry for this," he said, reaching inside her hoodie and yanking several hairs from her head.

"Ouch!" she screamed, pushing him away. "Are you crazy?" Jack was relieved to see that, just as he'd hoped, the pain had brought tears to Samantha's darkened eyes. He glanced sideways at Henry who twigged his plan. "Again, I'm sorry," said Jack, treading on her foot. Samantha grabbed her foot and hopped up and down, a torrent of foul language gushing from her mouth. Henry chose this moment to drop the saddle on her other foot.

Samantha yelped and collapsed to the pavement. "Arrrgh!" she cried. "The losers have gone insane!" Jack crouched and dabbed at the tears of pain that were now streaming down her cheeks with Henry's tissue. "Maniac!" she cried. "Get off me! Get! Off! ME!"

"Hold still, Sam ... almost done ..."

"Arrrgh! You're dead Jack Tracy! Dead! Dead! Dead! There's no place on Earth you can hide!" As the boys walked away, Samantha's tirade fading into the background, they experienced a warm feeling that signified one thing: mission accomplished.

When Jack arrived home, he went to the medicine drawer in the kitchen and removed a bottle of headache pills. He emptied the few remaining pills down the sink and placed the tear stained tissue inside the bottle along with the strands of Samantha's hair. Then he filled the bottle with water as Perkin had told him to. Finally, he screwed the cap back on and lifted its contents to eye level. Henry entered the kitchen. "I've hidden Perkin's saddle at the back of your wardrobe. Mrs. T. won't find it unless she goes snooping for weird stuff in your room."

"Thanks, Henry. Now I just have to return to Perkin and find out what we need to do with this concoction."

"Do you want me to stay over again tonight?"

"No. I'll be fine. I'm starting to get the hang of this tunnel travelling thing."

"Okay, if you're sure. I'll head off home before my parents forget what I look like ... which, come to think of it, wouldn't bother them that much. Good luck getting back to The Dark Matter ... and text me later if you need me!"

Jack said goodnight to his mother and closed his bedroom door. A thunder storm grumbled in the distance and raindrops thudded against his window. He lay down with Henry's cricket bat for reassurance. Annoyingly, every time he felt himself making progress with his questions, another thunder clap would distract him and he'd have to start all over again. *This is hell*, he thought. *I'll never get back to Perkin tonight if this storm keeps up.* Then a terrifying thought occurred to him. *What if the*

Snatcher-Gar comes for my essence tonight? He felt for the medicine bottle in his pocket and wondered if its contents would protect him against the creature's trance-inducing magic. *No. Perkin told me I had to return once I'd collected the ingredients ... then he'll tell me what I need to do with them.* He pulled his duvet up to his nose and watched the flashes of lightning periodically illuminate his room. *Maybe I should have asked Henry to stay over after all.*

A colossal thunder clap was accompanied by what sounded like a bird flying into his window. He sat up and stared at his curtains. *It's not the Snatcher-Gar*, he reassured himself, *it's just a bird or something and it might be injured.* He got out of bed and stood beside the curtains. Steeling his courage, he pulled them apart slowly – Jack could see nothing beyond the rain-sodden darkness and his own startled reflection. "I'm just being paranoid," he muttered, as something else SMASHED into his window. Jack jerked backwards and collapsed onto his bed. As he watched, an invisible presence, presumably a finger, began to write something in the condensation on the window. Jack held his breath as the words, SEEK OUT THE WINGED SHAMAN PENDANT AND TAKE THE INGREDIENTS TO IT, were written out before him. The message was signed with the letter P.

Jack jumped back into bed and pulled the duvet over his head. Another loud thunder clap rang out. Jack curled into a foetal position and began muttering, "The Winged Shaman? The Winged Shaman? What's the Winged Shaman? And how can I possibly find it*?" Has the message even come from Perkin? Sure, it's been signed with a 'P' but ... Oh, who else could it be from?*

Flashbacks of how he'd discovered the meaning of Cerca Trova filled his mind. It occurred to him that, should he survive the night, the internet might again come up trumps regarding this Winged Shaman. As usual, his curiosity flexed its muscles and dragged him from his bed. Moments later, he was creeping downstairs to his mother's study. The storm continued to rage as he switched on the computer and waited for it to boot up. It flickered on and illuminated the room in a reassuring glow.

It didn't take Jack long to find the 'Winged Shaman Pendant.' It had a number of websites dedicated to it. It was owned by the British Museum. He clicked onto one of the links towards the top of the list. Moments later, he was staring at a photograph of the solid gold pendant. Just 8cm in height, it resembled a tiny birdman with tail feathers and outstretched wings. He read how the ancient Aztecs believed that the Winged Shaman would enable a person's soul to leave their body and travel to other worlds. The idea of a soul moving between worlds fit snugly with what Perkin had told him. It looked menacing and it occurred to Jack that there was something distinctly gargoylish about its appearance. He shuddered. Jack had always wanted to visit the British Museum. Now it seemed he had a very good reason to go.

EIGHT

The Winged Shaman

When Jack awoke the following morning, the events of the previous night flooded back. He reached across to his bedside table and grabbed a computer printout of the Shaman. He gazed at it for a moment before sending a text message to Henry: 'Mt bus stop 10?'

'Cool,' replied Henry.

Jack shoved the medicine bottle containing Samantha's hair and the tear stained piece of tissue inside his coat pocket. He went downstairs and entered the kitchen. Mrs. Tracy was on the phone when he reached in and took a banana from a bowl on the counter. "I'm going out for a bit," he said.

"Oh, yes? A bit of what?" she asked, placing her hand over the receiver.

"I'm meeting Henry. We're going to a museum … to improve our minds."

"I expect you'll be gone all day then?" she said, smiling.

The boys ran a gauntlet through vandalised streets and hid in a clump of bushes beside the bus stop. Henry gazed through the shrubbery at the graffiti-covered walls and broken car windows. "The gangs have turned the neighbourhood into a no-go zone for uninfected kids."

"Good as. That's why we're going into town … to track this thing down at the British Museum." Jack unfolded the printout of the Winged Shaman and showed it to his friend.

"Great!" said Henry, "a spooky-looking thing that looks like it could make things *worse*."

"Perkin told me to take the ingredients to it … it's all we have."

"As usual, we're *so* impoverished."

Neither boy had been to the British Museum before. They walked along its black perimeter railings, once ornamental and magnificent, now worn with the passage of time, and through a gate into the museum's grounds. Facing them was a quadrangular building wrapped around a large courtyard. Along the front of the British Museum are forty-four

Romanesque columns, proud and intimidating, each the circumference of a mighty oak. They give the impression of entering a gladiatorial arena rather than a place of learning. "Impressive," said Henry.

"Massive," replied Jack.

They climbed the steps that led to the entrance, passed through the glass doors, and found themselves in an expansive lobby awash with tourists. A group of Japanese visitors had congregated close to the entrance. Their female tour guide bolted off carrying an umbrella raised above her head. Her eager party followed like ducklings in pursuit of their mother. The boys glanced at each other and fell into their slip-stream. They followed them across the stone lobby and into the museum's central courtyard area.

Jack and Henry gazed up into the glass dome that covered this vast enclosure. "Wow!" said Henry. "This place looks like something out of a science fiction movie. It's like we've arrived at a moon station."

"I know. It's impressive." Jack glanced to his right and spotted a circular information centre. They made their way towards it. Jack took the printout of the Winged Shaman from his pocket and approached a woman behind the counter. "Excuse me," he said. "Do you know where I can find this?" He shoved the picture of the Shaman under her nose.

"Oh, yes," she replied, "it's in Gallery 24 ... just the other side of this central area." The helpful woman even pointed in the right direction.

On their way, they passed a souvenir shop and Henry spotted some pyramid shaped chocolates. They seemed to exert a magnetic pull on him. "No, Henry!" said Jack. "Let's do what we came to do ... there'll be plenty of time for touristy treats later."

"You think? And what if what we came to do ends up being the last thing we *ever* do?"

They entered Gallery 24 – and stopped just inside the entrance. "It's *massive* in here ... must be the size of a football pitch," muttered Henry. Gallery 24 was chock-a-block with glass display cases containing South American artefacts. The first things to capture the boys' attention, however, were two papier-mâché models dangling from the ceiling. One was a red demon, the size of a teenager, sitting on a horse and holding a sword above its head. The other was a giant locust being ridden bare-backed by a skeleton.

As Jack gazed up at the hanging objects, Henry tugged on his sleeve, causing him to jump. "WHAT?" Jack asked.

"This room is huge, Jack. How are we supposed to find that small shaman thingy?"

"... You hear that?" Jack muttered.

"Course. I'm not deaf. Tourists are noisy people."

"No ... that *whispering*," said Jack, stepping into the room.

"Where are you going?" asked Henry. "And *no* ... I don't hear whispering." Jack didn't reply. He moved deeper into the room as though pulled by an invisible thread. "Speak to me," said Henry. "You're really wigging me out again." Jack walked on, paying no attention to Henry or to the ancient artefacts about him. He continued to the far-right hand side of the room and to a wall-mounted display case. The display was entitled 'Journeying to other worlds and dimensions.' Jack scanned the various golden objects that hung from hooks at the rear of the cabinet ... then he raised his hand, and pointed to the artefact they'd come to find.

"Look ... there it is, Henry ...the Winged Shaman ..."

"How did you know where it was? Have you been here before?"

"You know I haven't. It was like ... like it was calling to me."

"You're hearing voices?"

"No ... not exactly. I can't explain it." Jack placed his nose up against the glass. "In a weird way ... it's kind of beautiful," he said, as the condensation from his breath clouded his view.

"To be honest, it just gives me the willies," replied Henry, gazing at the palm sized object over Jack's shoulder. "Has it stopped whispering to you?"

Jack listened for a moment. "... *Think* so," he said, scrutinising the small golden object. The Shaman had a square head and penetrating eyes that stared in opposite directions. On either side of its head were large jutting circles with a spiralling effect in them. The spirals reminded Jack of the tunnel of light he'd travelled down ... *Right before those questions flew at me.* He dispelled this notion and remembered what they had come to do. "... No time like the present," he muttered, retrieving the medicine bottle from his pocket.

Henry looked around. "If you're sure about this ...the coast is clear." Jack held the bottle directly in the gaze of the Shaman. Several seconds passed but nothing happened.

Jack looked at the contents of the bottle. The tear stained tissue and the strands of Samantha's hair (which floated in the tap water) looked just the same.

"Is that it? Are we done?" asked Henry.

"I don't think anything happened, Henry. Surely *something* should happen. I'll try unscrewing the lid." Jack removed the cap from the bottle and once again held it in eye-shot of the golden shaman. Instantly, the spirals on either side of its head began to turn, churning out a faint red mist. Jack felt a sudden chill. "Are you seeing what I'm seeing?" Henry opened his mouth but made no sound. The mist poured from the spirals and seeped through the glass display case and disappeared inside the medicine bottle. *It looks like a genie returning to a bottle*, thought Henry. Jack grasped the bottle in his shaking hand and wondered how much mist could fit into such a tiny space. This unusual sight had caught the attention of the security guard on the other side of the gallery. He returned the diary he'd been scribbling in to his breast pocket and made his way over.

As soon as the last traces of mist had vanished inside the bottle, Jack quickly screwed the lid back on. The liquid was now glowing red and the previous contents had vanished. "I'm impressed," said Henry, "and we haven't been sucked into hell-fire, which is a bonus." A clanking sound suddenly rang out from the other end of the gallery. They gazed up at the red demon on its horse – the 'exhibit' was now swiping at the chain that fastened it to the ceiling with its sword!

Jack gulped so hard he practically swallowed his Adam's apple. "Henry, I don't think it's supposed to be doing that …" Henry glanced in the direction of the approaching guard. The guard's startled reaction confirmed Jack's hypothesis. A final blow severed the chain and the horned demon bobbed in mid-air high above the gallery. The demon pulled back on its reins and the horse reared up on its hind legs and produced a thunderous neigh – display cases shattered, and thousands of glass shards bounced across the gallery's polished floor. Tourists gasped and ducked for cover. The demon swung about, pointed the tip of its sword at Jack and *flew* at him. Henry grabbed Jack and bundled him to the ground. The demon careered over their heads and smashed into the wall, tumbling from its mount. The boys scrambled to their feet and made off towards the nearest exit. Meanwhile, the demon jumped on its horse and took to the air. It flew low and swiped at the crouching, panic-stricken tourists. Jack and Henry headed out of Gallery 24 and up a marble staircase. Three huge bells, silent for centuries, sat beside the staircase. The bronze bells thundered to life – bonging, chiming and tolling as though marking the end of time. Jack and Henry winced and clasped their hands to their ears as they scurried up the stairs. They ran into the next room and came to a halt at a circular viewing gallery in the floor. This strange hole, about the size of a large paddling pool, revealed people milling about on the floor below. "It's too far to jump down, Henry!" They turned to their right and headed off down another long gallery.

The demon gave chase.

The boys bobbed and weaved in and out of the display cases in a desperate attempt to avoid the demon's slashing blade. The creature flew in a straight line and simply ploughed through anything in its path. Some of the display cases were smashed, others completely upturned by the creature as it swiped, lunged and stabbed at the fleeing boys. At the far end of the gallery, three life-sized Buddhas sat in a row along a wall. The solid jade objects began chuckling, their fat bellies wobbling around like pink jellies. The boys froze momentarily and glanced at each other. This strange sight was the least of their worries – the demon was closing in on them, fast. A security guard, acting on instinct, hurled his stool at the flying beast. Much to his surprise, he scored a direct hit; horse and devilish rider came crashing to the ground. Jack gave the wide-eyed security guard the thumbs up before bolting down a narrow-carpeted corridor with Henry in tow. They ran along it and came to a dead end. "There's no way out!" said Henry, struggling for breath. A sign on the only exit read, 'Gallery closed for refurbishment.' The demon picked up its sword and scampered down the corridor towards them, shrieking and waving the weapon above its head. Jack and Henry huddled together with clenched fists.

"Oh God, Henry … I'm so sorry!" Just then, the locked door opened and a workman in a yellow hard hat appeared. The boys seized the opportunity and bolted through the door.

The workman heard the demon's terrifying cries and quickly closed the door behind them. "What the going on!?" he asked.

"The exhibits … they're revolting," replied Henry, "and, whatever you do, don't open that door!"

"I 'adn't planned to mate!" They made off down a flight of stairs. At the bottom of the stairwell was a fire door. They barged through it and ran out of the museum into the sunshine.

NINE

Preparation

A twig snapped close by. Perkin's hand moved towards the hilt of his sword lying beside him on the river bank. Squinting sideways into the dawn light, he saw a rabbit scamper into the bushes. He took hold of a length of twine and pulled a small wooden cage from the water. Several tiny fish flapped about inside. Perkin raised an eyebrow and lowered the cage back into the water.

Several nights had passed since Jack's last visit and Perkin feared for him. If Jack had found and evoked the magic of the Winged Shaman, the consequences may have proven too great an obstacle for the boy. Perkin gazed out over the water and sighed. The First Evil's latest campaign to push humanity over the edge into anarchy could only be thwarted by someone able to breach the Priory's walls. This boy, the first to somehow find his own way into The Dark Matter, may be the only hope of preventing mankind's final descent into wickedness. It therefore came as a great relief when he heard a familiar voice behind him. "There you are!" said Jack. "This thing weighs a ton." Perkin turned to see Jack heaving the heavy saddle towards him. Perkin grabbed the saddle and placed it on the ground. "It's good to see you," he said, trying not to sound too surprised. "You received my message?"

"You mean the window writing? Yes, I did ... spooky but effective."

"And?"

"And I found the Winged Shaman," announced Jack, proudly. "It's on display at the British Museum. I took the ingredients to it as your message told me."

Perkin smiled and shook his head as though he'd been a fool to doubt this boy's abilities. Jack retrieved the medicine bottle from his pocket and handed it to Perkin. "There was this demon thing on a horse, "Jack went on, "it did its best to slice-and-dice Henry and me, but we managed to get away somehow."

"You awakened a protection spell on the Shaman, one designed to prevent its secrets being revealed. You have done well," he said, placing his hand on Jack's shoulder. Jack's face lit up with pride. Perkin removed the lid of the medicine bottle. He sniffed its contents and handed it straight back to Jack. "Drink it now," he said.

Jack's expression suggested that he wasn't in the least bit thirsty.

"You must trust me, Jack. Drink it." Jack put the container to his lips … and drank. "What a relief …" he said as he emptied the last droplets into his mouth, "it doesn't taste of anything."

"You are protected now. But this protection is only effective against the magic of the Snatcher-Gar that is sent for you. That mind enchantment is intended to last the entire nine months of your stay at the Priory but, be warned, should they suspect that someone is not fully within their control, they will use the enchantment again. If this happens, you will be lost to them. Sorry. I have no wish to alarm you my young friend." Jack walked slowly to the edge of the river bank. He sat down and hugged his knees tightly to his chest. Perkin stood beside him. "You are capable of achieving far more than you imagine. Although, when the Snatcher-Gar comes it will be the truest test of your courage thus far. No human child has ever undertaken the journey to The Priory of Chaos in their natural state. You must not display any fear in the claws of the beast; if you do, it will know you still possess your mind."

"So, screaming for help is out of the question then?"

"It will be the last cry for help you make."

"I told you!" said Jack, picking up a stone and hurling it into the water. "I'm not a hero! I can't help freaking out sometimes. I'm not like you. I'm not a warrior."

"You don't think warriors know fear? All living things are programmed to fear. It's as important to our survival as the water we drink or the air we breathe. It is how we react to our fear that determines whether we behave as heroes or not."

Jack shook his head and skimmed a stone across the top of the water.

Perkin sighed. "It's not as difficult as you might imagine … turning fear to your advantage. Come with me and I will show you."

As they walked, Jack asked, "Who are you really?"

"A friend … for now, that is all you need know."

"Are you human? You look human."

Perkin smiled. "My story is not without interest, going back as it does into the mists of time. I have good reason to despise The Priory of Chaos … but this is not the time for my story. We must focus on your quest."

"Are you sure you've got the right person? How can I be quest material?"

"You've already proven yourself capable of overcoming great challenges."

"I've just been incredibly lucky so far. If that workman hadn't opened

46

the door at the museum when he did …"

"It was not luck but intuition that dictated your route through the museum. It was intuition that led you to that door moments before it was opened. You have the gift, Jack … the gift of intuition. You must learn to trust it."

Jack shrugged. "Apart from helping Samantha, I don't know what else is expected of me."

"You care for her deeply … she's lucky to have such a friend."

"I'm the lucky one … she's a far better person than me. She believes in things … and she fights for them."

"You believe in something too, Jack.'

"Really? And what's that?"

"Doing what is right for the greater good. And as for your quest, I can only repeat that your world now faces its greatest threat since the wars of the early 20th century. As I said, at that time it was German children who were the main targets of the Priory's harvest."

"Are you saying that The Priory of Chaos was responsible for the Second World War?"

"Oh, yes. Wherever there is conflict and chaos, the Priory's graduates will have played a central role."

Jack remained silent for the remainder of their walk. As did Perkin, who thought it best to allow his young ward time to absorb the enormity of his situation.

They reached the gap between the two cliffs where Jack had stumbled and almost fallen to his death. "Again, I ask you to trust me. I will not allow any harm to come to you. I need you to feel *actual* fear if I'm to help you to understand it."

Actual fear … I don't like the sound of actual fear, thought Jack. Perkin grabbed him and forced him towards the edge of the chasm. He held onto Jack's belt and lowered him so that his back was horizontal with the edge.

Jack was now looking straight down into the ravine hundreds of metres below. "Arrrh! What are you doing!?"

"I will try not to drop you. In the meantime, tell me how you feel?"

"Terrified! How do you think I feel!?"

"Where do you feel the terror?"

"Please Perkin, stop! Just let me up!"

"Where is the fear, Jack? In what part of your body?"

"Every part!"

"Please try to be more specific."

"… In my stomach! … In my belly! Please, I can't breathe."

"Do you feel it anywhere else?"

"… In my arms and legs … it's making me shake. Perkin, I'm going to fall!" he cried, as some stones came away from the edge and tumbled into the abyss.

"At this moment, your fear is chasing you, Jack. You are its victim. It wants to turn you into a cowering wreck."

"It's doing a great job! I have no choice … I can't help how I feel!"

"You do have a choice. You must stop running and fight back."

"But I don't know how!"

"Are you getting angry, Jack?"

"Yes!" he said, grabbing at Perkin's arms behind him.

"Who are you angry with?"

"You! I'm angry with you."

"Then your anger is wasted. I'm not your enemy. The fear that is coursing through your body is your enemy. I want you to direct your anger at it. Have you ever seen a bull before it's about to charge?"

"Yes, I suppose so, but …!"

"It huffs. It grunts. It uses the muscles in its belly to crush and then expel its fear. The more it huffs and grunts from deep within its abdomen, the more determined, angry and powerful it feels. I want you to do the same. Blow the fear from your belly in short sharp bursts, Jack. Imagine you are the bull, preparing to charge and tear your opponent limb from limb." Jack gritted his teeth, and did as he was told. At first, he merely felt as absurd as he did petrified. Then, as he continued to expel the air powerfully, from deep within his abdomen, he began to generate a sense of relief. It was as if the butterflies he felt swarming in his belly were being forced out, expelled with each huff and snarl – and one thing was clear, as the butterflies diminished, so did his fear. "That's it, Jack! Replace your fear with determination, the determination you are now creating!"

"Ok. I get it! I understand what you're saying …"

Perkin pulled Jack up and hugged him close. "Forgive me my young friend, but it was a useful lesson."

The adrenalin now coursing through Jack's veins (the adrenalin he had created) now gave him the courage to ask the question he'd been putting off. "When?" he said, "when will the Snatcher-Gar come for me?"

"It will be soon. There will be thunder and lightning when the time is upon you. The storms are created whenever the Snatcher-Gars pass from The Dark Matter into Earth's domain. A few nights ago, when I wrote that message for you, it was only possible because of the storms *they* were creating. That night, many children were harvested and taken to The Priory. We must be thankful you were not among them."

"Once I'm at the Priory, I will still be able to find you in the usual way

… using the tunnel of light?"

"As long as I have breath, you will be able to find me. And I will guide you."

TEN

The Snatcher-Gar cometh

Henry snuck downstairs and headed for the kitchen. His objective was a pre-dinner snack. A few minutes before, his mother had put the Sunday roast in the oven and left the vegetables boiling on the stove. She had just returned to the living room across the hall to watch the evening news with her husband. Henry slipped into the kitchen and raided the cupboards and drawers as quietly as he could. He retrieved a loaf of bread, a jar of peanut butter, a knife and a plate. As he tiptoed back past the living room, his father raised his voice, causing Henry to freeze like a rabbit caught in headlights. "What is it with the weather these days?" his father groaned. "Flash-floods and tornadoes in London? Whatever next? We never used to get storms like this. I blame it on global warming."

"I expect you're right," replied Henry's mother. "And there's another thunderstorm on the way again tonight. A big one, apparently." The phone rang. It startled Henry to his senses and he hurried upstairs to his bedroom carrying his booty.

"It's for you, Henry! It's Jack," shouted his mother from downstairs.

Henry picked up the phone beside his bed. "Jack? What happened? Is everything okay?"

"That depends upon how you define okay. I've spoken to Perkin."

"Oh, great. What certain death experience has the heroic one got planned for us now?" said Henry, holding the receiver under his chin and applying peanut butter to a slice of bread. Henry liked to eat when he was nervous (and when he wasn't).

"He told me to drink the potion," said Jack, darkly.

"He did *what*? Told you to drink the *poison*?"

"No. The potion."

"And did you?"

"Yes."

"What did it taste like?"

"I couldn't taste *anything*."

"Maybe you missed your mouth …" mumbled Henry.

"The Snatcher-Gar could come for me at any time. If something goes

50

wrong ..."

"We're the good guys? What could possibly go wrong?"

"Henry, if I end up as a gang member, you know it won't be *me*, don't you?"

"Of course ... look, who knows, it may be just a matter of time before a Snatcher-Gar comes for me. So, look on the bright side, we can give old ladies makeovers together."

"Not funny, Henry."

"I know. This is definitely the point in the conversation when someone should say, 'Failure is NOT an option.'"

"Henry, the Snatcher-Gar come during lightning storms ... so be careful."

"Superb! ... Have you heard the latest weather report?"

"No."

"We're in for a major storm later. My father was just saying that ..."

"I'll be going to The Priory of Chaos tonight. I just know it. When you wake up in the morning, you'll have been asleep for a few hours. When I wake up, I'll have spent *nine months in that place*. Perkin said that If I'm discovered ... if they realise I'm faking, I'll wake up tomorrow without a conscience ... a monster."

"Let's just believe it's going to work out ... we have to do that, Jack ... if only for Samantha's sake."

"Who'd have thought it? Henry Roscoe giving Jack Tracy a pep-talk."

"And there's more where that came from. You don't think I've peaked too soon ... you know, in the pep-talk department?"

There was a long pause.

"Jack? Are you still there?"

"... I'm here."

"I wish you wouldn't do that! Look, I'll be over first thing in the morning. And I know ... I just *know* that you'll still be you. You'll be back from Chaos Central with some new mojo that will snap Samantha out of her evil trance ... you'd never let Sam down."

"No, not intentionally, but ..."

"You've always wondered what it must be like to face some heroic challenge ... like those old guys did in the war. Well, this is your chance to find out." Henry tore off a chunk of bread with his teeth and chewed as he went on. "Perkin believes in you. And I do, too. You're like a snappy terrier that clasps something in its jaws and refuses to let go ... only, without the snappy part."

"Thanks? I don't think Perkin's too concerned about Samantha ... I know he's one of the good guys ... but ... it's like he's using her as bait."

"Of *course* he's using her as bait. It's the old 'your friend's in great

51

peril and you're her last hope' ploy. And oh! By the way, if you could also prevent the coming apocalypse, I'd be soooo grateful."

"I'm going to write mum a letter now ... you know, just in case ... I'll leave it in the bottom right hand drawer of my desk. If the worst happens, make sure she gets it. Try and make her understand, Henry ..."

"Good luck, Jack. I know I'll be seeing *you* in the morning. We're going on that school trip, tomorrow. Remember?"

"I'd completely forgotten about that."

"Your mum hasn't. She mentioned it the other day."

"I'd better write that letter to her."

"Keep the faith, Jack." The boys hung up and Jack sat down at his desk. He wrote the following:

Dear Mum,
If Henry has told you about this letter it means the worst has happened. I wanted to tell you about the stuff that's been going on but you wouldn't have believed me. You'd just have taken me to see Dr. Shingles. The thing is, I've been taken to a place against my will and brainwashed into being an evil person. I know it sounds like a very unoriginal excuse, but it's the truth. I'm sorry for anything psychotic I say or do. Please believe me when I say it's not me. Not the real me. I love you, mum. Your son, Jack

Jack lay on his bed and listened for any sign of the storm. *Stop fidgeting,* he told himself, *it has to think you're asleep!* Jack rolled onto his back and opened his eyes. *Didn't I try and dupe Santa once? That's right! I fooled no one and my presents were dumped on the landing. If Santa* Claws *realises I'm faking tonight, I'm gonna end up another unsolved crime, a half-eaten stat!* He wanted to leap out of bed and run. He also knew that the fate of humanity demanded that he lay still ... and let the thing take him to The Priory of Chaos.

Jack wondered if the weather forecasters had got it wrong. *Again.* Then he heard something. It was a long way off and had he been clearing his throat or shifting in his bed he'd have missed it. He closed his eyes ... listened ... *there it is again ... a storm.* He swallowed hard and remembered the old trick that his mother had taught him. After the flash of lightning, start counting slowly up from one. The final number you reach when you hear the thunder is the number of miles away the storm is. He saw another flash of lightning and began to count. He got as far as three ...

Three miles away, a bolt of lightning blazed across the sky, out of which a creature invisible to all but babies and animals soared into the night. This hybrid of mammoth bat and goblin had wings the size of a light aircraft's – and talons capable of snatching up a rhinoceros, let alone the boy it had been sent for. The Snatcher-Gar extended its colossal wings and flapped them several times, apparently enjoying a good stretch – tilted its cigar-like nose skyward and sniffed for the scent of goodness and humanity. It picked up a smell so unlike its own that its dark leathery face wrinkled in disgust – even so, it drew its wings close and dropped towards the ground like a guided missile in pursuit of its prey.

Jack's counting had led him to the terrifying conclusion that the storm must now be overhead. He stared up at his ceiling and wondered if the creature was out there somewhere. It was. Right above his house; its steady wing-beats batting away the rain. The Snatcher-Gar's eyes produced a sepia beam which passed through the roof and met with Jack's expectant gaze. Jack's ceiling appeared to dissolve to reveal the monster hovering above the house. Heart pounding, temples throbbing, Jack struggled not to betray his fear. The sepia beam vanished, and the Snatcher-Gar now believed that Jack had fallen victim to its trance. The creature was wrong. Its talons phased through the roof and hung from Jack's ceiling like a pair of macabre chandeliers. *I'm not going to lose it, I'm not!* He thought as he quietly forced air from a stomach tied in knots. *I feel sick. What if I throw up? Keep still, Jack ... just keep still. Play dead, play dead, play dead!*

Mercifully, Jack's eyes were shut tight when the creature opened its claws and looked poised to tear him to shreds. The claws reached inside Jack and salvaged the essence from his flesh like an oyster from its shell. Jack felt himself being lifted not only from his bed, but from his body as well. There were now two Jacks: the one staring lifelessly from his bed, and the one being carried off into the night sky.

ELEVEN

Journey to The Priory of Chaos

The Snatcher-Gar soared into the furious clouds. It held Jack tightly in his grip, something Jack found oddly reassuring. The creature had been known to drop children for sport. Their distraught parents finding a soulless, lifeless body the following morning. Jack was blissfully unaware of this and thinking how well he was doing when a bolt of lightning ripped through the atmosphere close by. The creature lunged at the streak of crackling silver, "What the …!" Jack whispered …*and I was doing so well!*

Jack opened his eyes to discover that the rain had stopped. He recognised the combination of humidity and pine only too well: they had arrived in The Dark Matter. He looked down and the sight took his breath away. In the distance, surrounded by thick forest on all sides, lay a fortress unlike anything he'd imagined. The fortress was encircled by three moats: each filled with molten lava that belched fire high into the air. Beyond the moats lay several tiers of battlements, out of which rose the citadel of The Priory of Chaos. The Snatcher-Gar was flying a kilometre from the ground, but the spire atop this great tower was higher still. Jack's eyes followed the glistening spire downwards, his gaze falling upon what appeared to be a cathedral. Even from this distance, Jack could tell it was the biggest building he'd ever seen. "A cathedral in the clouds …" he murmured.

At first, the sky around the citadel appeared to be teeming with bats. It soon became clear that these were not bats – but Snatcher-Gars transporting children to the Priory below. The creatures flew in a circular formation around the tower, each waiting in turn to land on what seemed an ever-descending, invisible conveyor belt. Jack was awestruck by this strangely ordered sight. After all, he was looking down upon the answer to 'those' questions. *Wow*! He thought, as a wave of euphoria crept over him. *I've found it … the cause of man's wickedness and cruelty. Me! Jack Tracy … and, if Perkin is right, I'm the first kid to see this place with his mind intact.* Jack's euphoria quickly melted away. This was where bullies and fiends had been created for millennia. Stripped of compassion and programmed for cruelty. He began to despise the sight before him. *How dare they do these things to innocent children!* He struggled to get more comfortable in the claws of the *thing* that had kidnapped him. It raised his talons and brought Jack up to eye level. He gazed down his long black nose at him and said, "Are thee struggling? Trying to free thyself, perhaps? Should I drop thee? The crows adore raw human flesh ... as do I. Does thee desire to be supped upon?"

Jack felt the creature loosen his grip. "No! I was just trying to get a better view of ... of your magnificent home," said Jack, thinking that this was the ugliest 'face' he had ever seen. The Snatcher-Gar screwed its features into what Jack thought may be a puzzled expression. *Oh, no ... I think I've given myself away already!*

"I see you've managed to get your human here in one piece, Gob! It makes a change," said another Snatcher-Gar, flying up alongside him.

"How dare thee utter such foul slanders, Phlem! My record is without flaw in the delivery tables."

"You molested the tables when the Keeper of Records was absent at the Harvest of Souls!"

"I'm starving," replied Gob, changing the subject. "And the stench of goodness in this boy sickens me."

"I'd happily swap it with mine – mine weighs a ton," replied Phlem, alluding to the boy in his claws. Jack struggled to get a look at the other boy. Annoyingly, the boy's back was turned to him. Then, as if the other boy had sensed Jack's curiosity, he turned and looked directly at him.

Henry!

NO! It can't be! Why didn't Perkin warn me? I would have shared the potion! Jack looked across at his friend and mouthed: "Henry?" Henry's eyes were different somehow, narrower and darker, and they gazed right through him. Jack swallowed hard. He felt more alone than ever.

Gob flew on ahead and joined the landing formation around the tower. Phlem and Henry fell in behind them.

As they descended towards the base of the citadel, Jack kept looking back, desperate to keep Henry in view. He now had something else to occupy his mind, something else to worry about besides his own skin – he had Henry and, whatever happened next, he was determined not to let him out of his sight.

Once they'd descended low enough, Jack could make out vast gothic arches in each of the citadel's four sides. He watched children being left outside these arches in groups of three. He felt his heart thump as he realised that, if he were the third child to be left in a group, he would be separated from Henry, possibly for good. "Please let me be number one or two," he whispered. "One or two. One or two," he repeated to himself. *Yes!* The Snatcher-Gar in front descended low over the heads of three newly deposited children and continued on to the next entrance. Jack looked down and watched these kids, two girls and a boy, walk purposely into the citadel. Now it was Jack's turn. The child in front, a girl of about 10, was lowered onto the dark cobbled stone.

Gob raised Jack up to his face and said: "Time to have that stench of humanity removed!" He deposited Jack on the ground beside her and flapped-off. Jack turned to see Henry lowered down beside him. Following a fleeting hesitation, Henry and the girl walked forward into the citadel of The Priory of Chaos and, against his every instinct, Jack did the same.

If the central area of the British Museum had made Jack feel small, the vision upon entering the citadel made him feel minute. The base of the citadel alone was large enough to contain a city. This was no city however, but a seething mass of staircases and landings that climbed, jutted and branched-off into the abyss above. Jack could see tiny creatures moving about on stairs and ramparts high above. The sight reminded him of the ant farm he'd once had. *Are they all children?* he thought, wishing he had a pair of binoculars.

At ground level, children were milling about in groups of three. Troublingly for Jack, there wasn't even a whiff of confusion about these kids. They all knew precisely where they were going. Jack was the only one who felt like curling into a ball of bewilderment. He slowed down a little, allowing Henry and the girl to walk half a step in front.

They approached one of the staircases which led up into the abyss and Jack felt giddy at the prospect of the climb before them. *I'll be exhausted within 2 minutes*, he thought. *And what about Henry?* Much to Jack's relief, Henry and the girl didn't go up the stairs but headed for a room beneath them.

All three entered the octagonal-shaped room. At its centre sat a monk, surrounded by hundreds of black and red candles. The monk wore a hood pulled low over his face, concealing his features in folds of dark cloth. *A Dark Monk?* thought Jack, trying to contain a shudder.

Henry approached him first. The monk raised an arm and, from the recesses of his baggy sleeve, produced a grey hand with freakishly long fingers. He placed his palm on Henry's head and fanned out his fingers – they engulfed Henry's head like a ravenous alien gobbling up its prey. Henry remained silent. He didn't even flinch. The Dark Monk withdrew his hand from Henry's head, and directed the newly 'charmed' pupil away with a flick of his wrist. Henry moved off and he did the same to the girl.

Now it was Jack's turn. His apprehension reminded him of his first trip to the dentist. Now, as then, his every impulse was to turn and run. He stood agonisingly still and couldn't help gazing into the inky depths of the hood: partly hoping, mostly dreading a glimpse of the face within. He

56

could see nothing but folds of cloth and shadow. He bowed his head, closed his eyes. Jack braced himself for pain but felt only a numbed probing. He opened his eyes to discover the monk gesturing impatiently for him to follow the others.

At the bottom of the staircase, Henry lifted his foot as if to embark on an impossible climb. He took his first step and rose several centimetres into the air, hovering briefly, before gliding slowly up the staircase. The girl did the same. *What if I can't do that?* thought Jack. *Maybe you have to be under the Snatcher-Gars' enchantment!* Jack paused at the foot of the staircase, captivated by the graceful ascent of his companions. Steeling himself, he lifted his right foot (which suddenly felt as if it were made of lead) and attempted to place it upon the first stair. *That's weird.* It felt as though he were stepping onto a cushion of rushing air. The next moment, he felt himself being carried up the staircase behind Henry and the girl. Balance wasn't even an issue – floating up these stairs felt like the most natural thing in the world. *It isnt!* thought Jack.

Up they floated along a seemingly endless trail of stairs and small landings. The higher they went, the more children they encountered and, unlike the new arrivals, these kids were nattering to one another. They were all dressed in identical dark green robes and carrying red leather pouches stuffed with books and papers. As they glided past, these kids ignored the new arrivals. Jack craned his head in an attempt to eavesdrop on them. "I don't agree," said a girl of about nine, "I think we should excel in inflicting mental torment … its effects last longer than mere physical cuts and …" She moved beyond ear shot. Jack looked at the back of Henry's head and shuddered at the thought of the space between his ears being programmed with such ideas. Two more boys approached, they were talking excitedly about something called 'The Broken Spirit Principle'. "I'm really looking forward to trying it out. I can't think of anything better than breaking someone's spirit," enthused one of the boys as they passed by.

They arrived at the main landing and their feet returned to the ground. Before them was a dark wooden door. Henry and the girl stood motionless before it. Jack's eyes settled on a tiny discoloration close to the door's handle. Something had been scratched into it. He leaned forwards and read: 'A.D. 1387-- NEVER THE SAME' had been carved in tiny letters. The letters receded as the door began to creak open …

TWELVE

Welcome to dread's classroom

The door opened, and the three freshmen walked through it. Jack had expected to come face-to-face with something hideous. He was therefore surprised by the sight of a small, undernourished boy of about 10. The boy's grey tweed jacket and shorts reminded Jack of the war urchins he'd seen in documentaries; the ones who had been evacuated from London during the blitz. His clothes were positively rag-like, crude stitching and lopsided patches were all that prevented them tumbling off his body. The boy remained silent as he backed into the room and beckoned them to follow with a single, scrawny finger.

It looked like a classroom in an ancient public school. It was oblong with rich oak panelling throughout. Portraits of eerie hooded characters adorned the four walls. In the centre of the room were eighteen desks set out in rows of three. The classroom had six doors leading from it, three down each side. At the far end, in front of the desks, loomed a pulpit surrounded by burning candles. Above the pulpit hung an enormous tapestry depicting a rotting apple with a serpent's head and tail protruding from it. The motto beneath it read: 'To corrupt is to ascend.'

They approached the first door on the left hand side. Outside of it sat another wretched child: a girl dressed in threadbare clothing of Elizabethan appearance. The ruff about her neck was frayed and blackened, and her face pale and gaunt. Jack felt like a voyeur intruding on a vision of tragedy. He looked around and spied a child sitting outside each of the six rooms that led from the classroom. Each child was dressed in a decaying garment from an era long since passed. It occurred to Jack that they might have been abducted from a fancy dress party. In his heart, he knew they had not. They followed their wretched guide through the last doorway on the left.

Their dorm was a semi-circular room with a single diagonal slit cut into the thick stone wall. It looked like the room had once been part of an outdoor turret, the slit being just large enough to shoot arrows through. It was certainly useless as a means of escape; particularly when you considered its dizzying distance from the ground. The walls and ceiling consisted of ancient stone slabs: grey and impenetrable. A meagre light

58

emanated from a wrought iron chandelier, containing a dozen or so withered candles.

There were three beds with basic wooden frames; a thin mattress with a black sheet covered each. On top of the sheet lay a dark green robe and a pair of sandals. The sandals reminded Jack of something a Roman scholar might have worn. Three ornate roll-top desks stood out as being particularly extravagant given the austere setting. *It looks as though a dungeon's been crossed with a university dormitory*, thought Jack, as a feeling of dread at the prospect of spending nine months in these surroundings pounced. His legs grew weak and he felt suddenly dizzy: *I have to hold it together* ... Jack looked at Henry for reassurance. But it was no longer Henry. Just a human shell that held Henry captive somewhere within. *I must get through this! For Henry's sake. For Samantha's. For all these kids.*

'Blitz Boy' took Henry by his arm and led him to one of the beds. He returned for the girl and then for Jack. Once all three were seated on their allocated bunks, he left the room and returned to his seat outside the door.

Jack was relieved to take the weight off his hollow legs. He was beginning to feel better. Not great obviously. But sort of numb. *I can cope with numb* ...

Henry and the girl sat staring into space. Jack tried to do the same but found himself staring at Henry. He wanted to get up and give his friend a good shake. The expression 'the lights are on but nobody's home' seemed despairingly appropriate. The same was true of the little girl. Beneath the blonde bob, her brown eyes were vacant and betrayed nothing of the person her parents had kissed goodnight a short while before. Jack leant back on his bed. It felt hard and inflexible. Even so, he yearned to lie down and close his eyes. Not just because he was exhausted but because he wanted to speak with Perkin about Henry. He remembered he was there to seek a cure for Samantha and experienced a fleeting optimism. After all, what would work for Samantha would surely work for Henry ... *right?* Jack heard footsteps on the stone floor of the central room. He immediately sat up straight and did his best to look as brain-dead as the others. Curiosity getting the better of him, he craned his head slightly in order to see over the tops of the desks in the classroom. He caught a glimpse of three children being led by their own tragic 'child host' into a room on the other side.

Within an hour, all six rooms contained their quota of three students apiece, eighteen in all. Henry and the girl stood up and began changing into the robe provided for them. Jack did the same. The robe was made from a curious fabric and felt alien to the touch ... as though tree bark had been interwoven with silk. They had been given a belt with a large bronze buckle. The buckle depicted the same apple and serpent motif that hung above the pulpit. Jack watched closely as Henry fastened the buckle and secured the belt around his waist. The garment was a perfect fit for him, as was the girl's. Jack secured his own belt as best he could. The result wasn't quite as neat as Henry's but it would have to do. A brass bell which hung above the door suddenly rang out and startled Jack. The others betrayed no sign of emotion. It was a timely reminder of just how precarious Jack's situation was. If he wasn't able to hold it together, he was doomed. After a few moments the bell stopped ringing. Henry and the girl stooped to put on their sandals. Jack did the same. Then they made their way out into the classroom and headed for their desks. Jack had no idea which desk was meant for him and held back until the others were seated. He wondered if Blitz Boy suspected anything and glanced back: Blitz Boy was staring at him in wide-eyed wonder. *That's it! Game over!* thought Jack. Blitz Boy shuffled fretfully in his chair – and then to Jack's immeasurable relief, looked away as though he hadn't seen anything. Jack sat down in the last remaining seat behind Henry in the second row. As ever, all he could do now was hope for the best.

Around the edges of the classroom numerous flaming torches sat in iron holders. They dimmed and went out, reminding Jack of a cinema auditorium just before the main feature starts. The only light source was now provided by the candles that illuminated the top of the pulpit.

The pulpit, which loomed some four metres above them, began to shake and rattle as though a train were passing beneath it. The rattling stopped and a cloaked and hooded figure rose up from inside. He was not dressed in a monk's habit – these were more the austere robes of a master at a medieval public school. He held a tall staff. A larger version of the Winged Shaman was perched atop it. The figure removed his hood to reveal a grey, corpse-like pallor, and ink-black eyes that shone like polished marbles. His long grey hair was matched by an even longer beard that tailed off to a point. Without uttering a word, he lifted his staff and banged it three times on the floor of his pulpit. The eyes of the Winged Shaman atop his staff shone a deep crimson. For several seconds, all the children, including Jack, sat mesmerised by the light. The glow vanished and the children exhaled as though they'd been holding their breath since they arrived. Then they shuffled in their seats and looked around like normal kids. It occurred to Jack that his classmates had just been 'activated'. The man in the pulpit spoke: "Welcome children!" he boomed. "I am Herute. I am to be your Dark Master. For the next nine months, I will be tutoring you in the sacred art-forms of wickedness and deception. I trust you will all be eager students. Let the Underlings seated about this room act as a warning. Like you, they had the promise of a glittering future ahead of them. They, too, were destined to take their places in the new world order, to revel in the torment of others. Look at the wretches now!" he boomed, crashing down his staff and causing the dozens of candles about his pulpit to flicker and cast terrifying shadows on him and on the tapestry behind him.

"Yikes," muttered Jack, his mouth remaining open. He quickly closed it. Herute continued, "The desolate souls seated around this room are doomed to spend all eternity here, tending to those of you who possess promise. But be warned," he said, lowering his voice, "if you do not study hard and become despicable children, you too will end up like them. Now return to your rooms and sleep, for tomorrow heralds a dark new beginning." With that, he banged his staff and vanished.

The children, of varying shapes, colours and ages, stood up and began introducing themselves as though it were the first day at any new school. Jack approached Henry from behind. He placed a hand on his shoulder and gently pulled him around to face him. The eternal optimist in Jack felt sure that, as soon as he spoke to Henry, his friend would remember everything. "Henry? It's me. It's Jack."

Henry lifted a chubby hand in greeting, and Jack shook it. "It's nice to meet you, Jack," replied Henry. "This is some place, huh," he continued, looking about him. "The best school in all creation, apparently. We're so lucky to be here. Don't you think?"

Jack lowered his voice. "Don't you know who I am, Henry?"

"Yes, of course I do. You're Jack. You just told me so." Jack's heart sank. It seemed as though his friend's memories had been wiped clean. Jack turned and made a bee-line for the relative safety of his bed. As he passed Blitz Boy, he felt the lad's gaze burning into him. He went straight to his bed and lay down in his robe. He closed his eyes and turned to face the wall. A single tear trickled down his cheek. *I must not cry,* he told himself. *I must question. I must find Perkin.*

61

THIRTEEN

Stranded and alone

The next morning, Jack opened his eyes and groaned. He had not visited Perkin. He had tried, but quickly found himself ambushed by sleep. Henry and the girl were already up and seated at their roll-top desks. They were reading a leather-bound book they'd discovered inside. "This is great! Listen to this," said the girl. "The Will is crushed and torn asunder if the torment is perpetual and precise."

"Love that!" said Henry.

"It doesn't sound like there's much *love* around here," muttered Jack, sitting up.

"I should hope not," said the girl. "I'm Claire. It's nice to meet you," she continued, closing the book.

"I'm Jack," he replied, feeling unable to return the sentiment. The bell over the door rang out and Blitz Boy hurried into the room. He began gesticulating wildly for them to follow him.

"What a vile, *pathetic* mess you are," snarled Henry, as he and Claire followed him out into the classroom. Jack rolled out of bed, still wearing his robe from the previous night. He pulled on his sandals and hurried after them. "Bullying this little runt is going to feel so good," said Henry as they made their way through the classroom. "Doesn't anybody else want to have a go?"

"Filthy scum!" said Claire, grabbing the boy's hair and pulling it hard. Blitz Boy opened his mouth to scream but made no sound. "The perfect way to start your day," rhymed Claire, as she skipped a little way ahead of them. "It's your turn to insult ... or attack him," she continued, stopping and turning to face Jack. Jack was appalled. He wanted to wrap his arms around the boy and protect him from these hypnotised monsters.

"Where are you taking us ... *boy*?" was the best he could muster. Blitz Boy replied by simulating putting food in his mouth.

"All right, breakfast!" said Henry. Jack almost smiled. *They obviously haven't erased his personality* completely *then*, he thought.

They followed Blitz Boy through the double doors and out into the Atrium of Staircases. Once again, as they made contact with the stairs, they rose into the air and floated on their way. Jack looked back at Blitz Boy who was standing on the landing, staring at him. The boy's sorrowful eyes followed him until he was out of sight.

The staircases were chock-a-block with floating children. Thousands of kids in groups of three: climbing, descending, rotating, pitching and crossing one another's paths but *never* making contact. Jack marvelled at the order and precision of it all. This was about as far from chaos as you could imagine. "Hypocrites!" he said, thinking aloud.

"Good for you," said Claire. "An insult for everyone!"

"You know, I think you're going to do really well here," said Henry, patting Jack on his back.

They approached a letterbox-shaped exit that had been carved out of the side of the citadel. The children up ahead floated through it and shot upwards. Jack drew a deep breath and wiped his sweaty hands on his robe. It occurred to him that this was some kind of culling process. "... You have *got* to be kidding me!" he murmured, as they floated through the rectangle and out into the open air. Jack couldn't resist the urge to look down. He regretted doing so. The distance between him and oblivion was considerable. He dragged his gaze back up and looked straight ahead. The view over the forest might have been breathtaking (had he any breath left to take).

Jack suddenly felt his body wheeling around and, following a fleeting panic, he was relieved to be deposited on top the citadel of The Priory of Chaos.

They were in a vast courtyard covered in black pebbles: the cathedral-like spires Jack had seen from the air towered over him now. The building comprised three segments: two gargantuan halls connected by a domed central lobby. The lobby was accessed through monstrous black doors that opened inward into an octagonal space. On either side of these doors, a battleship-size cannon was raised towards the heavens. Above the doors, a lantern emanated a deep purple flame. They walked under the lantern and into the lobby.

To their left and right, staircases led up into the two adjoining halls. They were directed by a hooded figure to follow the staircase to their left. They climbed to the top of the stairs and entered the Priory's cathedral – a vast space dedicated to the worship and propagation of Evil. They walked down the central aisle past a sea of stone pews and dedicatory plaques, all bathed in a shadowy, shifting light.

Halfway down the central aisle, they came upon statues of a dozen or so graduates of The Priory of Chaos. These bronze likenesses glorified some of the most repugnant people in Earth's history. Jack recognised three of them: Adolph Hitler, Joseph Stalin and Chairman Mao.

They sat on a cold, stone pew close to the altar. Looming high above the altar a dome contained a painting of the Four Horsemen of The Apocalypse. Each rider in turn represented Death, War, Pestilence and Famine. The horses alone upon which these harrowing figures sat were the size of a building apiece. Jack swallowed a lump in his throat and glanced sideways at Henry. His best friend was gazing up at the painting, and smiling broadly.

Under the dome and atop a platform sat three chairs. Two of the chairs were of normal size. The one in the centre looked like a throne, large enough to accommodate six grown men with ease. *Who, or WHAT, sits in that chair? I bet it's not daddy bear,* thought Jack, as his gaze fell to the altar. That's when he saw it: at the altar's centre, a Winged Shaman that looked identical to the one at the British Museum, albeit considerably larger, about the size of an owl. Jack had flashbacks of using the other Shaman to create the potion that now protected him. Then the penny dropped … *Of course! … A possible way of breaking Henry from his trance! If I collect some tears and hair from someone schooled here at the Priory, place them in a container with some water, then show it to the Winged Shaman on the altar, it might create a potion that will bring Henry back. It must!*

The organ fired up and spooky music boomed through the cathedral. The service that followed was not unlike a service in a regular cathedral. It was only the nature of the hymns that differed slightly, with titles such as: Onward Gory Soldiers, Praise Be To Those Who Discriminate and, How Sweet The Coming Apocalypse. The sermon, entitled 'Pouring Scorn on Innocence', left much to be desired and Jack was pleased when it was time to leave. The three chairs that had been given pride of place above the altar remained empty throughout.

As they made their way back up the aisle towards the main entrance, Jack kept turning his head and gazing back at the Shaman. Pretty soon it appeared no bigger than a speck in the furthest reaches of the cathedral.

They left the cathedral and crossed the central lobby to find themselves in another vast space – the dining room. Row upon row of wooden tables stretched into the distance. Straw had been strewn on the ground, tons of it, creating a sea of yellowy-grey. They approached a table and sat down on the bench beside it. Each table had its own server crone. Withered and hunched, these decrepit old women had filthy, pockmarked faces. Their crone was tending to the contents of an iron pot beside her. She lifted the pot and walked around the table, filling their deep wooden bowls with goodness only knew what. Jack watched the other children who displayed no hesitation in tucking in. *It looks harmless enough* … He dipped his wooden spoon into the bowl and sipped the black concoction. It had a slight metallic tinge to it perhaps but, all things considered, it wasn't all bad.

FOURTEEN

Sticks and stones

Back in the classroom, a number of items had been placed on the desks by the Underlings. These included: several sheets of parchment, a quill pen, a bottle of ink and 'that' red leather-bound book. Jack sat down at his desk and read its front cover: *Evil: Its Many Forms and Applications.* He ran his fingers over the letters. They had been woven in gold thread and felt silky smooth – *threads of pure gold?* he thought. The book was hefty and ancient, like something you might see under a glass case in a museum. *I bet this thing would blow people's minds back home,* thought Jack, feeling a pang of excitement at the notion of liberating it. He opened it and discovered numerous notes scribbled in the margins – including the occasional date. One such entry, which caught his attention read: 'Edward Rex, anno domini 1483. A true friend and master. May he flourish and reign forever.' Jack was no expert on English history, but he knew the story of the boy King Edward V. The twelve-year-old monarch had vanished from the Tower of London in that same year, 1483, along with his younger brother, Richard. The pair would never be seen again. *It couldn't actually be talking about* that *Edward Rex? Could it?* The heavy wooden doors behind them flew open and in marched Herute – his footsteps pounding the stone floor with a ferocity that caused the torches along the walls to rattle in their iron holders. His long shadow loomed large as he made his way towards the pulpit at the front of the classroom. "I was delayed," said Herute, already sounding at the end of his tether. "The pulpit delivery system has failed. While it's true that the sacred institution in which you are seated is called The Priory of Chaos, the one thing that will *not* be tolerated here is chaos!" He climbed to the top of the pulpit and stood before the class. "The pulpit delivery system will be repaired forthwith, or heads will roll. I speak with a literal tongue," he said, glancing at the skinny necks of Blitz Boy and one or two others of his ilk. Then he straightened his robe and began flicking through the pages of the book in front of him. "Time to close your minds, children," he continued, as the torches around the room dimmed, once again causing the candles about his pulpit to cast eerie, hypnotic shadows on his face. "Open your book at chapter one: 'Infliction; Its Many Aims and Purposes.' Now," he continued, "the first thing we need to cement into your rotting little minds is the importance of identifying potential targets in others. Targets come in two distinct forms. Are there any suggestions as to what these two targets are?" Seven of the eighteen children raised their hands. "You!" boomed Herute, pointing at a boy with close set eyes and acne.

"My Lord and Master," began the boy, "would the two targets be the left and right cheeks?"

"Address me as, *sir*, boy," snapped Herute before bellowing: "No! The answer I seek is further reaching and altogether more visionary." Revelling in the sound of his own voice, Herute went on, "Each of these two main targets has SCORES of sub-targets beneath them. So, who else would like to guess at what these two targets might be?"

"The left eye and right eye, sir?" said a tanned girl with a cut-glass English accent. "After all," she continued, "beneath the eyes are many more potential targets ... a whole body of targets in fact! And what could be more visionary than eyes, sir?"

Herute puffed out his chest and rolled his eyes. "The two main targets are mental and physical! Let us begin by focusing on the bigger of these two targets. Who would like to offer a suggestion as to which one of these two targets, mental or physical, is the bigger? Yes, child?" he boomed, pointing to a plump boy in the second row called Henry.

"That would be physical targets, sir ... after all: sticks and stones may break my bones but words will never harm me." Henry sat back in his chair and looked very pleased with himself.

"Nonsense," said Herute, running his fingers down his long grey beard. "Sticks and stones may break bones but bones heal quickly, particularly in the young. No. By far the biggest target available to us is the mental one: the target of the mind. And the weapons we use to strike at this target are words. Words! Words with spiteful, scathing overtones! Words that will enter the subconscious like seeds and grow into confidence destroying trees! Remember children, physical wounds heal but emotional wounds fester. The greatest damage is always inflicted using words with biting and negative overtones. Are there any questions?"

Jack had a question. But should he risk asking it? It was one of those occasions when his curiosity gave his free will a good thrashing. He cleared his throat and raised his hand ... "Why, sir?" he said. "Why is identifying a person's insecurities and then attacking them, a good thing?" Jack bit his bottom lip – *I wish I had a bit more willpower.*

Herute gazed down at him. "It appears we have a lateral thinker in our midst. When you're returned home boy, your sole purpose will be to eradicate confidence in others, rout their self-esteem, and replace it with

67

dread and insecurity. Once enough of this work has been done, you will be able to rise above and subjugate your fellow man … assume your rightful places amongst the highest ranks of the new order. Does that answer your question, boy?"

"Oh, yes," said Jack, "perfectly, sir." If Jack could have pulled a lever and reduced The Priory of Chaos to rubble at that moment, he would have done so. And, if what Perkin had told him was true, if there really was a way to prevent these monsters achieving their goals, then now, more than ever, he was eager for the challenges that lay ahead.

FIFTEEN

New allies

After the most anti-educational day in the history of the universe, Jack climbed into bed. He resolved to shut out the horror and think about something positive: the Shaman on the altar. The prospect of returning Henry to his old self was just the tonic he needed. It instilled within him the most comforting feeling imaginable. But how was he going to find his way back to the cathedral and the Shaman when nobody was around? And even if he managed to do so and create the potion, how would he get Henry to drink it? The task suddenly seemed not only daunting but, dare he think it, impossible? Just then, he felt a tap on his shoulder. He turned over to see Blitz Boy standing over him like a ghost on a haunting. Jack glanced over at Henry and Claire who appeared to be sleeping soundly. "What is it?" whispered Jack. The boy put a finger to his lips and motioned for him to follow. Intrigued, Jack climbed out of bed and accompanied the diminished figure to an empty wooden bookcase at the back of their dorm. The boy slid it silently to one side to reveal a waist-high arch that led into a 'wardrobe' once used to store weapons and munitions. Jack crouched and slid through the entrance on his knees.

Inside, languishing in the stench of decayed gunpowder, he discovered an Aladdin's cave of curiosities lit by a number of candles propped against the walls. Amongst the objects were parcels wrapped in brown paper and several wooden toys, including: a Spitfire, a U-boat, and several crudely painted World War Two soldiers. Blitz Boy pulled the bookcase back into place and sat crossed-legged on the stone floor opposite Jack. He picked up his Spitfire and handed it to him. Jack took the tiny plane and simulated landing it on the ground. As he did, Blitz Boy's face was transformed by a magical smile. This was the first time Jack had seen an expression other than woe on the wretched boy's face. "Thank you," whispered Jack. The boy opened his mouth to speak but, once again, he failed to produce a sound. He cleared his throat, his lips parted slowly and then, with no little effort he croaked, "Did … did we win?"

Jack looked puzzled. He said, "Did we *win*? Did we win what?"

"The war … did we beat 'em … did we best the Nazis?" Even by the

standards of his current predicament, the question was seriously weird. "…
Yes. Of *course* we beat them." Blitz Boy threw his arms in the air as if to
shriek but then clasped his hands to his mouth and rolled onto his side
giggling into his palms. The sight and sound of his mirth was infectious
and Jack couldn't help giggling himself. Moments later, the laughter
subsided, and the grim reality of their situation returned.

Jack said, "Have you been here … you know, since the *Second World
War*?" He dreaded the answer he knew was coming. "Yes, gov," said Blitz
Boy, his voice sounding a little stronger now. "I was being evacuated with
my kid sister, Sheila. We was going to stay with some kind folks on a farm
in Cornwall. Mummy said they was kind anyway. I fell asleep on the train
at Kings Cross … trouble up the line, see … a bomb someone said. And I
was tired, what with all the worry … so I shut my eyes. Next I knew I was
here … they told me I'd failed … that I weren't good enough for their dark
schooling and I'd be here for all eternity … as their slave." Blitz Boy's
eyes filled with wonder. "You're the *first* … how?" he said, reaching up
and pointing to Jack's forehead.

"You mean … how did I get here with my own mind? I'm not
altogether certain … but I'm here to help if I can. These monsters must be
stopped."

"Stopped? Oh, I don't think they can be stopped … My name's Ken by
the way … Ken Breeze and I'm at your service! Perhaps," he continued,
"the war isn't over then, after all?"

"It's nice to meet you, Ken. I'm Jack Tracy and the war against tyranny
is pretty much an ongoing thing it seems. But, there's someone who thinks
the Priory can be stopped … a warrior in the forest, his name's Perkin and
we could both use your help."

Ken sat upright and saluted. "It would be an honour and a privilege to
help you, gov," he said.

"Thank you, Ken. I've never felt so alone. Henry, the other boy in our
dormitory is my best friend … I think I know a way to release him from his
trance but it means getting inside the cathedral when no one's around."

Ken unfolded his legs and drew his knees up to his chin. He remained
silent, the cogs clearly turning behind his sad grey eyes. "The cathedral?"
he said, finally. "I know how to get to the cathedral, all right. I go there
sometimes to scavenge for food in Friar Dark's lodgings in the north
transept. But I stay out of sight and daren't venture into the cathedral
proper. What's in the cathedral that can help you?"

"The Winged Shaman … you know … the one that sits on the altar?"

Ken's eyes opened wide. "I know the Shaman all right … it sees
everything!

They say it's cursed, that it has the power to cast children into Hell!

70

What do you want with it?"

"I don't know anything about a curse, or being cast into Hell ... but I know the Shaman is one of a pair. Back home it has a smaller brother in the British Museum."

"You mean the British Museum weren't blown up in the blitz?"

"It was still standing the last time I saw it ... well, just about."

"I went there on a school trip. I remember them mummies ... don't recall seeing one of them shamans though."

"There is one there ... and the one in the cathedral could be the key to breaking my friend from his trance. Henry's a great guy. You'll like him if we can get him back to his old self. I need him back, Ken. I don't know if I'm going to get through this without him."

"I can take you to the cathedral, there's a way down through the pulpit delivery system ... it's not very nice mind."

"I don't care how nice it is ..." Jack suddenly looked deflated.

"What is it?" asked Ken.

"It's Claire. She's always with him. It's as though they're joined at the hip. Even if we can make the potion and it works, I can imagine Henry freaking and Claire raising the alarm."

"We can take Henry with us ... to the cathedral."

"But why would he come?"

"To offer me in a blood sacrifice at the altar!" said Ken, clapping silently.

"I appreciate your enthusiasm, Ken ... but the idea is slightly flawed, particularly where you're concerned."

"Sacrifice ...it happens to us sometimes. It almost happened to me once ... but I got away."

Jack shook his head. "I don't understand."

"Sometimes the students try to do us in ... to impress their Dark Masters."

"So, you're saying we should lure Henry to the cathedral with the promise of sacrificing you at the altar ... to impress Herute? It's a bit grisly ... even by the standards of this place."

Ken shook his head, "That Henry don't like me one bit ... he'll love the idea."

"No. It's too risky. What if something goes wrong? Henry's a big guy. He's strong ... stronger than me. If the worst happens, I may not be able to stop him."

"I'm a fast runner, gov. Henry may be strong but he don't look quick."

"No arguments there."

"Look, if you mean to get to the cathedral, best do it soon ... before the pulpit delivery system is fixed. The Dark Masters hurtle along down there at ungodly speeds. They'd be one less hazard to avoid."

"All right ... I'll try and get Henry on his own tomorrow ... dangle the carrot of your sacrifice under his nose. Right now, there's someone else I need to talk to urgently. And I can only do that when I'm lying down and concentrating. It's time for bed," said Jack, grabbing Ken's hand and shaking it warmly.

***

The tunnel of blazing light appeared, followed by the same questions. Jack knew the drill and braced himself for a thud followed by a smarting bottom. There was no thud. No smarting bottom. In fact, he was taken aback by an ever-so-gentle landing. *That was a serious improvement,* he thought. Then he looked down at his crossed legs. They were transparent! As were his arms, chest and stomach. He could see through himself to the dirt and leaves beneath. "I'm dead! I'm a ghost!"

"You're not dead ... not yet," came Perkin's (mildly) reassuring words from behind him. "There is nothing to fear, Jack. It is the essence of your essence that has returned here."

"Okay ... if you say so, but ... I'm feeling a bit ... freaked," said Jack, gazing through the palms of his hands.

"I've been given to understand that the dilution is perfectly safe," said Perkin. Jack stood up. "It's really good to see you!" he said, trying out his transparent legs.

"You too, my young friend. It's good to see you safe and well. How was your journey to the Priory? Clearly you avoided detection by the Snatcher-Gar. Kept your wits about you."

"Yes. The creature suspected something ... but another Snatcher-Gar distracted it. I was lucky again, I guess. Perkin, Henry's there! Henry's at the Priory with me!"

"I am sorry for your loss, Jack."

Sorry for my loss. "... But ... surely there's a way to break Henry from his trance? Using the Winged Shaman in the cathedral?"

Perkin shook his head. "It's too great a risk. There is so much we need to accomplish."

"The risk is mine to take. You once told me to trust my instincts. Well, my instincts are telling me I need Henry's help."

Perkin smiled. "Be that as it may, we must begin our journey now," he said, motioning towards Vargo.

"Where are we going?"

"We must travel north. I have it on good authority ... the very same as led me to you in the woods ... that there are Beings in the northern forests who mean to assist us."

"Beings?"

Perkin took hold of Vargo's reins and climbed into his saddle. "At present, that is all I know. Come!" he said, extending his hand and helping Jack up onto the horse. "Now we ride and see how far we can get before you awaken at the Priory and, when next you return, we can continue our journey from that point." With that, they galloped off into the night.

SIXTEEN

The First Evil

High above the southern forests, a great carriage hung suspended from ropes below eighteen members of the Snatcher-Guard. This elite troop carried their illustrious cargo with pride, flapping their immense wings in perfect unison towards The Priory of Chaos.

Upon the doors of the sky-bound carriage, the gold initials T.F.E. glistened in the light of the twin moons. Inside, a lavish compartment was separated by a blood-red curtain. On one side of this curtain sat two Dark Monks. These monks were not wearing the usual black habits but robes of crimson and purple. Around their necks were draped resplendent chains of office. Their names were Sinosa and Salcura and they held the highest rank in the Dark Order: Master Priors. Their eyes were closed but they were not sleeping. All those anointed into The Order had their eyelids permanently sealed during the Ritual of Welcomed Darkness. From a young age, Dark Monks are trained to see only despair and confusion in living things. The greater the surrounding despair, the more illuminating their world. This ensures that their calling to spread misery and dread remains all consuming.

Between the Master Priors sat a woman with masses of black, curly hair. She squirmed between her captives, trying to make herself as small and inconspicuous as possible. On the other side of the curtain sat a throne with the same freakish proportions as the one in the cathedral. On this throne sat a being as old as time, a monster, hollow of compassion and beyond all redemption. The First Evil was a cloven-hoofed colossus that, like the Snatcher-Gars that served him, had been remembered in the nightmares of Priory students for millennia. And so, when ancient scribes were charged with writing the Bible, they imbued their 'evil one' with the attributes of The First Evil. The First Evil's red, perpetually angry face grimaced and his lips parted: "Tell me again what this Reader has seen," he said from beyond the curtain, his voice utterly bass, no hint of treble whatsoever.

"The Reader has spoken of a child, Sire … a child of Earth who has visited the southern forests," said Sinosa.

"A *human* child?"

"The information is scant, exalted one," added Salcura. "As yet, we have been able to extract few details from this Reader. Her pain threshold is wanting, my Lord. She passes out under the most rudimentary of tortures."

"When we reach the Priory, have the Reader brought to my throne room …I will question her myself. Any occurrence, inexplicable in nature, must be viewed with suspicion. We are too close to take chances."

"Rest assured, Sire. The Law of Misdirection is holding fast on Earth. Adult humans remain in a state of oblivion regarding the sudden changes to their young."

"Indeed, My Lord. When they finally behold what has become of their offspring, it will be too late."

The First Evil attempted a smile. He said: "I yearn for the day when Earth's fathers turn against their sons – Earth's mothers against their daughters. The very heart of humanity corrupted from within."

"This time, there is nothing to stop us, My Lord. How can the humans prevent that which they cannot see happening?"

A party of senior monks and tutors had been assembled atop The Priory of Chaos as a welcoming committee. They had been summoned from their beds and, amongst them, an exhausted Herute was doing his best to look as alert and respectful as possible.

The First Evil's carriage hovered several metres from the roof of the citadel. A cloven, dinosaur-size hoof appeared from within the carriage and came crashing down upon the ground. The assembled committee bowed from the base of their spines. The First Evil straightened to his full height of four metres; five including his black, twisting antlers. He looked down upon the assembled party and sneered as if looking for someone specific to slaughter. The committee remained still, their bodies bent double in servitude. Much to the relief of everyone present, The First Evil thundered inside the building.

The First Evil's throne room was located behind the altar in the cathedral. As well as his throne, nestled amongst sumptuous drapes of black and red satin, the room contained a long, dark table. Around this table, strategies concerning the ruination of humanity had been planned and executed for millennia. On the wall behind the table, was a celestial map depicting Earth's universe. At its centre, like a fly caught in a celestial web, sat planet Earth; its continents colour coded to show the extent of the Priory's current harvest of children. The First Evil lurched past the table and climbed some steps to his throne. The Master Priors entered and

75

bowed their heads. "Do you wish to question the Reader now, my Lord," asked Sinosa.

"Yes … and I'm hungry, have food sent up."

"Any preference, my Lord?"

"Mammoth eels."

"As you wish, Sire." A messenger was dispatched from the kitchens to the aviary to fetch two Snatcher-Gars strong enough to carry a cauldron of the prehistoric eels. Gob and Phlem had recently returned from Earth. They'd left their latest victims (Jack and Henry) at the arrival point, and were looking forward to a bucket of raw horse flesh and some manure wine.

As they rose up towards the aviary's top tier, a server crone bellowed after them: "You two! Gob and Phlem! Come with me! You're needed in the kitchens!"

"What is it now?" groaned Gob, floating back down.

The woman clasped her hands together and looked towards the heavens. "The First Evil is here!" she cried, "He's here and he's starving!"

Gob fixed her with his most malign gaze. "Starving you say? Starving! Pick another! Are thee blind, woman? Am I not too comely to die? Take only Phlem. He's fat and he alone will provide an ample meal for our Lord. My tender flesh would surely give The First Evil indigestion!"

"He doesn't want to *eat you*, imbecile … the pot of eels is large and must be carried to him in the throne room!"

"Truly," said Gob, "you are a despicable old crone. Why did you not speak of this earlier? Can you not see that Phlem lacks my courage? Thanks to your thoughtlessness, he may succumb to lasting psychological trauma!"

The Reader was manhandled into the throne room, and stood trembling before The First Evil. "Do you know me, Reader?" he asked her.

She nodded quickly.

"Then you will want to please me. Is that not so?"

The woman's mouth gaped, fish-like, as if trying to produce a sound.

"IS THAT NOT SO?" boomed The First Evil, with such ferocity she could smell his foul breath from ten paces.

"Yes, yes, my Lord. It is so!"

"These visions concerning a human child, tell me of them?"

"I saw …"

"Yes?" The doors to the throne room flew open. Gob and Phlem flapped in carrying an enormous cauldron. They were accompanied by several fussing crones who directed them to place the cauldron down in front of The First Evil. The crones shooed the Snatcher-Gars into a corner and dragged the Reader several paces back. The First Evil rose from his

76

throne and fell upon the cauldron – his antlers plunged into the water and stabbed at the eels with savage twists and thrusts – a fountain of water and churned eel erupted, drenching the room and its terrified spectators.

After several minutes of frenzied feeding, The First Evil picked up the cauldron and poured its watery remains over his head. "I am refreshed!" he bellowed, before sending the cauldron crashing to the ground. The three crones moved forwards and began wiping water and slime off his muscular red torso. "Desist!" he said, stepping towards the Reader. The red giant bent down and brought his head close to hers. A coconut brought close to a walnut.

"You were saying?"

"The, the vision!" she babbled. "It was of a human child whose essence was able to reach the southern forests."

"Without the assistance of a Snatcher-Gar?"

"Yes!" replied the Reader, nodding so hard that she practically stabbed herself with her chin.

"How can this be?"

"I do not know."

"... This child ... is it a male or female?"

"My vision revealed only its shadow ... I could not be certain. That is everything I know, please ..."

The First Evil turned to Sinosa. "Have this Reader imprisoned in the dungeon. Inform me at once should she receive more of her *visions*." The reader was dragged from the room and a crone motioned for Gob and Phlem to remove the cauldron. The First Evil sat down on his throne and pointed at Phlem. "You, Snatcher-Gar," he said.

Phlem collapsed to one knee. "Yes! Your most magnificent and exalted Highness."

"Tell me *Snatcher-Gar* ... have you heard any rumours within the aviary?"

"R, rumours, My Lord?"

"That a child brought here by one of your kind may be ... *different* from the others?"

Salcura immediately spoke up: "My Lord! You're not suggesting that this child, if it even exists, could actually be within the walls of the Priory? Such a thing is inconceivable."

The First Evil ignored him and studied Phlem closely. "Speak up."

"Different? In what way, your most treasured Highness?"

"The child ... it would know its own mind."

"Know its own mind! I have heard of no such rumour, my Lord! The Master Prior is surely correct ... such a thing is impossible. Any Snatcher-Gar carrying this child would have smelt its fear ... and supped upon its flesh!"

"Nonetheless, should you hear of anything suspicious within the aviary, anything at all, get word to me at once. Is that understood?"

Phlem nodded eagerly.

As they made their way back to the kitchens, Phlem was puzzled by Gob's silence. It was wholly out of character. He had failed to utter a single moan or put-down for several minutes. There was a reason for this of course. Gob had been thinking about the strange boy who had, ever so fleetingly, struggled in his claws. Looking back, this child had undeniably shown a flicker of emotion: anger. Could this boy be the one the Reader spoke of? Gob now fretted over his predicament. After all, what terrible fate might befall the Snatcher-Gar who brought an intruder to The Priory of Chaos? A Snatcher-Gar who had failed in his duty to destroy it? Gob's thoughts turned to the destruction of one such human: Jack Tracy.

SEVENTEEN

How's this for a plan?

One second Jack was on horseback with Perkin, galloping through a forest, the next, he was being rocked by two sets of clammy hands and being told to "Wake up!" He opened his eyes and discovered his room-mates gazing at him in astonishment.

"What is it?" he asked.

"You were fading away!" said Claire.

You're got to be kidding! I must have been transparent in my bed as well as with Perkin. "I was *what*? Fading away?" said Jack, a picture of innocence.

"Yes, you were," said Henry, stroking his chin.

"Come to think of it," said Jack, "I was having the strangest dream."

"What on Earth about?" asked Claire.

"On Earth?" replied Jack, thinking fast. "That's just it ... we're not *on* Earth are we? So, clearly, if we dream about fading away in this astonishing place ... that must be what happens to us."

"Is that what you were dreaming about then, fading away?" asked Henry.

"Yes. Absolutely."

"I've dreamt about food every night since I arrived," sighed Henry.

"That would explain this then," said Claire, stabbing a finger into Henry's belly. Jack changed the subject. "What time is it?" he asked.

"Time that little slave turned up for some abuse," said Henry. "The little cretin is obviously skiving off. We should give him a good thrashing when he eventually *does* show," continued Henry, thumping his fist into his palm.

"He deserves worse," replied Jack, remembering the sacrificial plan he'd hatched with Ken before bed.

"What do you suggest?" asked Henry.

"I'll think of something suitably grisly and let you know," replied Jack, wishing Claire had been someplace else.

It was obvious there was something different about the morning service in the cathedral. For a start, the upper tiers were practically overflowing with Dark Monks and Tutors. "What's all this then?" mused Henry, as they made their way down the aisle towards their pew.

"It looks as though all the Dark Monks are here," mumbled Claire, gazing up at the army of cloaked and hooded figures. They had encountered few Dark Monks since arriving – and were yet to see a single face beneath those oversized hoods. They were about to have their first good look. Two Dark Monks came floating up the aisle towards them with their hoods down. "Look, guys! Dark Monks can float anywhere. Not just on stairs," beamed Claire.

"I hope they teach us how to do that … otherwise, all this exercise will be the death of me," mused Henry.

"Quiet!" whispered Jack, as the sinister figures floated close. He needn't have warned them. The faces of Dark Monks had a silencing effect on all who gazed upon them for the first time. With their grey complexions and permanently closed eyes they resembled upright, floating cadavers. As they floated past, the monks turned their heads towards the gawping children, placed a finger to their grey lips and communicated a silent 'hush.' *I'll never make another sound*, thought Jack, as they quickened their pace and moved in silence towards their pew.

They sat down. Jack looked up at the thousands of Dark Monks seated above him in the rafters. It felt as though they were looking down and judging him. He didn't like the feeling one bit. He distracted himself by thinking about his latest visit to Perkin. They had ridden for several hours. The further north they'd travelled the darker the woods had grown. Jack had heard animals shrieking and occasionally seen things dart about in his peripheral vision. Just before he'd been rocked back to consciousness in the dormitory, Perkin had told him they didn't have far to travel now. He said they were going to find two brothers: one a wizard and the other a craftsman. That's all Perkin knew. And even of these scant facts he seemed uncertain.

Jack was startled back to the present when everyone stood up and clasped their hands in prayer. A commotion could be heard coming from behind the altar. Jack gazed over the tips of his fingers as The First Evil lurched into view. The sight of this red giant, until now just a biblical legend in his mind, caused his dizziness to return. Jack's head swam. *It's him! It really is him! My legs … I can't feel them … what if he knows I'm different … I need to sit … just hold on … for a few seconds more …* The First Evil sat on his throne. Sinosa climbed to the top of the pulpit and, much to Jack's relief, the congregation was seated. "Firstly," said Sinosa, "I'd like to offer humble thanks for the presence of our Lord, The First Evil, at our morning service." He paused briefly before bellowing, "HATE!

WHAT IS IT TO HATE!? To hate is to embrace all that is wicked in the universe ..."

Sinosa preached about the benefits of hatred for a further forty five minutes. During the sermon, Jack experienced a mixture of boredom and annoyance. *If he says the word hate one more time*! he thought. In fact, Sinosa used the word *one hundred and forty seven* more times but Jack thought it wise to keep his objections to himself.

Once the sermon was over, The First Evil rose from his throne and stood before the altar. Jack was no longer bored or annoyed, he was electrified – every hair on his body now standing to attention. The red giant gazed into the cathedral. He sighed and said, "'How do I hate thee? Let me count the ways.' I'd like to thank Sinosa for including my favourite sonnet in his service. It is a morbid joy to be here once again in this cradle of evil. Looking about this edifice, I see many fine young souls who will do their best to bully, intimidate and inject fear into the hearts of all they meet when they are returned to Earth. When you grow, I know you will make me proud by promoting war and fanaticism, by creating divisions and causing as much chaos and unrest as is within your power. Sadly, once you are returned to Earth you will no longer remember me or what I'm telling you ... but the spirit of my words will remain in your hearts. This spirit will guide and protect you until the time of the coming apocalypse, when you will join me in the kingdom of everlasting death." Jack gulped so loudly he thought he may have given himself away. It didn't help that The First Evil then paused as if distracted by something. "And now I must take my leave. When next we meet, I shall be standing before you on Earth. When that day comes my children ... victory will already be ours!"

Jack finished breakfast first and placed his wooden spoon inside his bowl. Claire was talking to an older boy across the table, picking his brains about some punishment involving cupboards full of exposed nails. Jack seized his opportunity. "Henry, why don't we make our way back to the classroom?" Henry had finished his breakfast and was growing bored. He glanced at Claire still nattering away, shrugged and stood up.

As they approached the exit to the dining room, Jack threw caution to the wind. "I've heard a fab way some students earn praise from their Dark Tutors, Henry. And it sounds like fun, too."

"Fun you say? Go on."

"You know you wanted to punish that vile slave for skiving off this morning?"

"Yes."

"Well, how about sacrificing him before the altar in the cathedral tonight?"

"Is that permitted?" asked Henry, practically jumping up and down.

"Oh, yes. The Dark Masters look upon it as a sign of initiative, apparently."

"I like it! We can get rid of that kid and impress Herute. Hold up. Let's wait for Claire, she's gonna love the idea."

"Why share the glory with Claire? Not to mention the gory," said Jack, his fingers crossed behind his back.

"I do admire your reasoning."

Just then, Claire pitched up. "Sorry boys, I got talking to one of the second month students … I tried to get some juicy info out of him about upcoming topics."

"Find out anything interesting?" asked Henry.

"Not much. Apparently, it's forbidden to discuss anything too advanced with the new arrivals. Have I missed something?" she asked, sensing Henry's excitement. "No," replied the boys in unison.

"If you say so," said Claire, raising an eyebrow.

EIGHTEEN

Discrimination

When they arrived at the classroom, Ken was back on his chair outside the dormitory. "There you are," snarled Henry. Then he trod on Ken's foot. "This will teach you," he continued, gradually applying more pressure. Ken scrunched up his face but made no sound.

Jack grabbed Henry's arm. "Come on, Henry. Let's sit down. Herute will be here any second."

Henry bent over and whispered in Ken's ear. "We'll deal with you later … make you sorry you were ever born."

Herute burst into the classroom and thundered towards the pulpit. He climbed the stairs at its side and flicked through the pages of the book before him. The seconds ticked by. Eventually, Herute sighed and said, "Not only has the pulpit delivery system *not* been fixed, but I was awoken last night, deprived of my slumber and dragged outside in the early hours. I won't enlighten you with the details but I'm exhausted. So, you'd better be vile children or the consequences will be severe. Now, where were we? Chapter two: The Joy of Discrimination. Dis-crim-in-ation, the syllables, so playful, they dance on one's lips," he said, as once again, the torches dimmed and his menacing features were illuminated by the candles around his pulpit. "To discriminate children," he continued, "means to cast negative aspersions on, well, anything. The possibilities are endless. It's all about differences. Would anyone care to suggest where these differences may lie?"

A boy at the back of the class said, "Different opinions, sir?"

"You're certainly right about that, boy. People who have different opinions should not be tolerated. What fate should befall such individuals?"

"They should be boiled alive!" shouted Claire.

"Indeed they should, child. You, my dear girl, were born five hundred years too late. I regret that boiling punishments are no longer tolerated on Earth. Of course, once our work at the Priory is complete, and The First Evil is able to set foot on Earth, you can look forward to a time when boiling is once again commonplace."

"It'll be so great," mused Claire, turning to high-five the boy behind her.

"So, in the long-lamented absence of boiling, what else might be done with people who display abhorrent differences of opinion to our own?" Once again hands went up all over the classroom. There followed a slew of suggestions recommending that they should be punched, kicked, spat at, robbed, tormented, blown-up, head-butted, drowned, run-over and dropped from a great height.

Herute spent the rest of the day delving microscopically into the art of discrimination. Finally, he said: "I would like you to write a two-thousand-word essay on why discriminating against others is so important." Then he took his leave. Jack picked up his quill pen. *Ok*, he thought, *the only way to get through this is to treat the exercise as a sick joke. I'll write down the vilest, most despicable things I can imagine. In this place, I'm bound to get an A grade.*

Jack deliberately rushed his essay and finished before anyone else. He stood up and headed back to his dorm. "Follow me, boy!" he barked at Ken. Henry and Claire were still working in the classroom when Ken sat beside Jack on his bed. "The plan's afoot," Jack whispered in Ken's ear.

"It's a *foot* …?" said Ken, in astonishment.

"It's set for tonight. Just as you thought, Henry really jumped at the chance to sacrifice you."

"I told you he would."

"All we need now are some tears and a few strands of hair from someone who's been schooled at the Priory."

"I was schooled here, once. And then they decided I wasn't worthy of their schoolin' and woke me from my trance. I can cry real easy, too … I only have to think about how much I miss mum … and my little sister, Sheila. I've got loads of hair," he said, yanking out a few strands.

"Thanks, Ken. We're also going to need a container … to put your tears and hair in."

"Leave it to me, I'll take care of everything," said Ken.

"I don't know how to thank you."

"There's no need to thank me, gov, honest."

"There's still time to back out … rather than put you in danger, we could find another way."

"'In for a penny, in for a pound,' that's what my uncle Arthur always used to say."

"Well, if you're certain you want to go ahead, have all the ingredients ready by midnight. As soon as Claire falls asleep, we'll put the plan into action … and get Henry back from the dark side."

NINETEEN

The sacrificial lamb

It was approaching midnight. Henry was lying in bed wide-eyed, barely able to contain his excitement at the prospect of sacrificing Ken. Jack climbed out of bed and crossed the room to check that Claire was sleeping soundly. He leant over her and looked at her upturned face. Her expression, one part frown, three parts sneer, gave Jack the willies. Henry bounced out of bed. He picked up his robe and tiptoed into the classroom.

The five Underlings were slumped on their chairs, sound asleep. Henry pulled his robe over his head and secured the belt about his waist. Jack approached him and whispered, "I've told Blitz Boy that if he guides us to the cathedral, there'll be a reward in it for him."

"There's going to be a reward, all right," said Henry, producing a short dagger from beneath his robe. *What the ...! Where'd he get that?* thought Jack.

Ken made his way towards the pulpit and motioned for the boys to follow. He carried an oil lamp, and had a sack which dangled from his shoulder. They climbed the stairs to the top of the pulpit; Ken knelt and opened a trapdoor; the boys watched as he descended a ladder into the darkness. "After me," said Henry, pushing Jack aside. The stench of damp and mildew made them cringe. The further down they went, the higher the stench climbed their nostrils, settling at the back of their throats like a rotting sponge. Down they climbed, following Ken's tiny flame beneath them.

Ken climbed off the ladder and carefully negotiated his way around a small ledge. He knelt down, removed a wooden vent, and disappeared through the narrow entrance. Henry and Jack hurried after him and his precious light source. They crawled on all fours through a maze of black, water-stained tunnels until they reached another vent. Ken removed it and motioned for the boys to crawl past him into another darkened area. Ken followed them in and replaced the vent.

He held the lamp above his head to reveal thousands of reflective dots, telescoping into the distance. "Are we in a diamond mine?" Jack pondered out loud. "I wish we was," replied Ken. "Stick close to me on the path and they shouldn't attack." Neither Henry nor Jack liked the sound of that but there was a job to be done. Ken removed the sack from his shoulder. He felt around inside it and withdrew a fleshy creature that resembled a lobster without a shell.

"Is it snack time already?" said Henry, licking his lips.

"It's not for you, governor … it's for them," said Ken, turning a screw on his oil lamp and increasing its flame. The light crept into the cavern, illuminating hundreds of gigantic spiders in their webs. "Those are the black ones," he said, pointing to colossal black spiders on the left side of the cavern. "And them over there are the black and tans," he continued, highlighting spiders with black bodies and ginger legs on the other side. "It's rare that they eat us kids. That's not to say they don't have an appetite for us mind … that's why we keep 'em sweet with these little beauties," he said, tossing the wriggling creature to the spiders on his left. It landed in a web the size of a sail. Within moments, several spiders were making their way towards it. These monstrous arachnids had legs as long as Jack's and fangs the size of daggers.

Henry produced his dagger, "If they come near me, I'll have 'em," he snarled, in typical Priory of Chaos fashion.

Jack said, "Somehow, I think you might need a bigger weapon … like a sword … or maybe a rocket launcher."

They walked deeper into the cavern. Jack and Henry hunched up close to Ken. The spiders had an air of acceptance about their human visitors. It said: "Pay the toll and we *probably* won't eat you."

They left the cavern and entered a narrow tunnel. Ken turned to face his two companions, "I've got just the one left," he said, holding up the sack. "Now stick close by me 'cause they ain't keen on the light." Jack looked up. Spiders were clinging to the roof just centimetres above him. All three boys crouched low and moved swiftly through the confined space.

Jack and Henry skated around a sharp bend and bumped into Ken. Ken steadied himself and said, "This is it! This is the Way-Point that'll carry us up to the cathedral. Follow me in and make sure it's head first. Got it? Head first!" The boys nodded. Ken dove into the hole as if diving into a swimming pool and disappeared. Jack did the same.

Henry paused, the shadow of a spider looming behind him. Henry had never learnt to swim, let alone dive. *I'll have to leap in feet first.* As he did, the spider vomited a silky line which wrapped itself around Henry's neck! Henry dangled in the hole, gasping for breath. With his knife, he slashed at the spongy web above him – once, twice, three times, and, on the fourth attempt, it came apart and Henry plunged feet first into the darkness.

Up ahead, Jack was plunging *head first* into darkness. The darkness undulated and Jack suddenly found himself shooting upwards, head first, towards the roof of the citadel. Henry, on the other hand, hung upside down and screamed as he rocketed *feet first* after him. Jack had risen so far that it occurred to him he might miss his 'stop' at 'cathedral level' and be hurled from the roof. It came as a relief, therefore, when his flight path began to undulate, banking left and right, right and then left, before wheeling sharply to the left and launching him head first into a darkened room.

Thud!

Jack found himself lying face down on top of Ken. Another thud followed, louder than the first. Henry was now lying on top of them both. Jack and Henry heard a muffled whimpering beneath them. "Quick!" shouted Jack, "That's Ken! Get off me, Henry!" The boys scrambled to their feet. Ken was lying spread-eagled on the ground, face down, like a human starfish.

"Is he dead?" asked Henry, casually. Jack bent down and rolled Ken over. "Ken!" he said, shaking him. Ken coughed several times and sat up looking bewildered. "Ken, are you all right?"

"Is *he* all right? What about me? And who's *Ken*?"

"That's his name," snapped Jack.

"It has a name?"

Jack helped Ken sit up.

"Thanks, thank you. I'm all right," said Ken. "I'd planned to let the big guy go first … something soft for us both to land on … but in all the excitement."

"Where are we?" asked Jack.

"We're under the altar," replied Ken, crawling over to a vent and pushing it open. "You wait here. I'll have a quick look around and make sure the coast's clear." Both boys nodded at him. Ken crawled out into the darkened cathedral. It was deathly quiet and icy cold. Ken popped his head above the pulpit and peered in the direction of The First Evil's throne room. A dim light ebbed towards him into the murky cathedral. Ken trod carefully on the cold, ancient stone as he made his way towards it. He crouched outside the throne room and pressed his ear to the heavy wooden doors. He could hear the faint murmurings of a conversation within. Having satisfied himself that all was as well as could be expected, he made his way back to the open vent beneath the altar.

"Coast's clear," he whispered into the vent. The boys crawled into the cathedral and stood before the altar. Henry grinned and whipped out his dagger.

"No!" said Jack. "There's a better way …" He produced the bottle that contained Ken's hair and tears. "If we expose this to the Shaman on the altar, it will be transformed into poison. I got the formula from the back of 'Evil: Its Many Forms and Applications'. I've done my research and this method will impress Herute much more than just stabbing Ken," said Jack, rolling his eyes.

"Alright. Sounds interesting," said Henry, snatching the container from Jack. "What do we do with it again?" he asked.

"I'll show you," replied Jack, making his way to the Altar Shaman.

The three boys stood before the owl-size Shaman. "Remove the cork," said Jack, his heart heavy with expectation. Henry removed it.

Yes, yes, YES! thought Jack, as the spirals on either side of the Shaman's head began to churn out red mist just as they had in the British Museum. "How cool is this!" said Henry, as the container consumed the mist.

"*Very,*" said Jack, triumphantly.

Once the last of it had disappeared inside, Jack told Henry to replace the cork. Henry gazed at the newly created red liquid, then he grinned at Ken and said, "You look very thirsty."

"I *do?*" replied Ken, looking at Jack. Jack grabbed the phial from Henry's grasp.

"What do you think you're doing!" cried Henry, attempting to grab it back. "What's going on? I've smelled a rat from the start!" The boys didn't answer. "Right then," said Henry, "I'll just have to do it my way." He pulled the dagger from his pocket and glared at Ken. Ken took a step back, lost his balance, and collapsed onto his bottom. "You're history," snarled Henry, raising the dagger above his head. Jack removed the cork from the container and threw its contents at Henry's open mouth. Henry screamed and clasped his hands to his face as though it had been splashed with acid – then Henry fell to his knees and wiped the 'poison' furiously from his lips. Jack and Ken looked on as Henry froze, drew an enormous breath, and collapsed onto his side. There he lay, groaning and whimpering, for a good minute before falling silent.

Jack stepped towards him. "Henry … *Henry*? … Is that you?"

TWENTY

Back from The Dark Side

Henry rolled onto his back – kicked out with his legs and slid backwards along the ground, smacking into the altar. He gazed around as if woken from a terrible nightmare. His gaze found Jack and his expression brightened a little. "J ...ack?" he mumbled. "Where are we?"

Jack knelt and placed his hands on his friend's shoulders. "It's okay, Henry. We're in The Dark Matter ... at The Priory of Chaos."

"And that's *okay*?"

"Oh man it's good to have you back!" said Jack.

Henry glanced sideways at the dagger on the ground. He looked up at Ken. "I'm sorry ... I think I was going to ... I had no control ... I ..."

"Listen to me Henry ... it wasn't you, it was your evil twin," Jack reassured him.

"It's all right, gov. No harm done."

"What can you remember?" asked a curious Jack.

Henry looked down and thought for a moment ... "Everything. The journey here ...Herute, Claire, floating about on the stairs, the 'food' ... I think I'm going to be sick ..." Henry turned onto his side and began to heave.

"Governor, no!" cried Ken. "You can't vomit at the altar ... I mean, that's GOT to be bad luck, hasn't it?"

Henry sat back up, wide eyed. "You mean ... there's still some bad luck we haven't used up yet?" Just then, a shaft of light flooded the area behind the altar and footsteps crashed in their direction.

"Quick!" whispered Ken, crawling back through the open vent. The boys followed him in and Ken replaced the grating.

The First Evil and Sinosa stood before the altar. "It was nothing, My Lord ... just some vermin searching for food," said Sinosa. The First Evil drew air slowly through his enormous red nostrils. "... I thought I could smell a human presence." The boys moved away from the vent and crawled deeper into the darkened recess beneath the altar. There they sat, huddled in the dust-filled darkness.

Thirty minutes had passed and the voices outside had long since gone.

Ken whispered, "I reckon the coast's clear."

"We have to go back out there?" said Henry.

"Well, we can't stay in here forever ... not much of a life, is it?"

"Can't we get back to the classroom the way we came?" asked Jack.

"No, gov. That Way-Point's a climber. We'll have to return using the one outside on the roof."

"Won't we be seen?"

"The whole place is sleeping. There won't be any guards about ... no need for 'em."

The boys crawled back into the empty cathedral. "Wait!" Jack whispered. "There's something I have to do before we leave." Jack held up a potion phial he'd made using a pepper pot from the dining room. "I plugged the holes using bits of moist bread. It's got my tears and hair inside it." He approached the Altar Shaman. A minute later, another potion had been created. Jack turned to face the other two, and smiled.

"For Samantha?" asked Henry, his voice filled with hope.

"For Samantha!" replied Jack triumphantly, fastening the lid and pushing it down inside his robe's deep pocket.

"So, Perkin lied to you. You didn't have to come here to help Samantha – another trip to the British Museum would have done the trick."

"Maybe. But we were going to be brought here anyhow. So, whichever way we look at it, we owe everything to Perkin."

Henry shrugged.

"Who's Samantha?" asked Ken.

"A good friend who needs to be brought back from the dark side a.s.a.p. – before she kills us," said Henry.

They moved swiftly through the cathedral, ran across the pebbled courtyard, and made for the Way-Point that would carry them down the side of the citadel.

The Atrium of Staircases was eerily devoid of life as they passed through it on their way back to their dorm. They pushed open the classroom door as quietly as they could and tiptoed inside.

Having checked that Claire was sleeping soundly, Jack pointed towards Ken's hideaway behind the bookcase. They made their way inside. Ken lit a candle and slid the bookcase back into place.

"Great den," said Henry, crossing his legs in the cramped space.

"It's not much ... but it's the closest thing I got to home," replied Ken.

"We'll all be going home soon enough," said Jack.

"I don't have a home on Earth no more. Mum and dad ... they'd be long gone by now."

"What about your sister?" asked Jack.

"Sheila? If she's still alive, she'll be an old lady. She would have forgotten about me years ago."

"I doubt it," said Henry. "I bet she's thought about you at least once a day since you disappeared."

"You think so? Not that it matters much … I'll never be going home. This isn't just my essence," said Ken, holding up his hands, "This *really is* me."

"If I've learnt anything it's that anything's possible," said Jack smiling at Ken.

"Talking about getting home, what's the latest news from Perkin Central?" said Henry.

"I was with him last night. We were riding north." Jack leant back on the palms of his hands. "Perkin's planning something, Henry."

"Oh, that's just great. The three words in the English language most likely to strike dread into the heart of any kid: 'Perkin's planning something.' Does he think we're superheroes or something?"

"No way… he just believes there are people willing to do the right thing …whatever the cost, I guess."

"Oh, I get it … he means *billionaires* like us?"

"Yes, billionaires like us!" said Jack, raising his hand above his head. The other two boys high-fived him. "And now it's time for bed," said Jack. "The sooner I complete my journey with Perkin, the sooner we can get out of this place."

TWENTY ONE

Endareolfs

The tunnel spat Jack out but, thanks to his transparent form, he sank to the ground like a slightly weighted balloon. He sat completely still for a moment, savouring the contrast of an outdoor environment. *All right, that's enough nature appreciation ... where's Perkin?* He stood up. "One small step for man, one giant leap for mankind," he muttered, launching himself forward as if enjoying zero gravity. His leap took him to the side of a tree.

"There you are," came Perkin's familiar voice from behind him. Jack turned to see his friend sitting atop Vargo. The powerful white horse drew up alongside Jack, whereupon Perkin reached down a hand and helped Jack float up onto the saddle behind him. "There is no time to spare," said Perkin. "As you know you might vanish at any moment." Without any further ado, Perkin kicked his heels into Vargo's sides, and the horse thundered off at breakneck speed.

Some thirty minutes later, when Perkin slowed Vargo to a trot, Jack gazed about in wonder and asked, "Where *are* we?"

"We have reached the Woods of Despair."

"That's an odd name for a wood. Let's hope whoever chose it was rubbish at choosing names."

"I fear its reputation may be well earned ... those who have spent time here have not fared well."

"So pleased you brought me," said Jack, his eyes widening. Perkin brought Vargo to a halt. They sat deathly still and listened ... and could hear nothing. No birdsong. No birds. No animals. No buzzing flies. Even the wind had gone AWOL.

"Where is everything?" muttered Jack. Just then it grew darker, like someone had turned a dimmer switch. They looked above them – the branches of the trees were creeping and knitting together. "I'm guessing this happens *a lot* in The Dark Matter," said Jack, swallowing hard.

"I've never encountered anything like it."

"Please tell me this isn't your first visit to the Woods of Despair."

"It *is* my first visit. I was taught to avoid these woods at all cost ... there are dark forces here, Jack ... tales that tell of ..."

Jack interrupted him. "Unless they're happy tales, I'd rather you didn't tell me till later."

"I've been given to understand that the dark powers here are our allies … that they are expecting us."

"Expecting to kill us maybe," muttered Jack.

"No, I've received word that we have a common enemy in The First Evil. But that is all I know. Until recently, I thought the existence of endareolfs a myth. Their kind disappeared millennia ago. Needless to say, I have never met one."

Jack gazed into the darkness. *"Endareolfs?"*

Perkin reached down and retrieved what looked like a stick from his saddle bag. Moments later, he'd lit a torch.

"Did you hear that?" said Jack.

"Whispering?" replied Perkin.

"There it is again. Where's it coming from?"

"… All about us."

"What are the voices saying?"

"Hush. Listen …" said Perkin.

"Nightmares – welcome – to – your – nightmares – welcome – to –"

Jack saw Henry scamper from the darkness, his friend's face drenched in blood. Claire was close on his heels holding a mallet. She swung it over her head as Henry vanished into the side of the horse. Jack gazed about in vain for his vanished friend and Claire. Then he felt someone tugging on his robe. Gazing down he saw Samantha, her eyes filled with terror as she plunged down into a bog of quicksand.

"Help me, Jack!" she pleaded before she too vanished. A Snatcher-Gar flew directly at them. Jack braced himself but like Henry it passed through them and disappeared. Another materialised, and then another, all swooping and vanishing just as quickly. "S, sword," stuttered Jack.

"There is no need, the giant bears are but apparitions … sent to flame the embers of our despair!"

"Giant bears!?" said Jack, looking about frantically.

"I was brought close to death by one once. They are a feature of *my* nightmares. Whatever you're seeing Jack, it's not real! Close your eyes!"

Perkin kicked Vargo's ribs and they shot forwards, torch raised high, into the woods. Giant bears rushed from the darkness. They reared up on their hind legs, bellowing and swiping at Perkin with their great paws. Voices whispered of their destruction, their defeat, their doom.

As quickly as it had left, the light returned and the apparitions ceased.

They were within a tight cluster of trees. An area beside them pulsated like a room revealed by a flickering bulb. At once, a stone dwelling materialised.

93

"It appears we may have found them, Jack … the endareolfs."

"Are you sure *they* didn't find us?"

"I can be sure of nothing in the Woods of Despair." Perkin drew his sword and jumped to the ground. "Wait here," he continued, walking towards the dwelling moulded within the trees.

"Where's the door?" asked Jack.

"A timely question …" Perkin used his sword to remove some of the creepers that were all about the dwelling like a rash. In a flash, one of the vines shot forward and took his sword from his grasp. Perkin stood helpless as he watched his sword passed from vine-to-vine above him.

The wind in the trees picked up and seemed to whisper: "State your business here, hu-man."

"My name is Perkin Beck. I seek the endareolfs. I was told they could assist my companion and I on our quest."

"… State your quest."

"The annihilation of The Priory of Chaos."

"Who is your young companion?" the trees whispered.

"Jack Tracy. The only human child to find his way to The Dark Matter unhypnotised." A section of the ivy parted to reveal an impossibly tall, willowy figure. Jack leaned forward on Vargo, *Is that something's stretched shadow?*

The stretched shadow spoke: "Jack Tracy? We have been ex-*pecting* you," it whispered, taking a long stride out into the open. Jack gazed up, open mouthed – it had large, saucer-shaped eyes and a tiny round mouth … its expression one of never-ending surprise … *or fear*, thought Jack. "What's wrong?" The looming figure whispered, "you gawp like it's the first time you have beheld an endareolf."

Jack shook his head. "Uh … I think I'd remember if I'd seen another like you …" The endareolf nodded slowly. "I am The Wizard Margrin … and this is my brother, The Craftsman Grinmar," he continued, as another endareolf edged into view. "The Wizard and The Craftsman!" said Perkin, removing a glove and extending a hand for them to shake.

"It has been many years since I placed a spell on Earth," said Margrin, solemnly.

"But our patience has been rewarded, brother. For the fates have delivered us a young hero of *truly* indomitable spirit."

Jack looked back and forth between the two brothers. "What *me*? Are you joking?"

"Are you not here? … Alive and vital and ready to embrace the task ahead?"

"I am here … and to be honest, I'm just hoping to get through this in one piece."

94

"Your humility suits you well," said Grinmar.

A penny dropped. "… Was that you? … That day in the British museum … the whispering that led me to the Shaman?"

"Oh, yes. We have had an eye on you, Jack Tracy. And been present a number of times to assist you in your short life." Jack thought for a moment. Then he shrugged and smiled broadly as if he'd always *known* somehow that someone was looking out for him.

"You look hungry. Come in, come in …we've rabbit stew and fresh bread."

Margrin placed a hand on his brother's shoulder. "Jack's essence is quite diminished. It's best he does not eat in his transparent form."

"You're the wizard, brother of mine. I bow to your superior knowledge in such matters."

Inside the cramped dwelling, they sat in chairs hollowed from trees that rose up to join with the thatched roof. All around, nooks and crannies were crammed with unusual ornaments fashioned from gold, silver and platinum. "You can never have too much precious metal about, Jack," whispered Grinmar, who had noticed him staring at his creations.

"I suppose not," said Jack, shuffling in his narrow seat trying to get comfortable. "Why do you whisper all the time?" he asked, feeling positively wedged in.

"Why? … Because we are in hiding," whispered Grinmar.

"In hiding? From who?"

"The First Evil. Who else?"

"Is he looking for you?"

Grinmar shuddered. "I very much hope not. He doesn't know we exist … and it's our intention it should remain that way."

"Which is why the voices of our kind have evolved into whispers."

"And … what about your faces?" said Jack.

"What? They don't meet with your approval?"

"It's just that you look so…"

"So shocked? Hunted, perhaps?"

"Well, yes," said Jack.

"We should not trouble our hosts with too many personal questions," said Perkin.

"It is no trouble," said Grinmar.

"I agree. We are glad to satisfy *this* boy's curiosity," added Margrin.

"You see Jack," continued Grinmar, "our ancestors were once in the employ of The First Evil. They were commissioned to make The First Evil's plan of a university of chaos possible."

Perkin leant forwards. "Your kind made The Priory of Chaos possible? How?"

"Our ancestors, with their grasp of magic and the manipulation of matter, were tasked to construct a gateway ... one that would allow the Snatcher-Gars to travel to-and-from Earth with the souls of its children. The Winged Shaman that our ancestors created made this gateway possible," said Margrin, regretfully.

"When the gateway was opened, a great celebration was thrown for all six thousand six hundred and seven members of the endareolf community. The party was held atop what is now known as The Priory of Chaos," added Grinmar.

"Back then it was called The Fortress of Darkness. The party was an opening of sorts. A celebration of this newly created institute for the advancement of evil on Earth ... the newly-bred Snatcher-Gars were to collect the first Earth children that very night."

"So, there they were, our ancestors, gathered on top of the citadel, dressed in their finest robes, awaiting their celebration." Grinmar sighed. "There was never going to be a celebration. The first duty of these newly created beasts, the Snatcher-Gars, was to exterminate our entire species by dropping them from the skies about the citadel."

"Only they hadn't reckoned on the ingenuity of one of our forebears. He had magic by him that provided him dominion over his Snatcher-Gar assassin," said Margrin.

"And over those close by," added his brother.

"And so it was that a small band of endareolfs escaped. We are their descendants ... and the last of our kind."

"As a species we have felt persecuted for thousands of years. We also carry the burden of what our species has enabled The First Evil to do ..."

"And we've been waiting for our chance to avenge that terrible night ... and put things right," said Margrin.

"Some home brew for our solid guest," exclaimed Grinmar. He fetched a wooden bottle and three crystal goblets.

"Thank you," said Perkin, taking a sip of the alcoholic brew. Jack licked his lips. Perkin said, "You heard Margrin. You should not eat or drink in your current state. Besides, we should avoid any possibility of your returning to the Priory in a state of inebriation."

Jack shrugged.

"So how are you fitting in at The Priory of Chaos? Nobody suspects your freedom of thought?" said Margrin, his whisper betraying his excitement.

"No. Well, *yes*. Our underling had me sussed from day one. His name is Ken ... he was taken during the Second World War."

"He has not given you up to them?"

"No. He's become a good friend and an ally."

The brothers nodded at each other. "Good at inspiring camaraderie," said Grinmar.

"Indeed. Just as our early observations suggested."

Remembering how limited their time could be, Perkin decided to cut to the chase: "How do you propose to help us and, at the same time, avenge your ancestors?" Grinmar stood up and approached a richly polished chest in the corner of the dwelling. He opened it to reveal a Winged Shaman of the same owl-like proportions as the one in the cathedral.

"I was led to believe there were only *two* authentic Shamans in existence. The one in the cathedral, and the one that I recently learned is in the British Museum on Earth," said Perkin.

"Just two? An understandable misconception," said Margrin.

Perkin leaned forwards in his seat. "Alright. So how can this third Shaman be of use to us?"

"Are you aware of the differences between the two known Shamans?"

"Differences?" said Perkin.

"How could he be aware?" said Grinmar "The true nature of the Shamans has been kept secret and passed down through generations of endareolfs alone."

"Let me explain," said Margrin. "*Two* original Shamans were forged to create a gateway that allows the Snatcher-Gars to travel to and from Earth. The first Shaman was forged using elements taken from The Greater Good ... and the second is made from pure evil," Margrin went on, his whisper filled with regret.

"The 'good' Shaman was transported to Earth where it has remained ever since – one half of the celestial gateway," said Grinmar.

"While the other half of the gateway, the *evil* Shaman, sits atop the altar in the Priory's cathedral."

"The precise locations of the two Shamans are vital in creating the gateway that allows the Snatcher-Gars access to Earth. The only way to destroy the Earth Gate, thereby putting an end to the kidnapping of Earth's young for good, is to reverse the positions of the two Winged Shamans."

"And then activate the imploding sequence with a spell," said Margrin.

Jack shook his head. "How can I possibly take the Altar Shaman back to Earth without arousing suspicion?"

"By replacing it with this beauty," said Margrin, walking over to his brother and polishing the third Shaman with the sleeve of his black cloak.

"You're not suggesting I take *that* thing back to the Priory with me? Where would I hide it?"

"Show him, Margrin," whispered Grinmar.

The wizard closed his eyes and began to recite a spell ...

Shaman without, Shaman within
Shrink or grow, for con*cealing*,
For if it's found, humanity's bound,
To be sucked into hell and torment profound ...

With that, the Shaman shrank to the size of the one in the British Museum.

"Think you can conceal this?" asked Grinmar, placing the tiny Shaman in the palm of his hand and passing it to Jack. "Our ancestors were not fools, Jack. They knew The First Evil may betray them."

"They had no idea of the true extent of his treachery ... although his name might have provided them a clue."

"So they created this third Shaman and imbued it with magic of its own. This Shaman is the only hope you have of switching the positions of the Earth and Altar Shamans without arousing suspicion."

"And what will that do?" murmured Jack, gazing trance-like at the tiny shaman in his palm.

"As we said ... it will destroy the Earth Gate."

Jack swallowed hard.

"Do you realise the heavy weight of responsibility that now hangs on your shoulders, Jack?" said Grinmar.

Jack nodded slowly.

"Listen to me, boy," said Margrin. "You must switch the two Winged Shamans. All three Shamans can be shrunken and enlarged with the alteration spell." He handed Jack a piece of parchment with the words of the spell written on it. Jack opened his mouth to ask a question but, before he could utter a syllable, he vanished.

TWENTY THREE

Lost royalty

"That's it! Break his legs!" Claire yelled in her sleep. Her sickening cries had startled Jack and pulled him from the endareolfs' dwelling. Jack pushed the tiny Shaman and parchment down inside the pocket of his robe and looked over at Henry. Henry had been woken by Claire some time before. He was sitting up in his bed, arms folded, scowling in her direction. As soon as he realised Jack was back and unscathed, he smiled and unfolded his arms.

Jack climbed out of bed and pointed towards Ken's hideaway. Then he leaned around the door into the classroom and tapped Ken on his shoulder.

The three boys made their way inside the secret den.

"I hope this is a progress report," said Henry, rubbing his hands expectantly. "If I have to spend much longer with Claire, I'll throttle her, even in my enlightened state."

"We certainly are making progress," said Jack, struggling to contain his excitement. "Look at this," he continued, producing the tiny Shaman from his pockct and resting it in the palm of his hand.

Henry and Ken gazed at it blankly.

"Who'd have thought?" said Henry. "The Priory's got a gift shop after all. Next time you stop by there, pick me up a Claire action figure would you? Oh! And a hammer."

"This is it guys … this is the key to preventing the Priory carrying out its master plan," continued Jack, grasping the Shaman between his thumb and forefinger and holding it under Henry's nose.

Henry went boss-eyed. "I'm not convinced you've grasped the seriousness of our situation here, Jack."

"Look, I'll show you …" Jack placed the tiny object in his lap, cleared his throat and read the words from the parchment:

Shaman without, Shaman within
Shrink or grow for con*cealing*,
For if it's found, humanity's bound,
To be sucked into hell and torment profound

99

The Shaman mushroomed to owl size and sat heavily in Jack's lap.

"O ... kay ... nice trick, but shouldn't we be making them *smaller?*" said Henry, as Ken scrambled backwards and bumped his head on the wall.

"It's all right, guys," said Jack. "This one's just a decoy. Let me explain. According to the endareolfs, the only way to shut the gate that allows the Snatcher-Gars access to Earth is to reverse the positions of the two Winged Shamans. The one on the altar in the cathedral must be taken to Earth. The Shaman in the British Museum must be brought back here and placed on the altar. This third Shaman will ensure that the Priory has no idea that we've nabbed their original and taken it back with us."

"Wait a minute. Wait a minute!" said Henry. "This means that someone will have to return to The Priory of Chaos with the museum Shaman."

"One step at a time, Henry," said Jack, scratching his head.

"Oh yeah, one step at a time ... edging ever closer to oblivion," said Henry.

Just then, they heard a tapping on the other side of the wall. Jack and Henry looked startled. "It's all right, governors. Three taps followed by a pause and two further taps means ... it's them!" said Ken.

"*Them?*" replied Jack, covering the Shaman with his robe.

"The Underling Renegades," said Ken, tapping out a coded response. As he finished, a slab of rock began wobbling back-and-forth before being dragged through the wall to create an opening. The face of a pale, raven-haired boy poked through. "The king desires an audience with these two," he said, looking at Jack and Henry with a mixture of apprehension and disbelief.

"The *king?*" said Jack.

"Don't tell me they've got Elvis here ... I honestly don't think I could cope," said Henry.

"I am Peter McIvor," said the boy, "and I have been sent to escort you to an audience with King Edward the V ... of England." His tone was superior and direct.

"King Edward the *what* of *where?*" said Henry.

Jack said, "I think I know what he's talking about. I found an inscription in my book. Henry, do you remember when we went on that school trip to the Tower of London? Our Beefeater guide told us the story of 'The Princes in the Tower'.

"The only thing I remember about that trip was my Tower Cheese and Bacon Burger – enormous it was, with loads of ..."

"Henry! I know you're frightened but ... anyway, I think he's talking about King Edward ... the boy king who was imprisoned in the Tower of

London by his Uncle Richard ... 500 years ago! The story sounded so tragic ... it *actually* stayed with me." Jack gazed at the den's ceiling, inches from his head, and tried to remember the details of what he'd heard. He said, "The young king vanished from the Tower of London with his little brother ... and neither of the boys were ever seen again. Their uncle Richard was crowned king shortly after they disappeared. It's thought that Richard had his young nephews murdered."

"That's our King Edward, all right," said Ken, impressed with Jack's knowledge of history. "And what Richard did to them, having them brought here ...well, it was *worse* than murder if you ask me."

"What should we do?" asked Jack.

"Oh, the king's harmless enough. He's been here much longer than I have ...some five hundred years longer. I heard he was made an example of ... being a king and all ... and turned into an Underling as soon as he got 'ere. The story goes that he refused to wait on the students and went into hiding. He leads the Renegade Underlings. They live in the spaces between the walls of the citadel. The monks gave up searching for him centuries ago. They probably think he was eaten by the spiders or starved to death."

"If they're free, why haven't you joined them, Ken?" said Henry.

"There can only be one hundred renegades. It's what you might call the law. They keep the numbers down ... less chance of 'em being discovered that way."

"Should we go with him?" asked Jack, motioning towards the messenger.

Ken nodded enthusiastically. "I can't think of a single reason why not. You could do worse than make an ally of King Edward."

"Give us a minute, would you?" Jack said to Peter McIvor.

"I'll be waiting for you just through here," the raven-haired boy replied, pulling his head back through the opening. Jack recited the alteration spell under his breath. The Shaman shrunk and he put it in his pocket.

The boys crawled through the hole into a narrow space between two walls. Peter McIvor was dressed in the tattered finery of a medieval courtier: a filthy ruff, a crudely stitched red tunic and drainpipe pants that made his legs appear horribly thin and bow-legged. He picked a lantern off the floor and walked ahead of them.

Several hundred metres along, McIvor stopped and tapped out another code on a section of wall. A circular slab of masonry was pulled away from within, creating an entrance. McIvor doffed his cap but said nothing as they made their way past the three 'door-lings' and continued along another narrow passage. Jack and Henry's apprehension was growing with every step into this maze of corridors. Jack grasped the tiny Shaman in his sweating palm. The burden of losing it, or someone taking it from him, now rested heavy on his mind.

"It's all right, governors," said Ken. "We're almost there … there's nothing to worry about."

McIvor once again paused by an innocent looking section of wall. He placed the lantern on the ground and turned to face Jack and Henry. He approached (the now normal and scruffy) Henry and attempted to smarten him up as best he could. Then he turned to Jack and did the same, pulling on his robe and making sure his belt was correctly fastened round his waist. "You will address the king as Your Majesty. You will not speak to the king unless he speaks to you, first. Is that clear?" The boys nodded. McIvor straightened his own tunic and tapped on the wall. The stone wall slid apart to reveal the king's chamber: a long, narrow cavern with fifty wooden stumps down each side. Upon the stumps sat the ninety-nine assembled Renegade Underlings. At the far end was a raised platform, upon which stood a crude throne cobbled together from bits of old wood. Upon the throne sat a straight-backed boy, dressed from ruff-to-toe in tattered black velvet. He was as pale as a ghost with curly, golden locks held in place by a lopsided crown. McIvor motioned the three boys forward.

They walked through the narrow room, the curious gaze of the Renegade Underlings burning into them. These Underlings were wearing the same rag-tag finery as McIvor. It occurred to Henry they looked like sad harlequins who had been dragged through the countryside in their Sunday best. "Approach!" said the boy monarch, beckoning them with a languid wrist movement. The boys came to a halt before the raised throne.

The boy king leant forward. He looked down and studied the apprehension on Jack and Henry's faces. "There is nothing to fear," he said, warmly, extending a gloved hand for them to kiss. The boys took his hand and shook it in turn. The king looked puzzled but said nothing. Then he asked, "Have you come to deliver us?"

"To deliver you …Your Majesty?" said Jack, taken aback by the boy's nobility and ease.

"Yes. Are you not the students that possess their own minds?"

Jack and Henry looked at one another.

"There is little that comes to pass in this university of evil that escapes my attention. You were observed in the cathedral, three nights ago … using magic before the altar. You're fast becoming legends amongst the Underling community. They say you are messiahs come to free us from our torment."

Jack glanced at Henry. "Uh, we're definitely *not* messiahs … we're just

102

kids ... trying to do what's right."

"And pray, what *is* right?"

"The Priory ... it must be stopped ... or else our home, the place we all come from ... it will become a living nightmare."

"You have something important in your pocket?" continued the king, looking at Jack's concealed, fidgety hand. "Is it a weapon?"

"No," replied Jack.

"Reveal the object," said the boy king, firmly.

Jack hesitated but, realising he had little option, removed the tiny Shaman from his pocket.

The king stretched out his hand ... "Show us ..."

Jack took a step forward and placed the Shaman in his palm. "Indeed, it is an object of questionable beauty," said the king.

"It's our only hope of preventing the destruction of our world – of your old kingdom, Your Majesty," replied Jack.

The king smiled. "You should know that you have an ally in me, young sir," he said, handing it back. The king rested his head in his hand. "We have remained dormant here for so long. What is the year in our kingdom?" he asked, raising his head and looking straight at Jack, his blue eyes filled with a dulled curiosity.

Jack told him the date.

"And pray tell. What fate awaited my destroyer ... *Uncle* Richard?"

"He was killed ... at the Battle of Bosworth Field, I think."

"... I see. Killed by whom?"

Jack had known the answer once, but it escaped him now. He thought hard. The king appeared to be of the opinion that an answer would be worth the wait. And wait he did.

"I know this," said Jack, racking his brains. "It was something to do with ... with the Tudors," he muttered, "Henry the 8th's father ...? Yes, that's it! It was Henry Tudor ... he became King Henry the 7th It was Henry the 7th's army that killed your uncle ... on the field of battle!"

"Young master Tracy ... there would have been a time when news of my uncle's brutal demise would have been greeted with much festivity. But now? The years have mellowed us, we think."

"So, Richard wasn't what you'd call a *great* uncle, then ... Your Holiness," said Henry.

"It was Richard who locked us in the Tower. Our uncle was much taken with the dark arts, seduced by witches, portents and so forth. He discovered a way to communicate with those loathsome beasts, the Snatcher-Gars. One evening in November, he escorted my brother and I to the roof of the White Tower. It was a clear night and we were to observe the celestial heavens ... a particular hobby of my dear brother. I remember that cold November night as if it were yesterday. How our uncle laughed as the monsters descended from the heavens and carried us from our kingdom. Alas, my brother did not survive the journey here. He died of fright … and was dropped for the crows."

"I'm sorry, Your Majesty, sorry for your loss," said Jack.

"He was one of the lucky ones. Taken to the bosom of our Lord and eternal peace therein … something *we* may never find."

"You have a strong faith in an afterlife?" asked Jack.

"I do. Is this something you lack, Master Tracy?"

"… I have faith in the intentions and actions of good people. Therefore, I thank you for your kind offer of help. Apart from our good friend Ken, we are all alone here."

"Nonsense! Your ranks are swelling, young sir," said the king, standing. "You look tired. And I have demanded enough of your time. McIvor, escort our visitors back to their dormitory." The king addressed Jack. "May God go with you and protect you. And may he also protect you with the hearty appetite," he said, glancing at Henry.

"Thank you, Your Holiness," replied Henry.

"Poor boy … he imagines I'm the Pope. Never mind. Carry on!" he said, turning and ascending his throne.

As they made their way back to the dormitory behind McIvor, the boys were unaware of a bat-like creature circling the citadel. Gob was using his acute sense of smell to locate Jack. Ever since he'd overheard The First Evil question the Reader about this child, the 'one who may know his own mind', Gob had been fretting over his probable involvement. If it was this boy, who Gob now felt certain had shown a spark of anger as he'd carried him to the Priory, his position was grave. He needed to discover more about this child, if only to put his mind at ease. This was why he was about to take a huge risk and interrogate the boy himself. He had expected it to be a straightforward abduction. He'd simply have to locate and remove the boy from his dorm …

What's this? The boy is on the move?" thought Gob, snot bubbling from his nostrils and plummeting towards the forest below. "How can he be on the move at *this* hour? All humans are confined to their dormitories!" The implications of this triggered a tidal wave of dread and curiosity, and Gob went into free-fall like a hawk dive-bombing a rabbit. He phased through the thick outer walls of the Priory, taking the most direct route towards Jack's scent.

A pupil studying late in his dorm, saw a black shadow shoot through his room. The boy shuddered as Gob phased through him on his way towards his quarry.

On the level below, a girl was fast asleep and dreaming about her new life as Head Bully at her school back on Earth. In her dream, she had thrown a brick at her victim's head. As the girl collapsed with a shattered skull, a Snatcher-Gar flew past and disappeared through the gymnasium wall. *Unusual place for a Snatcher-Gar,* mused the dreaming bully.

"The king seems like a great guy," said Henry, as they made their way back down the narrow corridor behind McIvor.

"I agree," said Jack. "You know, I think things are finally starting to go in our favour." Just as Jack finished speaking, Gob's head appeared through the ceiling above them. The Snatcher-Gar held back and eavesdropped on their conversation. "I can't wait to see Samantha ... give her the potion and get her back to her old self again," said Jack.

"I'm looking forward to hearing the old Samantha's take on all this too," said Henry.

What's this? thought Gob. *They* both *know their own minds ... two intruders! And the fat one was brought here by Phlem. I can't wait to share the news with him!* And with that, Gob's eyes narrowed as his claws swung open ...

Jack and Henry's world became a blur as Gob picked them up and spun like a tornado towards the roof of the citadel. Half a minute later, Ken turned and looked behind him to discover that his two companions had simply vanished.

The boys found themselves dumped unceremoniously onto the roof of the citadel – their worlds continuing to spin. "You've been such *bad* little humans," said a high-pitched, rasping voice that Jack recognised immediately.

Jack sat up and attempted to focus on the creature standing atop its clawed feet. "What do you want?" he asked, groggily.

"What do I want? WHAT DO I WANT?" replied Gob, hopping with rage. I want NOT to be cut up and fed to the wolves of the forest! I want not to end up as a garnish on The First Evil's cauldron! And thanks to you, these things are now a distinct possibility. I should just gut you here," he continued, walking towards the boys.

"Wait!" cried Jack. "If, if you kill us, you will be doomed for sure," he continued, trying desperately to think of a way to buy them some time.

"Wait you say? Why should I wait? I must surely destroy and then dispose of the evidence?"

Jack grasped at a half-formed idea: "I knew!" he said, "I knew you'd realise that something was different about me. It was inevitable ... what with your ... your incredible intelligence!"

"It's true. My intelligence is incredible."

"That's right! So realising how intelligent you arc, I took out an insurance policy."

"An insurance policy? Against my intelligence? What manner of policy? It must have been expensive!"

We're billionaires ... thought Henry.

"A letter ... I've written a letter. It's held by one of the Underlings ... not our own Underling ... that would be too obvious."

"Letter you say? Who's the letter for? What does the letter say?"

"It's for The First Evil. It explains everything about my journey here. It ... it mentions you by name!"

"It mentions me by name?"

"Yes," interrupted Henry, making sure he still possessed the power of speech.

"What despicable lies! You do not know my name. How could you? We were never formally introduced."

Jack was now trying frantically to remember the name that he'd heard the other Snatcher-Gar call this repulsive creature. He knew it was something short that had struck him as being entirely appropriate. Unless he could remember it within the next few seconds, they were Snatcher-Gar meat. *Snot? Blot? Glob? Fob? Sob? Rob? GOB!* The relief that Jack experienced was indescribable. "I do know your name!" he shouted.

"Well?" said Gob, his talon raised and ready to gut him.

Jack looked into the creature's eyes ... "Gob! Your name is Gob and if *anything* happens to me, or my friend, The First Evil will know your name too."

"That's right!" yelled Henry, crawling to Jack and throwing a protective arm over him. Gob lowered his claw.

Uncertainty now rocked the Snatcher-Gar. *What if they speak the truth? Are they not resourceful? The first to infiltrate The Priory of Chaos.* "You are so troublesome! Of all the Snatcher-Gars, you had to pick me!" he screeched.

Jack and Henry looked at each other as if to say 'It was us who picked *him*?'

"Gob must have time to think. To consult with his colleague, Phlem." Gob was sure to say the name 'Phlem' loud enough to be overheard by the two boys. "It was Phlem who carried the fat one here," he continued, motioning in Henry's direction. "Did you hear that humans?"

"Yes, we heard that," replied Jack, appalled but not surprised at the beast's lack of loyalty to his friend.

Henry said, "I'll write a letter to The First Evil as soon as I get back to my dormitory ... tell him it was Phlem who brought me here."

"As I say, I will consult with my esteemed colleague, PHLEM ...and we will decide how best to deal with this matter."

He was about to flap off and leave them on the roof when Jack, feeling they actually had the upper hand for once, said: "You're not going to *leave* us up here are you? How would we get back to our dormitory without getting caught? If that happens, we'll *all* be for it," he said, narrowing his eyes at Gob. Gob shook his head and swore before grabbing them both and plunging back down inside The Priory of Chaos.

TWENTY FOUR

Hunted!

In the First Evil's throne room, the twelve elders of The Priory of Chaos sat with their heads bowed. At the top of the table, and positioned either side of The First Evil's empty chair, sat the Master Priors, Salcura and Sinosa. All twelve monks looked fidgety and sheepish. "Heads must roll for this," said Salcura, gazing down the table.

"Such a development was inconceivable. None of us could have foreseen it," added Sinosa.

"The Reader HAS seen it." The double doors to the throne room flew open. The First Evil thundered in, his bullish bulk swaying from side-to-side like a drunk lurching towards a bar. He headed for the table and brought his enormous fists crashing down upon it. "Why is the Reader not here!" he bellowed. "I have no interest in what this assembly of clerks has to say. Send for the Reader, now!"

"The Reader is being held in the cathedral, my Lord," replied Sinosa, motioning to a Dark Monk to fetch her.

The First Evil seated himself at the head of the table. "Tell me," he said, through gritted teeth. "How was this new information extracted from the Reader? Can it be trusted?"

"We have been starving the Reader, my Lord. She was promised food in exchange for information we might find of value. It was made clear that, should she waste our time, she would be boiled alive in Snatcher-Gar urine."

"Prepare the urine," said The First Evil, as the Reader was manhandled into the room.

Even though seated, The First Evil towered over her waif-like form. He narrowed his eyes, and fixed them on her. "You have new information? Concerning the child visiting the forests?"

"Yes, your Majesty ..." she replied, breathlessly.

"Well?"

"I saw the boy, my Lord ... in the Woods of Despair."

"*Boy*? It has a gender now?"

"My vision clearly revealed a boy, my Lord."

"And pray tell ... what was this boy doing?"

"He was meeting with ..." the Reader paused and gazed towards the ground.

"Yes?"

"He was meeting with two endareolfs." Many of those present experienced a cold shudder as they heard the woman speak the name that should never be spoken. "That's impossible ... the endareolfs were culled to extinction millennia ago," said The First Evil, his voice betraying uncharacteristic concern.

"Yes, my Lord, I know, but ..."

"And yet you dare to stand here and lie to me, your Lord and Master!" He reached out and grabbed her by her throat.

"It's true!" she spluttered.

"My Lord," said Sinosa, "If the Reader is extinguished, she will yield scant information."

The First Evil drew her close, "How sure are you of your vision?"

"I'm certain of it," she gurgled.

"Pray, what was the subject of their conversation?"

"I do not know, my Lord. My visions are as silent as they are fleeting ..."

"Can you not lip read?"

"No, my Lord ..."

The First Evil released her and looked at Sinosa. "Dispatch the Snatcher Guard to the Woods of Despair," he ordered.

"How many battalions, my liege?"

"How many, this fool asks. Send them all! Uproot every tree. Burn every bush. Extinguish anything with a pulse. If the endareolfs are there, find and destroy them. Bring their bodies to me. The child may prove a trickier quarry – returning to Earth as it surely is between excursions. In the meantime, place a twenty-four hour guard on the Altar Shaman."

"Yes, My Lord."

***

The next morning the boys awoke with renewed positivity. They didn't feel so alone now they had a king and his entourage looking out for them. Not to mention gaining the upper hand over a Snatcher-Gar. Quite a coup, Jack had thought, as he nodded off the night before. During breakfast, they had been unable to discuss the new developments thanks to Claire plonking herself between them.

"I must say, you two are in remarkably good spirits this morning. I hope you're not keeping anything from me?" said Claire, as they glided through the Atrium of Staircases on their way to the morning lesson.

"We wouldn't dare keep something from you," said Jack.

"As if we'd ever do anything that stupid," added Henry.

As they approached the landing, they saw Ken standing outside the classroom. He was pacing up and down and looking more troubled than usual. "Oh, look!" said Claire. "The runt's in a right state. Wonder what the waste-of-space has done now?" The boys sensed that something was terribly wrong. "He's probably just terrified because he knows we're due back," said Jack.

"You think so? If that's true then we're obviously doing something right," replied Claire, rubbing her hands in glee.

"You should be afraid, runt!" Henry yelled in his best pantomime villain voice. "No. Let me deal with him, Henry. I could use a good laugh," said Jack, grabbing Ken by an earlobe and pulling him a little way along the corridor. "You two carry on," said Jack, glancing back at Claire.

"Seems rather selfish of you Jack," remarked Claire. "So, carry on then!"

In the shadows between their classroom and the one next door, Jack grabbed Ken gently by his throat and pushed him up against the wall. "What's wrong?" Jack asked him.

"We've got serious trouble, gov. I've just received a message from the Underling Renegades."

"And?"

"And The First Evil has only gone and placed the Altar Shaman under guard."

"Is that normal?"

"I've never heard of such a thing. Not in the seventy-five years I've been here ... and it gets worse."

Jack braced himself.

"They've dispatched the Snatcher Guard to the Woods of Despair."

"But why?"

"It's the forest where you met the endareolfs ... they're after 'em."

Jack's legs turned to jelly. "Oh God, Ken ... what have I done?"

"You? You've done nothing wrong. It's that Reader."

"Reader?"

"Yes, the mystic. She's been spilling the beans. One of the king's Renegades spied on her being interrogated. The brave lad heard everything through a vent in the ceiling of the throne room."

"What did he hear?"

"Apparently, the Reader saw you talking to them tree dwellers in a vision."

"Did she hear what they told me about switching the Shamans?"

"No, thank goodness. But they're on to you, gov. They know you've been visiting the woods."

"Do they know I'm here? At the Priory?"

"Not yet they don't. Not for sure anyhow."

"We're going to have to steal the Altar Shamans and get out of Dodge as soon as possible!"

"It's not going to be easy ... not with that guard hanging about."

"There has to be a way."

"I'll put on my thinking cap." Just then, a group of students walked past and glared at them. Without uttering another word, Jack and Ken returned to the classroom.

The torches dimmed and Herute made his customary entrance from beneath the pulpit. "A bad morning to you all," he said. Then he paused, grabbed a stack of papers and tossed them into the air. The papers separated and came floating down all about the previously tidy classroom. "Oh! The joys of anti-social behaviour!" boomed Herute. "Although, before you start behaving like primates, don't forget that anti-social behaviour is to be restricted to the Earth realm." The children all nodded in agreement. Jack removed a sheet of paper that had settled on his head and looked at it. 'Embrace The Chaos' was the title at the top of the page. *I'm doing my best*, he thought.

"So! What is the difference between anti-social behaviour and chaos?" asked Herute, even though he was looking forward to enlightening the class himself. "I'll tell you," he continued, ignoring the hands that had shot up. "Anti-social behaviour comprises those small pockets of unrest that combine to create chaos as a whole. Now, who would like to suggest a typical example of anti-social behaviour?" Several children put up their hands. "You child," he said, pointing to a boy at the back of the classroom.

"Hanging out in gangs and breaking stuff!"

"Adequate answer, boy. It's important that you congregate in groups of like-minded hoodlums and defile as much property as you can. But, moving away from property and possessions, what is the main target we're endeavouring to destroy with intimidating, loutish behaviour?"

"Windows, sir?" said a girl next to Jack.

"*Windows?*" muttered Jack, rolling his eyes in contempt.

"I concur with your response," Herute said to Jack. "I presume it means you can do better?"

Jack knew exactly what answer this odious teacher wanted to hear. He drew a deep breath and said, "Peace of mind, sir ... we're hoping to destroy people's peace of mind."

"I feel a commendation coming on," said Herute, dipping his hand into his pocket and retrieving his note pad.

I really have got to get out of this place A.S.A.P. thought Jack, while doing his best to look chuffed. Herute grabbed his lapels with his thumbs in that superior manner of his. "We absolutely CANNOT permit individuals to go about their lives with any peace of mind whatsoever. Feelings such as contentment and security must be stripped bare and replaced by uncertainty and distress. Positive emotions *are* the enemies of chaos. They are to be crushed without hesitation and without mercy!" Jack was now pondering the likelihood that the gang in his neighbourhood had been taught the tools of their trade right here in this very classroom. He quickly dispelled the idea when he remembered that literally *thousands* of classrooms like this one existed at The Priory of Chaos. He was once again overwhelmed with a sense of purpose. These classrooms would remain empty *forever* if he had anything to do with it. Jack was startled from his thoughts by the sound of Herute bashing the pulpit with his staff and raising his voice. "This brings us to the MAIN FUEL of anti-social behaviour. This fuel was developed here in The Dark Matter by Friar Cirrhosis for a single purpose: to rot humanity from within. This glorious substance unburdens humans of their inhibitions and encourages them to spray their environments with acidic bile. Now children, the poison to which I refer is ...?"

At least a dozen hands shot up. A boy in the second row, whose father had been an abusive alcoholic, was practically hanging off his chair at the prospect of answering the question. Herute ignored him and pointed to a disinterested girl next to him. The girl picked some dirt from beneath her fingernails and said, "Alcohol, sir."

"That's right, ALCOHOL! In the pursuit of anti-social behaviour, alcohol is an invention of unrivalled genius. You are therefore to encourage your peers to drink as much alcohol as possible. However, I advise you to limit your own intake as chaos is best orchestrated with a clear head."

The next couple of hours crawled by for Jack and Henry. Jack in particular had started to feel like a hunted animal. *Hunted animals should be on the move,* he thought, as he sat there, trying desperately not to betray his growing anxiety. The seconds felt like minutes and the minutes like hours before the lesson was finally over.

TWENTY FIVE

Rags, buckets and Shamans

The wait felt like an eternity, but the sound the boys had been waiting for could now be heard: Claire's snoring. Ken put his head around the door and peered into the darkened dormitory. He was keen to see if Jack and Henry were ready for their group meeting and eager to tell them the plan he'd hatched for switching the Shamans. Jack saw the outline of Ken's head silhouetted against the burning torch on the far side of the classroom. He climbed out of bed and beckoned him in. Henry got up and all three crept towards the den.

Once inside the tiny hideaway, they sat cross-legged in a circle. Ken unfolded what appeared to be a large brown rag. "Who's that for?" asked Jack.

"It's for you," said Ken, handing it to him.

"What am I supposed to do with an old rag," he asked, taking it.

"You're supposed to wear it. An hour from now, the Underling cleaners will be doing their scrubbing duties in the cathedral. This means making sure the altar and everything on it is spick-and-span. I know you're going to want to switch the Shaman yourself – wearing these clothes is the only way that's going to be possible."

"Well done, Ken," said Jack. "You've saved the day again."

Ken smiled warmly.

"Well?" said Henry. "Where's my tramp's costume?"

"You don't look like an Underling cleaner, you're too well fed," said Ken.

"That's a joke! I'm starving."

"You don't look starving," Ken pointed out.

"It's okay, Henry. You stay here and keep an eye on Claire."

"Great! My all-time favourite activity: Claire Watch."

"We'll be back before you know it," said Jack, pulling the filthy garment over his head. "How do I look?" he asked.

"You've looked worse ... but smelt a lot better," said Henry, grimacing.

"And you're going to need to look worse now," said Ken, scraping his hand along the dusty wall and smudging the resulting filth on Jack's face and neck.

Ken tapped on the wall: three knocks followed by two knocks. The usual section of wall began to wobble to-and-fro and then disappeared to reveal the exit. Jack was about to crawl through the narrow space when Henry grabbed his shoulder, "Good luck," he said, "… you *can* do this, Jack."

Jack smiled, "Thanks, Henry."

On the other side of the wall, Jack was greeted by a troop of a dozen Underling cleaners: filthy, emaciated and pungent, they were dressed in rags similar to his own. The children were holding wooden buckets by handles made from twine. A little black boy emerged from the group and handed Jack a bucket. Jack took hold of the twine handle and gazed down inside it. He saw several centimetres of grey water with two sponges floating on top. "The Altar Shaman should fit inside the bucket nicely," said Ken.

Jack removed one of the sponges. "Has anyone got a penknife?" he asked. The Underling cleaners shook their heads. Jack turned to see Ken disappearing back inside his den. He emerged moments later with a penknife. Jack unfolded it and used the rusty blade to hollow out a small space in the sponge. He handed Ken his penknife and retrieved the tiny Shaman from his pocket. The urchins looked on as he inserted it into the newly-hollowed space in the sponge. "It's a perfect fit," he said, placing the sponge (and the Shaman concealed within it) back inside the bucket.

The Snatcher-Guardsman who'd been assigned to protect the Altar Shaman stood proud and motionless before the altar. As a member of the elite Snatcher-Guard, his black chain-mail was highly polished and protected his folded wings as well as his body. He looked like a giant, gothic ornament. At his side hung a sword encased within a bronze scabbard. This member of the Guard was in a foul mood. While the rest of his battalion was out slaughtering anything with a pulse in the Woods of Despair, he had been ordered to stay behind on guard duty.

As the party of cleaners approached, the Guardsman's hand fell to the hilt of his sword. He was itching to raise his spirits by embarking upon a bloody purge of his own. The muffled sound of The First Evil raising his voice in his throne room behind him made him think again.

As the Underling cleaners neared the altar, they huddled around Jack. The group passed under the gaze of the Guardsman who looked down upon them with disdain before raising his long nose into the air. Jack was jostled to-and-fro within the 'scrum' and emerged to find himself nose-to-nose with the Altar Shaman. It looked like an exact copy of the one in the

114

British Museum, albeit its larger brother. He put down the bucket and, having withdrawn the empty sponge, began to swab the face of the Altar Shaman with it. A moment later, he looked nervously over his shoulder at the Guardsman. The Guardsman, who seconds before had satisfied himself that Jack posed no threat to the Shaman, once again stood facing into the main body of the cathedral. Jack knelt down and, as he rinsed out his sponge, he mouthed the alteration spell over the sponge that contained the tiny Shaman. The decoy Shaman inside the sponge enlarged and banged against the inside of the bucket! The Guardsman looked around. Jack stood up and began to wipe the area around the Altar Shaman. With a lump of fear now wedged in his throat, Jack once gain glanced over his shoulder. The Guardsman glared at him before looking away, his nose hoisted by an invisible line of self-importance towards the rafters.

In Jack's personal space, there were now *two* owl-sized Shamans. He felt dizzy at the idea that, within the next few moments, he was going to have to swap them over. Having glanced over his shoulder one last time, his heart beating flat-out in his chest, he lifted the Altar Shaman off its velvet plinth and placed it to one side. He crouched and, wiping away the beads of sweat that threatened his vision, he grabbed at the now enlarged decoy Shaman in the bucket. *It can't be! It is ... it's wedged inside!* He lifted his leg and placed a trembling knee on the edge of the bucket. *Pull Jack! ...* The decoy Shaman began to move. *A firmer tug, Jack ... just a bit more ... come on ... come on ...* It slid free and Jack lifted it out and gave it pride of place on the velvet plinth. Then he picked up the Altar Shaman; the tips of his fingers flat and aching as he lowered it carefully inside the bucket. He whispered the alteration spell and the evilest object in all creation was reduced to the size of a thimble and shoved inside a sponge. *Mission accomplished.*

Just then, voices and footsteps could be heard approaching from behind the altar. Jack glanced about at the Underlings. They looked petrified. The reason for their anxiety became clear as The First Evil's horns and then his enormous head loomed over the altar and gazed down at him. "What have we here? A filthy Underling?" observed The First Evil. Jack gazed up into the First Evil's blood-red eyes – his legs grew weak and he reached out for the pulpit to steady himself. The First Evil peered closely at the decoy Shaman. He tapped it with a long black fingernail and then, to Jack's exquisite relief, he moved away.

As Jack and the Underling cleaners made their way back up the cathedral's central aisle, they could hear The First Evil's cloven hooves thundering up and down behind the altar. He was clearly restless and returned several times to peer at the decoy Shaman. Then he slumped down upon his throne above the altar. "I've overlooked something," he muttered, before standing and heading back into the throne room.

Inside the throne room, Sinosa was seated at the table and signing documents. "I sense that something's troubling you, my Lord," he said, as the red giant leant on the table and glared at the celestial map.

"There's something ... something I've overlooked." The First Evil made his way towards his main throne and sat down. He rested his head in his left hand and remained motionless for several minutes. Then he looked up and bellowed: "Bring me the Reader! Bring me the Reader NOW!"

The cleaning party had left the cathedral. They had glided down a maintenance Way-Point and disappeared inside the fabric of the citadel. Once they were out of sight, Ken sidled up to Jack and attempted to look inside his bucket. "Did you get it, gov?"

Jack nodded ... "I got it."

"He got it!" shouted Ken, making a fist and punching the air. The others gathered around Jack. Some patted him on the back while others waited in turn to shake his hand.

"Thanks, guys," said Jack. "I couldn't have done it without you. I thought we were mincemeat when The First Evil pitched up."

"You fooled him. He didn't suspect a thing he didn't!" said Ken.

"I don't know how I didn't freak ..."

"What are you going to do with the Altar Shaman," asked the black boy whose bucket he'd used.

"With any luck, I'll be using it to do good."

"You think there's good in it?" the boy asked, wide eyed.

"Probably not," said Jack, retrieving the sponge and pulling out the Altar Shaman. The Underling cleaners gasped at the sight of it.

The Reader was standing before The First Evil. "I'm going to ask you a simple question, Reader. In response only one word will pass your lips. The word will be 'yes' or 'no'. Nod if you understand."

The Reader nodded.

"The boy you saw talking to the endareolfs ... was he ... transparent?" The Reader's face contorted with apprehension.

She opened her mouth and, through quivering lips she whispered, "Yes!"

The First Evil stood and raised his massive fists into the air ... "The boy is here!" he bellowed, "He is at The Priory of Chaos!"

Several metres above, the Renegade Underling assigned to spy on the throne room, spat out the piece of bread he'd been chewing and scurried off as fast as his skinny legs would carry him.

116

TWENTY SIX

The net closes in

The Snatcher-Gar Aviary had changed little since its construction three thousand years earlier. A domed structure, that ballooned from the side of the citadel like a foul growth. It was composed of black meshing weaved around an ascending, festering cone of straw crammed with Snatcher-Gar nests.

Gob was pacing about his 'nest' near the top of the aviary. A rancid living-space, strewn with half eaten rodents and shiny objects he'd liberated from the homes of his victims. These included a rusted trombone and a hoard of costume jewellery, all partially submerged in the Snatcher-Gar droppings that were removed monthly and trodden into wine.

For the last twenty-four hours, Gob had been champing at the bit to tell Phlem about their involvement in the unfolding crisis. Phlem had been on a hunting break in the western forests and was due back any time.

"Where is the fool?" muttered Gob, peering westerly through the aviary's torn meshing for the umpteenth time.

A dot appeared on the horizon.

"Could it be the dot has a name?" mumbled Gob. "Would that dot answer to the name of Phlem?" Gob squinted at the approaching U.F.O. before turning his long black nose skyward and inhaling. "Such a foul stench … it is him!" he shouted, opening his enormous wings to attract Phlem's attention.

Phlem had enjoyed his hunting break. He'd caught and eaten several pig-size rodents. As pleasurable as that had been, it was not uppermost in his thoughts. The spectacle he had witnessed as he'd flown over the Woods of Despair had proven of far greater interest. The Snatcher-Guards' assault on the area was impressive and he was now eager to tell the regular Snatcher-Gars the latest news. He spotted Gob flapping his wings at him and imagined he was keen to hear news of these developments. He was wrong.

Phlem negotiated his way through a section of torn meshing and flew down close to Gob. He was about to relay his news when Gob stole his thunder. "We're doomed, Phlem!" screeched Gob. "Doomed! Everything

117

is our fault!"

"Calm thyself Snatcher-Gar! I have important news concerning developments in the Woods of Despair."

"Developments? Developments? There would *be* no developments if not for our foolishness!"

"What in The Dark Matter are you flapping about?"

"It was us!"

"What was us?"

"The intruders ..."

"What of the intruders?"

"We brought them to The Priory of Chaos!"

"Them? There is but ONE intruder and he has been visiting the woods of Despair."

"No! There are *two* intruders and they're here, within the citadel, because WE brought them!"

"Have you been at the excrement wine again?" asked Phlem, sniffing at Gob's breath.

"Listen to me! I've spoken to them. They've written letters about us to The First Evil. They're *black*mailing us."

"Calm yourself ... and tell me of these children?"

"They came from Barton Road in the province of Londinium. You must remember my ward that day ... the child smelt so *putrid* in its humanity that I wanted to vomit."

"I do remember. What of him?"

"It's him! He's the intruder! I knew I should have dropped him for the crows. But then, along you came with your great fat buddy and your insulting remarks. It's your fault! You distracted me! The fat one you were carrying is the second intruder!"

"There's no way the leaden child knew his own mind when I carried him here."

"Well, he does now! And a more opinionated ball of human blubber I never wish to meet!"

"If what you say is correct ... then our path is clear. We must at once molest the delivery tables and incriminate others in their transportation."

"And then ...?"

"Then we must kill the intruders and bury their stinking carcasses in the woods."

"But what of the letters they've readied for The First Evil?"

"Letters you say? I do not believe there are any letters – just the rantings of desperate children. You said it yourself, this human reeks of humanity. How would he benefit from our executions? He would not."

"The lying excrement! I should have gutted him on the roof ..."

"Do not trouble yourself with your own stupidity now. We must abduct and destroy them before The First Evil has a chance to question them. Do you know where the intruders be?"

"Those two could be anywhere! They treat the place like a holiday camp!"

"Once the delivery tables are molested, we shall seek them by their scents ... and dispose of them."

The spy from the ceiling grating in The First Evil's throne room finally burst into King Edward's chamber. He approached the king and fell on one knee, panting and struggling for breath. "Grave news, Sire," he spluttered. "The First Evil ... he knows, he knows that Jack Tracy is here ... he knows he's at the Priory."

The king sprang to his feet, "Send a messenger to warn them, immediately!"

When Jack and Ken returned from their mission to liberate the Altar Shaman, they found Henry and Claire asleep in bed. Jack, who had changed back into his robe inside Ken's den, climbed into bed clutching the now tiny Altar Shaman. He lay on his side staring at it in the diminished candle light. He couldn't believe he had such an important object in his grasp. This thing had sat atop the cathedral's altar for thousands of years. Now it was his responsibility. *One Shaman down ... one to go*, he thought, remembering the other one they must somehow liberate from the British Museum. Jack closed his eyes and his mind filled with the disturbing thoughts he'd been trying to shut out all day. *What has become of my friends in the Woods of Despair? Are Grinmar and Margrin okay? Not to mention Perkin.* Jack felt that Perkin could probably take care of himself (even faced with a battalion of the Snatcher-Guard). But the endareolfs? Notwithstanding their magic, they were old and vulnerable. Lying there, snug in the comparative security of his bed, Jack began to consider the dangerous notion of returning to their tree-dwelling that night. *Just for a quick peek*, he thought. *They may be injured and need my help. But I'll have no control over how long I'm there. If I'm captured ...* He let out a heavy sigh and resigned himself to getting some much needed sleep. His sleep would be short-lived.

TWENTY SEVEN

Time's up!

An army of Dark Monks had been dispatched and instructed to wait outside each of the classrooms housing the first-month students. Each Dark Monk had been directed to enter his assigned classroom at precisely 3am. Once inside, they would amplify their perceptive abilities, using them to glimpse fear or uncertainty within the sleeping students. The time was now 2.57am. Six hundred and sixty six monks stood poised to enter six hundred and sixty six classrooms.

The messenger that King Edward had sent to warn the boys had reached the outside wall of Ken's den. The panting Underling attempted to remove the stone slab with fingers drenched in sweat. "Please, please, please, come away," he muttered. "If I fail, all will be lost!" The stone suddenly slid several centimetres towards him and he dug his fingers into the grooves on either side of it …

Outside the classrooms, the Dark Monks, who were able to sense the passing of time to within a fraction of a second, moved closer to their respective doors; their freakish fingers bristling with anticipation.

The Underling messenger heaved out the stone. He crawled through the tiny gap into Ken's den and then made his way out into the darkened dorm. He tiptoed over to Jack's bed and shook him firmly by the shoulders. "Wake up! Wake up!" he whispered.

Jack, who had nodded off only moments before, woke with a start. "What is it?" he said, his eyes wide with bafflement.

"You must come with me, now!" said the boy. The urgency in the Underling's voice was such that Jack realised this was no time for questions. It was 3am. The monks entered the classrooms. The Dark Monk assigned to Jack and Henry's classroom walked past the Underling asleep on her chair and entered the first dormitory to his left. Once inside, the Dark Monk scanned the sleeping children for any trace of real emotion. He sensed nothing and headed for dormitory two. Meanwhile, in the boys' dormitory (number three), Jack was alerting Henry while the messenger woke Ken by yanking him off his chair and pulling him inside the dorm. Ken rubbed his eyes and peered into the darkness to see several hands beckoning him furiously.

In the dormitory next door, the Dark Monk had scanned the sleeping children and, having satisfied himself of their innocence, he headed swiftly back into the classroom. The 'sight' of Ken's empty chair outside Jack and Henry's dormitory made him suspicious. His suspicions were justified: four of the five children within, Jack, Henry, Ken and the Renegade Underling, were making good their escape through Ken's den – Claire's snoring fading into the background.

The Dark Monk entered their dormitory and glared in the direction of the two empty beds. Then he woke Claire by clapping his hands. "What is it?" asked Claire, gazing up into the face of (what looked like) a floating corpse. "A Dark Monk?" she muttered, and glanced over at the now empty beds. *That's odd*, she thought.

"Where are the others?" asked the monk, his voice flat, emotionless, empty.

"I was about to ask you the same question," replied Claire, rubbing the sleep from her eyes. Sensing the girl knew nothing, the Dark Monk began searching the room like a burglar with a strict time code. He flew towards Jack's bed, tossed it aside – nothing but darkened stone beneath. He moved swiftly to Henry's bed and sent it cart-wheeling the length of the dormitory. Again nothing. Claire leapt from her bed moments before the monk sent it screeching into the empty bookcase – the bookcase, which was hopelessly old, shattered into several pieces.

"Oh, look!" said Claire, pointing at the kennel-size entrance to Ken's den. The Dark Monk glided towards it as if carried by a sudden gust. He shrank to the ground and squeezed through the entrance like a large dog into a small kennel. Inside, he ran his long fingers over the walls, searching for an exit – his spatula fingertips soon discovered the grooves around the removable stone. The monk produced a menacing cry as he forced the stone into the narrow corridor beyond.

"Hello …?" said Claire, as she walked towards the den's entrance. "What's all this then?" She dropped to her knees and peered inside the secret hideaway. The monk was gone. She reached in and withdrew an object lying on the floor … *a plane?* She held Ken's Spitfire aloft. The tiny green plane's wings were broken and dangling from its side. Just then, two more Dark Monks glided into the dormitory. Claire stood up and turned to face them. "He went through there," she said, pointing down at the tiny entrance.

The boys had been high-tailing it behind the messenger for several minutes. "I must rest," said Henry, finally. "I just need half a minute."

"I agree," said Jack. "And maybe you should tell us what's going on?"

"I have grave news," replied the messenger, attempting to catch his breath. "The First Evil … he knows you're at the Priory. As we speak, an army of Dark Monks is searching the citadel for you."

Jack steadied himself against the wall. "You've got to be kidding … how does he know?"

"It was the Reader."

"What is it with that woman? It's like she's had it in for us from day one," said Henry.

"What now? Are we done for?" asked Jack.

"No gov … you're both going home," said Ken, his voice faltering with emotion.

"Home?" said Henry. "Are you about to provide us with some ruby slippers?"

"No," replied the messenger, looking at Henry suspiciously. "I'm taking you to the Earth Gate."

"The Earth Gate?" said Jack, "You mean we haven't got to be here for nine months before we can use that thing?"

"No one has ever been returned to their body before the nine month 'rebirth period' – but that doesn't mean it can't be done. Now that The First Evil knows you're here, it's your only hope. Besides, whatever happens when you pass through the Earth Gate, it's *got* to be better than what will happen should *he* find you."

"Really?" said Henry. "Even if the Earth Gate turns us into goo?"

"Certainly," replied the messenger, earnestly.

"The Gate is below the cathedral. We must move quickly. The monks will not be far behind – there's a Way-Point just around here!" The messenger sprinted around the next corner. He ran a short distance before dropping to his knees and removing a section of floor grating. "This Way-Point will deliver you to the Observation Room above the Earth Gate." The boys looked down into the darkness.

Sensing their fear, Ken stepped forward. "It's safe … it's just like the other one. Remember? I'll show you …" With that, Ken dived in and vanished. The messenger spotted the Dark Monk's shadow creeping up the corridor behind them. He whispered, "You must go now! I'll lead the monk away."

Jack grabbed Henry's head and pushed it towards the opening. "Come on, Henry. You know the score with these Way-Points, it's head first!" Henry dropped to his knees and Jack rolled him into the space, and then dived in after him. The Underling replaced the grating and sprinted off, whooping and cheering to draw the monk's attention. It worked. The Dark Monk glided over the floor grating in hot pursuit.

Inside the throne room, the red giant pounded up and down before his throne. Sinosa entered. "What news of the intruder?" asked The First Evil, slumping down onto his throne.

"The news is not good, my Lord. It appears there are now *two* intruders."

"Two? How can this be? Are we to be infested with these spies? Where are they? Why are they not cowering before me?"

"We're still attempting to locate them …"

"FOOLS! How is it you cannot find two frightened children?"

"It appears they were warned, Sire. They escaped through a hidden passage that leads from their dormitory into the walls of the citadel. It's possible they're being assisted by a rogue Underling. We are tracking them, it's only a matter of time."

"And what news of the endareolfs?"

"We have made some progress there, my Lord," said Sinosa, proudly. "The Snatcher Guard has discovered their tree dwelling in the Woods of Despair. It had been camouflaged by potent magic but thanks to their ceaseless dedication …"

"You've discovered their dwelling? Am I supposed to be grateful? WHERE ARE THE ENDAREOLFS?"

"They are on the run … our trackers have indicated they are being assisted by a skilled woodsman."

The First Evil slumped deeper into his throne and began to stroke his long, red chin. "These children must not be permitted to leave the citadel. Send the Monk Guard to the Earth Gate. Halt the return process. They are clearly resourceful and may attempt to use it." The First Evil stood up. "Follow me," he said, as he headed into the cathedral, a nervous Sinosa in tow.

The First Evil stood before the altar. He picked up the decoy Shaman and said, "This Shaman is forged with blood from mine own heart. Blood the colour of oil …the essence of undiluted evil." He lifted the Shaman to his eternally angry face and sniffed it. He features contorted as through he'd smelt something repellent. "The Altar Shaman …it has been thoroughly handled … by human hands!"

"That's not possible my Lord. The Underling cleaners are instructed never to bring their flesh in contact with it. It would be sacrilege. They would not dare!"

"Like it was not possible that the boy could be here at the Priory?" replied The First Evil, placing the Shaman back on the plinth. He grabbed Sinosa around his neck and lifted him into the air, his grip tightened before he hurled the Master Prior's body into the rafters. "Send every available monk to the Earth Gate NOW! These children must not be allowed to leave the citadel."

The Way-Point delivered the boys into a vast circular area. It was metallic, like the inside of an alien spacecraft, the air thick with ghostly vapours of white and yellow. "Are we inside a giant pressure cooker?" asked Henry.

"No gov, we're inside the Observation Room. It has been created over thousands of years by them vapours coming from the Earth Gate below. Something in them vapours has turned the place all silvery."

"What's this place for?" asked Jack, waving the vapours from his nose.

"The Underlings like to come here and watch kids doing the one thing we can never do ...return home."

"I don't see anyone returning home," said Henry. "Unless we're vaporised first ... we're not vaporised, are we?"

"No, governor. The Earth Gate is below us."

Ken knelt and removed a sheet of slate flooring. The boys joined him and peered through it. The sight took their breath away. Several hundred metres below lay a gaping circular chasm the size of several football pitches. Within it, bolts of lightning streaked, crackled and exploded across a mass of swirling cloud. From the four corners about the Earth Gate, came a procession of children heading straight for it. These graduates of The Priory of Chaos walked unflinchingly towards the swirling mass that would reunite them with their bodies. As they reached its edge, they simply toppled in and vanished.

"My God," muttered Jack.

"I don't think God had a hand in its making," said Ken.

The orderly scene below was shattered as dozens of Dark Monks floated into the chamber. The boys watched in horror as several monks headed for the ends of the procession and halted the return process. Their colleagues began searching the queues for Jack and Henry. "What are we going to do now?" asked Henry. "We could never hope to get past that lot."

"You will if you jump," said Ken.

Henry rolled onto his back and buried his face in his hands. "That was the one suggestion I was hoping you weren't going to make." They heard footsteps approaching from behind. It was King Edward accompanied by an entourage of Renegade Underlings. The boys stood up.

"Your Highness," said Jack, surprised.

"Your Holiness!" said Henry, scrambling to his feet.

"I have come to bid you farewell ... and to grant Henry absolution it would seem. My friends, the courage you have shown in defence of all you hold true has made your King proud."

"I have the Altar Shaman, Your Majesty," said Jack, feeling for it in the pocket of his robe. "If we make it back, we must somehow swap it with the one in the British Museum in London. I have no idea how we're going

124

to do that ..."

"I have the utmost faith in you Jack Tracy ... and I wish upon you many doors of opportunity."

"Thank you. If all goes to plan, I'll be back with the good Shaman from the museum – bringing it here is the only way to destroy that thing," said Jack, motioning to the swirling mass beneath them.

"You may rely on my patronage when you return ... and now you must depart!" He directed the renegades forward to remove more of the flooring.

"This has got to be dangerous," murmured Henry.

The King shook his head defiantly. "Countless millions have passed through the Earth Gate. You will come to no harm," the king reassured him.

Jack turned to Ken and hugged him. "Thank you for everything ... we could never have come this far without you ... I will be back for you, my friend."

"I'll hold you to that, gov. And it's me what should be thanking you ..."

"For what?" asked Jack, astonished.

"For calling me your friend."

Jack smiled warmly and turned to Henry. "All those ready to jump into the Earth Gate and return home, raise your right hand and say, I".

"I" the boys shouted uncertainly. They drew deep breaths and inched towards the edge, whereupon the King nodded at two of his entourage who rushed forwards and shoved them over the edge.

The boys fell screaming into the swirling chasm.

TWENTY EIGHT

Back in one piece?

Mrs. Tracy had got up to refill a glass of water. As she made her way downstairs, she heard Jack cry out in what she thought was his sleep. *Poor boy. He must be having a horrid nightmare.*

The swirling mass of colour, vapour and smoke disappeared, and Jack's world turned pitch black. *Oh, no! I'm paralysed. I'm blind! I can't move my arms!* He struggled to open his eyes but couldn't. *Am I dreaming? Am I dead!? Something's gone wrong! I must wake up! Come on Jack, wake up!* Jack's eyes fluttered open to reveal a blurred vision of his bedroom ceiling. He sat up, bewildered, and realised he was wearing a strange robe. "What's *this* … it certainly isn't mine," he muttered, as the events of the last couple of weeks flooded back. He leapt out of bed and began searching the deep pockets of his robe for the Altar Shaman and the potion he'd prepared for Samantha. His hands fell upon the small Shaman and the pepper pot. *Yes!* He heard his mother coming back upstairs. He jumped into bed and pulled the duvet up to his chin. *Henry!* he thought, and reached for the mobile on his bedside table. *R U OK*? He sent the text message and lay still, grasping the phone.

'Ding!'

'Back but freaked,' came the reply.

Alright! We've both made it back in one piece. Jack climbed out of bed, drew back his curtains, and looked at the houses opposite. *Behind those doors are people with day-to-day problems … losing sleep over such small, everyday things! All of them oblivious to the evil that's gathering pace.* He scrutinised Samantha's bedroom window and wondered what she'd been up to. *Nothing too horrible, I hope. Once she's drunk the potion and returned to her old self, she's going to have a terrible conscience. What if she's maimed … or killed something?* He swallowed. His throat felt dry. He replaced the Priory's robe with a T-shirt and track pants and headed onto the landing.

At the bottom of the stairs, he almost tripped over the rucksack that his mother had packed for their school trip that day. *Oh, yeah! We're going on a class outing today. I'd completely forgotten.*

126

He went into the kitchen and poured himself some orange juice and sat down. He placed the pepper pot that contained the elixir that would return Samantha to her true self on the table. Jack gazed at it, swallowed hard, and thought. *I hope Samantha turns up for the class trip today. I think.*

***

In The Dark Matter, Gob and Phlem had been beside themselves with indecision. Should they stick to their plan and molest the delivery tables or come clean and beg The First Evil for forgiveness? Following a short discussion, they reached the conclusion that The First Evil was not big on forgiveness. So they decided to stick with plan A: the finger of blame would be directed elsewhere: the delivery tables would be molested.

Although Jack and Henry had escaped only minutes before, rumour and innuendo had spread like wildfire amongst the Snatcher-Gar community. A single question occupied their thoughts: who were the doomed Snatcher-Gars that had brought these troublemakers to the Priory? As Gob and Phlem made their way through the aviary in the direction of the Records Office, they tried to appear as 'normal' and nonchalant as possible. The whole business had caused such uproar that nobody paid any attention to either of them. If they had, they might easily have deduced that these two were guilty. "Keep going … and, if any fool looks at you, smile," said Gob, grinning at all and sundry.

"*Must* you look so happy?" replied Phlem. "It's wholly out of character. You'll arouse suspicion."

"I can't help it," said Gob, his grin becoming so pronounced that his cheeks ached.

The Records Office was located in The Pit. The Pit was dug out of a mass of filth ridden, decaying straw in the bottom of the aviary. The Snatcher-Gars reached the edge of The Pit and peered over its edge. "The Keeper of Records must be at large in the aviary," said Phlem, having scanned the area.

"Indeed, that thirsty Snatcher-Gar is addicted to gossip as much as he is excrement wine. Quick!" continued Gob, "this is our chance!" He shoved Phlem over the edge of the pit. Phlem opened his wings and glided to the straw covered ground below. He looked up and beckoned Gob to follow. Gob said, "I'll remain up here and keep a look out for you … no need to thank me … just proceed to the Keeper's desk and molest the records."

Phlem's face filled with rage. He rolled his eyes and walked towards a large desk piled high with recent log books. Once more he turned and looked up at Gob. "The coast could not be clearer! Go on!" mouthed Gob, flicking his wrist at the log books. Phlem felt as though he'd reached the point of no return.

He scanned the sides of the thick volumes for the date in question. "It was recently that we ferried the troublesome pair here," he muttered. *The records must be right here on this table, somewhere.* He placed a long black fingernail on the side of the stack of documents and began to scrutinise them more closely. Then he saw it. *The correct date!* He withdrew the colossal volume and having glanced about him, opened it. Pages were turned, flicked and discarded ... *Here the records be!* He turned to signal the good news to Gob. *Huh?* Gob had vanished.

Phlem turned back to the book only to discover The First Evil towering above him. "You have less than one second to point out the child you brought here," he spat.

"The fat one, Sire!" said Phlem, pointing to Henry's 'Barton Road, Londinium' entry. "Please, please don't kill me, my Lord! The child did not know its own mind when I carried it here! I would swear to it. It must have been its accomplice. The boy that Gob brought here! HE must have broken the fat one from its trance." Phlem dropped to his knees and clasped his hands together, "Please Your Majesty ... take pity on this innocent wretch!"

The First Evil bent down and pulled Phlem to his feet by his throat. "Where is the record of the other boy of which you speak?"

"It's here, Sire," gurgled Phlem, pointing to Jack's entry on Barton Road.

"And where is Gob?"

"He was up there a minute ago, my Lord," replied Phlem, flicking his eyes at the rim of the pit.

Gob was flying low and at speed under the forest's canopy. His 'danger radar' had been on overdrive all morning. *Gob must hide! Phlem will explain all to The First Evil. Phlem will be fine! Who am I kidding? The First Evil will turn him into Snatcher-Gar porridge! Tonight, I will find my way back inside to the Earth Gate. I will depart for Earth. I will find the boy. He cannot hide from me. I know his scent! I will kidnap him once more and take him to The First Evil in person. Beg his forgiveness!*

The First Evil had not turned Phlem into porridge. He knew that he might still need him. Or, more specifically, his nose – the only nose that knew Henry's scent. In the meantime, he had summoned his one remaining Master Prior to the throne room.

Salcura entered the throne room. He was relieved to see The First Evil tucking in to his favourite dish; a cauldron of giant eels.

128

The First Evil wiped his mouth with the back of his hand, and looked at Salcura. "You've heard the sad news of Sinosa's demise?"

Salcura nodded.

"And then there was ONE," continued The First Evil, pointing at him.

"As ever, I will serve Your Highness in all things."

"Convene the Council of Elders and appoint a fresh Master Prior to replace the one being cleaned off the cathedral's ceiling. Do whatever it is you people *do*."

"As you wish, Sire."

"You are aware that the spies have escaped to Earth?"

"I have been fully briefed, Your Majesty."

"It's difficult to imagine what harm these children can cause us. It isn't as if anyone on Earth will believe their babblings. Nonetheless, I find myself troubled. The emergence of these endareolfs and the fact that the spies may have tampered with the Altar Shaman ..."

"What do you suggest, my Lord?"

"The intruders must be found and brought back to face questioning and punishment. They may also know the whereabouts of the endareolfs."

"What would you have me do, Sire?"

"Activate the Sleepers."

"The Sleepers, sire? Would it not be simpler to send Gob and Phlem to retrieve the children? They have their scents after all. It's only a matter of time before Gob is captured. Even without him, Phlem will doubtless find the intruders together."

"Snatcher-Gars are not the brightest of beasts. They were not bred for intelligence. This situation calls for a more delicate touch. If the Sleepers fail to locate them, we may have no choice but, for now, activate the Sleepers and send them in search of the fugitives. We know where they live ... Barton Road ... in the province of Londinium."

TWENTY NINE

The Sleepers

In AD 1, three Dark Monks had been chosen for their tenacity and spite. They were carried through the Earth Gate by Snatcher-Gars. The consequences to these Dark Monks would be severe. Should they survive the journey, they would be disfigured beyond recognition and confined to deep meditation for millennia – their internal organs needing hundreds of years to re-form. They remained in this wretched state, cut off from all life and secreted in a cave deep below London until 1682. This was the year that Sir Christopher Wren was commissioned to design the Royal Hospital in Chelsea – on a site directly above their cave.

The Royal Hospital is not a hospital – it is a grand building that looks more like a palace. It was built to house retired soldiers – soldiers who had given all for king and country from the seventeenth century to the present day. Along its wide corridors, dressed in red coats adorned with medals, walk the few surviving heroes of World War Two.

When the building's architect, Sir Christopher Wren, began to visit the site, the Dark Monks picked up on his creative vibe. They went further, infusing his mind with visions of the building, containing their beloved cathedral, atop The Priory of Chaos. These visions became reality when Wren built the central part of the Royal Hospital – which was to become a smaller version of the cathedral, central lobby, and dining room atop the Citadel.

The three monks had been meditating in a cave far below this site for two thousand years. All that time, the Shaman-shaped beacon they had carried with them had remained dormant. This beacon now began to glimmer in the dark – its eyes glowed and bathed the walls of the cave in crimson. As it flickered on and off, the beacon intermittently revealed the faces of the monks beneath their black hoods. The journey the monks had undertaken had melted their faces to mere husks of flesh. The monks opened the tiny holes that had once been their mouths and, for the first time in two thousand years, sucked in the stale, damp air. They exhaled and, on the cusp of their breath, came two words: "Barton Road."

When Jack entered the kitchen for breakfast the following morning, he found the sight of his mother going about her daily chores particularly comforting. "Good morning, son of mine," she said, as she ferried clothes from the dryer and placed them on the end of the ironing board. "You're looking a bit … what's the expression I'm looking for? … Oh, yes … shell-shocked. Is everything all right?" she continued, as Jack sat down and poured himself some cereal.

"I've just had a rough night, Mum."

"I heard you cry out. Were you having a nightmare?"

"… Of sorts."

"Really? What about?"

"… A place where children are taught to be wicked and brutal."

"It just sounds like your average comprehensive to me!" replied Mrs. Tracy, tickled by her own wit. "I don't know," she continued, "even the nightmares are complicated these days. Whatever happened to old favourites like falling from a great height or being chased by faceless monsters?"

"There was a fair bit of that, too, Mum," said Jack, shovelling another spoonful of cereal into his mouth.

"Have you and Henry made it up with Samantha yet?"

"No … we're hoping to do that today."

"Glad to hear it. These things shouldn't be allowed to fester for too long," she said, as she began ironing one of Jack's school shirts. Just then, the doorbell went. "I'll get it," said Mrs. Tracy. Moments later, Henry followed her into the kitchen.

"Guess who's here," she said. "Would you like some breakfast, Henry," Mrs. Tracy asked him.

"No thanks. I'm not hungry," replied Henry, sitting down next to Jack.

"Not hungry? Has the world gone mad? You're both acting very strangely this morning."

"There's nothing strange about my behaviour," replied Henry, crossing his arms and staring blankly into the middle distance.

For the next few minutes, the boys remained suspiciously quiet. In fact, the only sound coming from the table was the sound of Jack munching his corn flakes. "Where are they taking you on your school trip, again?" asked Mrs. Tracy, the silence getting to her.

"Sir John Soane's Museum, Mum."

"John Soane? Who was he?"

"An architect who used to collect old stuff," murmured Henry.

"He died like a hundred years ago and they turned his house into a museum," said Jack.

"Did he design anything I might have seen?"

131

Henry shrugged. "The teachers only tell us stuff on a need-to-know basis, Mrs T."

"I expect they've told you a great deal about the man if they're bothering to take you to his house. Whether the pair of you were paying attention is another matter."

"It's true. We have been a little preoccupied lately," said Jack.

"Preoccupied? I can't imagine with what."

"You *really* couldn't," said Henry.

"It wouldn't have anything to do with … the *Winged Shaman*, would it?"

Jack dropped his spoon into his bowl and Henry cleared his throat nervously.

"*What* did you say*?*" asked Jack.

"I seem to have struck a nerve. Oh, don't look so worried you two! I found this in your trouser pocket," she continued, producing the computer printout that Jack had made of the Shaman.

"Oh, that? It's nothing. Just some research I've been doing for a school project."

"Well, just as long as you're not getting involved in Devil worship," replied Mrs. Tracy, pulling a scary face. "Anyway boys, you'd better hurry. The coach leaves from the school gates in thirty minutes."

Mrs. Tracy had been wrong about the coach. It wasn't due to leave for an hour. The boys were the first to arrive at the departure point outside the gates. "Have we missed it?" said Henry, surveying the parking lot where the coach should have been waiting.

"I doubt it … it's only five to nine." Just then, a silver coach belched around the corner and came to a shuddering halt in front of them.

The driver, a squat man with grey stubble looked surprised to see anyone so early. "You're keen," he said, as the boys climbed on board.

"School trips … can't get enough of 'em," said Henry, as they made their way to the back of the coach and sat down.

"You've brought the mojo for Samantha?" asked Henry.

"It's right here," said Jack, patting his inside pocket.

"Great. All we need now is for Sam's evil twin to show … and then the 'fun' can begin."

It was 9.20am. The bus was gradually filling with children, many with injuries inflicted by the local gang. "It's seriously tragic," said Jack, surveying the parade of sad and bruised faces. "There's no sign of Samantha. If she doesn't show, we'll have to stop by her house later."

"Look forward to *that*," said Henry, as Mrs. Makepeace's red car pulled up beside the coach. The car door opened and Samantha climbed out. She was wearing a black leather jacket with a white skull painted on

132

its back. She stood straight-backed and surveyed her surroundings like an all-powerful empress.

"Didn't Samantha once start a campaign *against* the wearing of animal hides, Henry?"

"That's right, Jack, she did ... and now she's wearing an entire cow on her back." The differences in her appearance didn't end there. She was wearing thick black eye-liner, black lipstick and she had a large ... "Is that a *ring* through her nose?" asked Henry.

A hush descended as the girl everyone now feared climbed on board the coach. "Move out the way, fool," Samantha ordered a boy sitting at the front. The boy stood up and edged past her towards the rear of the coach. Samantha sat down and lit a cigarette.

"Can you believe this?" whispered Henry. Then she leant over the seat in front and puffed smoke into the face of their form teacher, Mrs. Heist. Mrs. Heist coughed and spluttered and couldn't understand why she was doing so.

Samantha finished her cigarette and stubbed it out on the sleeve of Mrs. Heist's jacket. Then she produced a black bag from inside her jacket and turned to face her petrified classmates. "It's time to pay the toll, losers. I'm talking every penny you have," she snarled. She walked down the central aisle of the coach. The terrified children dropped their loose change and valuables into her bag as she passed by.

"The sooner we rid the world of Samantha mark 2, the better," said Henry, as Samantha stopped in front of them. Sam put her foot on the seat between them and leant in close.

Under her breath she whispered, "Don't think I've forgotten about your little stunt the other day. You're both going to need coffins ... real coffins, real soon." The coach pulled away and Samantha returned to her seat, slapping heads as she went.

They arrived at the museum. Jack and Henry followed the class up a narrow pathway and through a black door into the grand old house.

They congregated in Sir John Soame's perfectly preserved sitting room – spacious and brimming with lush antiques and paintings. Their tour guide, a pretty girl with flame red hair and freckles, was standing before a large portrait of Sir John in his prime. The class gathered round her.

Jack and Henry were careful to position themselves so they could keep an eye on Samantha. The more the tour guide waxed lyrical about the "boundless talents" and "ceaseless spirit of preservation" of the "enduring Sir John," the more pained Samantha's expression grew.

"Samantha may have a point," whispered Henry.

At one point, the young guide appeared to lose her train of thought and, as she gazed up at the portrait for inspiration, Samantha yawned loudly. Then she produced a red marker and scrawled 'OLD DEAD FART' across the bottom of the painting. The children gasped. The tour guide appeared to thank her. "Don't mention it freckles," said Samantha, applying a few more to her forehead. The group then moved on to a galleried area which looked down upon the empty sarcophagus of King Seti 1st in the basement below. Once again, the guide enthused about the historical significance of the object. Midway through her account, she spoke about the hieroglyphs inside the sarcophagus and explained how they contained instructions on how the King could "Pass through the Gates of Death." At which point, Samantha muttered something about the guide "Joining him if she didn't put a sock in it."

Jack spotted a bottle of mineral water sticking out of Samantha's jacket pocket. He tapped Henry on his shoulder and pointed it out.

"I'm not that thirsty," replied Henry.

"No, not for us," whispered Jack. "If we can get it … we could add the elixir to it."

"I like it."

"Come on," continued Jack, edging around the outer rim of the group towards Samantha.

The boys were standing right behind her as the assembly moved off towards a staircase that led to the basement. As they reached the top of the staircase, Henry stood aside. "She's all yours," he whispered.

As they made their way down the stairs, Jack seized his chance and lunged at the bottle. As he did, Samantha turned slightly with the angle of the staircase and he was left grasping nothing but air. This annoyed him and terrified the children behind who assumed he had some kind of death wish. He took a deep breath and, once again, he leant forward … *bingo!* The bottle slid effortlessly from her pocket. Stunned by his own success, Jack quickly passed the bottle back to Henry who stuffed it under his sweater. At the bottom of the stairs, the boys noticed a men's room and quickly darted through its door.

"Quick!" Get the bottle out," said Jack.

Henry pulled it from under his jumper. "Unscrew the lid," continued Jack as he retrieved the Priory's pepper pot and unfastened its top. Henry held the bottle while Jack poured the contents of the pepper pot into the water. They watched as red fluid streaked through the water on its way to the bottom. "Give it a good shake," said Jack. "WAIT! Screw the lid on first."

Following a good shake, they inspected the contents. "Looks good to me," said Henry.

"She only has to drink a tiny amount for it to work its magic," added Jack hopefully.

134

They made their way out of the men's room and headed towards the ever-enthusiastic tones of their tour guide.

Ironically, they found the group huddled together in a small room in the basement called the Monk's Parlour. This eccentric little room contained a round, highly polished wooden table with a human skull on it. As Jack gazed through the door into the packed room, the objects that really caught his attention were the numerous plaster casts of gargoyles that Sir John had taken from cathedrals during his grand tour of Europe. *Friends of Gob? They're certainly hideous enough,* he thought. Once the guide had finished giving the children the full history of this peculiar little room, the group made their way back out past Jack and Henry. The boys waited on either side of the door for the emergence of Samantha.

She didn't emerge.

They poked their heads inside and watched her climb over a rope barrier meant to restrict access to the right hand side of the room. She sat down at the round table and picked up the human skull. Jack expelled his butterflies as best he could and entered the Monk's Parlour with Henry in tow.

Samantha was so transfixed by the skull in her grasp that she didn't even register the boys' arrival. Jack motioned to Henry to hand him the water bottle. Samantha looked up. "Just think ... one day we're all going to look just like this," she mused, holding up the skull. "And, in the case of you two, that day can't come soon enough."

"What a charmer," replied Jack. "We only came in here to give you back your water bottle. It must have fallen out of your jacket."

"What are you doing with that? Give it back right now," she said, thrusting out her arm.

"Henry's really thirsty. Do you mind if he has some?"

"Mind? Of course, I mind! I'm not having that pig infect my water. GIVE IT BACK!"

"Okay, keep your nose ring on," replied Jack, handing it to her over the rope barrier.

"Thirsty are you, Henry?" Samantha asked.

"Yes, very ..." replied Henry, fully aware of the tactics that Jack was now employing.

"That makes two of us," she replied, unscrewing the lid and placing the bottle to her lips. "Nice, cool ... water," she continued, chugging down several gulps. She wiped her mouth on her sleeve. "Is there something else I can help you ..." She wasn't able to finish her sentence. The water bottle crashed to the ground and she began to shake as though having a fit, causing the legs of the wooden chair to screech against the stone floor.

"Quick!" said Jack. The boys scrambled over the barrier and wrestled

Samantha to the ground.

"What should I do?" asked Henry.

"Sit on her!" said Jack, grabbing at her flailing arms. As Henry's bulk pinned Samantha to the ground, Jack stifled her cries with the end of Henry's jumper. She suddenly became quite still and began to whimper. Henry climbed off her. "Samantha?" Jack asked. "Is that … you?"

THIRTY

Conscience

Samantha gazed up into Jack's eyes. Tears rolled down her cheeks as she reached out for both her friends. "… What have I done?" she gasped as her memories came flooding back.

"Samantha? Is that really you?" asked Jack, his eyes wide with hope.

"Jack … *Henry* … I'm so sorry, I …"

"Listen to me Sam; whatever you've done or said … *none* of it was your fault. You were brainwashed at …"

"*The Priory of Chaos*?"

"You remember?" said Henry, swallowing a lump in his throat.

"Yes … that disgusting place! What's happening … I mean …"

"We'll explain everything later. Right now, we need to rejoin the class," said Jack, as a warder walked into the Monk's Parlour.

"Hey!" said the man of Afro-Caribbean descent. "What are you three doing behind there? It's not allowed!"

"Our friend passed out," said Henry, always quick with a plausible excuse. "Yes, she fainted," said Jack. "And she needs some water!" The man hurried from the room to fetch some. The boys helped Samantha to her feet.

Samantha gazed down at herself and grimaced. "What's *this*?" she asked, prodding at her leather jacket.

Henry folded his arms. "That's Ermintrude. The cow you're wearing."

"Gross!" Samantha removed her jacket and plonked it into Henry's now waiting arms. "I need to use the ladies room," she continued, wiping the tears from her eyes and gazing curiously at the black streaks left on her sleeve.

"It's just through here," said Jack, leading her out of the Monk's Parlour and taking her the short distance to the ladies W.C. Samantha went inside.

A moment later, a muffled scream came from beyond the door. Followed by a muffled "What the! – No way!" And "OH MY GOD!"

"Sounds like she's taken to her new makeover pretty well," said Henry, digging some dirt from beneath his thumb nail.

"Best not tease her about it, Henry."

The warder returned with Mrs. Heist in tow. Mrs. Heist, a thick set woman with short brown hair and half-moon spectacles, looked dutifully concerned. "Has someone fainted?" she asked.

"It's Samantha, Miss," replied Jack, "she's in the ladies room." Mrs. Heist barged through the door.

A few minutes later, she emerged with a pale and shaken Samantha.

"She's feeling a bit better now," said Mrs. Heist, looking relieved. "Would you boys escort her to the coach and wait with her? We'll be setting off in about twenty minutes."

"Yes, of course," said Jack.

The three of them sat down at the rear of the empty coach.

Following a long pause, Samantha sighed and stated: "There's a ring through my nose." The boys, who were seated either side of her, leaned forwards and peered at it. "It's a nice ring, Sam," said Jack.

"Maybe so but that's not really the point, is it? I'd be much happier if it were, oh, I don't know, *on my finger*."

"It looks pricey," said Henry.

Samantha shuddered. "It was £180. I … I got the money when … when I sold my grandmother's wedding dress." Her words had clearly caused her considerable discomfort. She drew a deep breath and went on, "I found the dress in the attic. Mum doesn't know it's gone yet." The boys could tell she was about to burst into tears. "Best not to dwell on that now," said Jack. "It'll just upset you. And as I said, nothing you did or said was your fault. You were brainwashed. Under an enchantment."

"That's right," said Henry. "They placed me under the same enchantment … and I tried to kill a kid with a dagger. A nice kid called Ken."

"You didn't though, I mean … you didn't actually kill him, did you?" asked Samantha, squeezing Henry's hand.

"No … Jack brought me back from the dark side just in time."

Jack winked at Henry. "Look Sam," he said, "We're going to need your help … that is, if you're up to it."

"Help? Doing what?"

Henry folded his arms and leant back in his seat. "Well, you know how you've spent most of your childhood on a quest to save the entire planet?"

"Yes …" she replied, perking up slightly.

"Well, now's your chance to *actually* save it."

"What have you two done now?"

Jack explained about Perkin, the endareolfs, and the plan to switch the Shamans. Samantha listened intently throughout and never once interrupted. "So, what do you think?" asked Henry, once Jack had filled her in.

Samantha blew her nose like a trumpeter heralding a new dawn. "I don't think, I *know*. It's payback time."

When they arrived back at Barton Road, Henry went straight home for his supper and left Jack and Samantha standing outside her house. "I'm not sure I can face my parents right now," said Samantha. "Can I come home with you for a bit? I'd really like to compose my thoughts first."

"Come on, Sam ... mum will be pleased to see you," he said, walking towards his front door.

"Hello Samantha, it's nice to have you back in the fold," said Mrs. Tracy, opening the front door and letting them in.

"Thank you, Mrs. Tracy. It's nice to be back." Just then the phone rang. Mrs. Tracy answered it. "Oh, Jean ... how lovely to hear from you!" said Mrs. Tracy, rolling her eyes.

"That's my aunt J," said Jack, pointing towards the living room.

"Be good," said Mrs. Tracy, as they made their way across the hall.

They sat down on the sofa. Jack sensed Samantha was in the process of composing her thoughts. He remained silent until she said: "Talk about weird. I've accomplished so much I hate in such a short space of time. I mean, I've joined the local gang. I'm the youngest member of the pro-nuclear lobby; we're talking bombs here, not fuel. I even managed to send off my first subscription to the 'Bring Back Fur' campaign ... I enclosed a slogan with it and everything." Samantha went silent.

"Well? What was it?" asked Jack.

"What was what?"

"The slogan?"

Samantha sighed heavily: "'Fur – Nature's natural insulator.'"

"Well, it's snappy ... and it almost rhymes," said Jack.

"Like me when I wrote it, I guess. On a serious point, if they decide to use my slogan, I will kill myself." Then she looked at Jack. "So ... I owe my restored sanity to you?"

"I've had a lot of help, Sam."

"It's obvious you were the ring leader. Without you the 'Save Samantha Campaign' might never have got off the ground."

"There was no way I was going to leave you like that."

"Thank you, Jack," she said, squeezing his hand warmly. "So," she went on, composing herself, "how are we going to go about stealing the Shaman from the British Museum?"

Jack plunged his hand into his trouser pocket and produced the tiny Altar Shaman. "We have to find a way to swap it with this one."

"Is that *really* the Shaman from the cathedral like you said?" she said, taking it from him.

139

"I sincerely hope so," said Jack.

"It's quite sweet really."

"It's made with the blood of The First Evil … it's pure evil."

"So? Any ideas on the swapping them over front?"

Jack shook his head. "Not a single one."

Mrs. Tracy opened the living room door and stuck her head inside. "Your aunty Jean is on her way over. Troubles are brewing!" she said, as her head disappeared back through the door.

"You obviously inherited your mother's gift for understatement. I'll be off then!" said Samantha, standing up.

"Are you sure?"

"Yes. I'm being a complete wimp about everything. I'm going home to tell mum about the wedding dress … and some other stuff that she's going to freak over. If I have to grovel for the next decade, so be it!" With that, she marched purposefully from the room. *Sam's really back*, beamed Jack.

That night, Jack lay in his bed wrapped in the comfy knowledge that Samantha was fine again. And it was largely due to his and Henry's efforts. *I can't believe we actually did it!* Jack felt proud of what they had achieved. Then he thought about Perkin and the endareolfs. He wanted so much to return to the woods and see his friends, to ask for advice and guidance. In his gut, he felt sure that Perkin was safe and protecting the endareolfs. *Perkin told me to trust my instincts. They're telling me it would be foolish to return to the tree dwelling. The First Evil is bound to have laid a trap for me there.* His thoughts then veered to switching the Shamans at the British Museum. *We don't have the first clue how to go about doing that. It's sealed inside a glass case! There will be people everywhere ... not to mention guards.* Then he remembered what King Edward had said: *'I wish upon you many new doors of opportunity.'* Maybe such a door will open. I hope so, he thought.

Little did Jack know but a more pressing problem was ascending from a cave below Chelsea in the shape of three disfigured monks. The monks phased through several hundred metres of limestone and clay and entered the chapel. They floated down the darkened knave towards the altar. The monk in the centre caressed the large gold cross on the altar with his freakishly long fingers. Then he ascended through the roof of the chapel with his two companion Sleepers in tow.

The Dark Monks, who had not ventured beyond their cave for two millennia, were greeted with clear skies and a full moon. They pulled their black hoods down over their grey faces and floated skyward.

As they drifted over London of the 21st century, they revelled in the angst they sensed below. The monks, who were able to communicate telepathically, floated over a Piccadilly Circus that thronged with tourists and commuters. *"Such advancements. The work of the Priory is almost complete."*

"The progress is greater than expected. The humans below us are riddled with indifference and selfishness – The First Evil's victory is surely at hand."

When they reached Barton Road, they floated down onto the pavement outside Jack's house. The tallest monk in the centre raised his right hand and the street lights for a kilometre in every direction went out. A large chunk of south London plunged into darkness. *"I sense a third child who is aware of too much ... a girl,"* the centre monk communicated telepathically to the other two.

"I sensed her some time ago. I will get the girl," replied the monk to his left, who then floated towards Samantha's driveway.

The monk on the right headed off in the direction of Henry's house while the tallest monk gazed up at Jack's bedroom window.

Moments later, he was levitating outside of it. Jack was asleep when he phased into his room. The Dark Monk stood beside Jack's bed. His head swivelled towards the door as he sensed Mrs. Tracy's love for her son across the landing. The ruined muscles beneath his skin attempted to supply him with a look of revulsion. Nothing doing. His expression remained unaltered. After a few moments, he leaned forwards and whispered an incantation into Jack's ear. Jack spiralled into a deep trance.

***

Salcura entered The First Evil's throne room. "The Sleepers have captured the spies, My Lord," he said.

"Both of them?"

"It ... it appears there are now three spies, Your Highness."

The First Evil looked at Salcura with such profound menace that he feared he may be indulging his last breath (he quickly took another). "Send three trusted officers of the Snatcher-Guard to retrieve them. Have the spies brought directly to me. Do you understand?"

"Yes, your Majesty."

"I need not explain the consequences should they not be in this room ...begging for their lives before the twin suns rise."

"They will be here, your most gracious Lordship," said Salcura, before bowing and leaving the throne room.

In the cave below the Royal Hospital, Samantha was the first to come round. She sat up drowsily and peered towards several flickering candles in the centre of the cavern. Enveloped in their glow, three hooded figures sat cross-legged in a circle, their heads bowed in meditation. Samantha leaned over and shook Jack. He slowly began to come round.

"Wake up, Jack! We're in deep you know what," she whispered.

"Where *are* we?" he said, searching the pocket of his boxer shorts for the Altar Shaman. His hands fell upon it and he breathed a sigh of relief.

"I'm no geologist, but it appears we're in a cave," said Henry, sitting up and rubbing his eyes. "And … oh, great … monks," he continued, squinting towards the candle light.

"My guess is we're still on Earth," said Jack, trying to offer the others a crumb of reassurance.

"That's optimistic, even for you," said Henry.

"I doubt if we'd be hidden away if we were already back in The Dark Matter."

"I suppose that makes sense … but how did we get down here?" said Samantha.

"They must have brought us," said Jack, motioning towards the figures.

"Are they asleep?" said Henry, dragging himself to his feet.

"There's only one way to find out," said Samantha. She made her way towards them. The boys glanced at each other and followed her tentatively. Samantha bent down and peered inside a hood. The look of horror on her face left the boys in little doubt: she had seen something they really didn't need to. She hurried back towards them and folded her arms as though in a huff. "They're monsters," she pronounced. "I think, before we can save the world, someone is going to have to save us … from them!"

Jack walked cautiously around the inside of the cave, seeking a means of escape – his gaze returning to the 'monsters' every few seconds. He discovered nothing but jagged rock in shades of red and grey. The cave was so small that he returned in no time carrying some garments for himself and his friends.

"What are they?" asked Samantha, shivering.

"Habits, I think," replied Jack, handing her one. She took the black robe and pulled it over the T-shirt and shorts she'd worn to bed. Henry and Jack did the same. "I take it you didn't find any exit signs over there," said Henry, folding up the long sleeves.

"Afraid not … there's no way in or out."

"We had to get in here *some*how," said Samantha.

"My guess is that they carried us in using similar magic to the Snatcher-Gars," said Jack.

"I agree," said Henry. "We're talking about some serious wall-phasing mojo."

"Which means we're probably waiting for Snatcher-Gars to pick us up and fly us back to the Priory."

"One way tickets to Doom Central," said Henry. The Sleepers stood up suddenly, and their captives retreated until their backs pressed against the wall. The shrouded figures floated upwards and disappeared through the roof of the cave. "They ignored us *completely*," said Samantha. "What do you think that means?"

"That they consider us a zero threat … and that there's no way out," said Jack. Just then, a long black nose phased through the wall behind them. "There you be!" All three turned and, once again, they staggered backwards. Gob's evil face glared down at them.

THIRTY ONE

The door of opportunity

"Thought you could hide from me inside this rancid cave? Did you think the damp sufficient to mask your odious stenches? And look! My prize has grown! No less than THREE spies have I apprehended this night!" Gob swept all three stunned children up in his claws and made for the surface. Within moments, they had passed through rock, clay, concrete, chapel and out into the open – their compressed lungs filling with freezing air as they soared skyward.

Jack was wedged up against Samantha in Gob's left claw. "Put us down, Gob! Put us down! I need to talk to you!" he cried.

"Talk you say? Talk! I have nothing to say to you. Actually … I have a GREAT DEAL to unburden from my chest!" Gob descended into Raleigh Gardens, a private, lovingly maintained park in the grounds of the Royal Hospital. He released the children from a safe yet spiteful height onto the recently mown grass below: all three landed on a steep incline and tumbled several metres. "You're lucky I need you as a peace offering for The First Evil, otherwise I would tear organ from flesh and turn this little wood red with you! Such is the trouble you've caused me."

"We've caused you? You started it, Gob. You took me, remember? I was in my bed … minding my own business. You kidnapped ME!"

"Just following orders. What's your point?"

"My point is … oh, it doesn't matter. You just said you need us alive as a peace offering. So," continued Jack standing up: "The First Evil hasn't sent you to bring us back?"

"The First Evil had no need. Gob has used his initiative. Gob is famed throughout The Dark Matter for his initiative, not to mention his underrated intelligence."

"Oh, really?" interrupted Samantha. "And what does your underrated intelligence tell you about the three disfigured monks who were holding us captive?"

"Monks, you say?"

"Yes. The one's you've just liberated us from."

"*Dis*figured monks you say?"

144

"Yes ... there were three hideously disfigured monks in that cave when we woke up."

"The Sleepers?" muttered Gob. "The First Evil sent the Sleepers for you!?"

"Think about it Snatcher-Stein," said Henry. "That cave has no way in or out ... at least, not for us. How do you think we got down there? Burrowed?" Henry then did a pretty good impersonation of a toothy mole.

"What has Gob done!"

"Something unspeakable in his pants by the sound of it," continued Henry, still flashing his molars

"There is but one thing for it! I must take you back and beg the Sleepers for forgiveness!"

"They didn't look like forgiving types to me," said Samantha.

"This girl is right! Her judgement of character is without flaw. I'm doomed! WE ARE ALL DOOMED!"

This is it! ... The 'door of opportunity' thought Jack, his brain slamming into gear. "There is only one thing for it," he said, "just one chance for you to save yourself."

"You know of a plan to save *me*, child?"

"To save us *all*, Gob."

Gob's nose started to twitch.

"What is it?" asked Samantha.

"Something approaches," said Gob, raising his nose skyward and inhaling. "...whatever it be that approaches ... it is not of this Earth."

"Look! It's the Sleepers," said Jack, pointing towards the full moon and three shadows highlighted against its glow.

"It's them! They're coming for us," Gob shrieked.

"Can't you out fly them?" said Samantha.

The rusty, worn-out penny in Gob's mind dropped: "Of course! I have great and powerful wings ... Sleepers can but drift!"

"Get us away from here and I'll tell you the plan ... the plan that's going to save us all!" shouted Jack. "Now Gob!" Gob scooped them up and ascended like a rocket, his wing beats rapid and furious, the downdraft stripping trees in Raleigh Gardens of their leaves and acorns.

The Sleepers spotted the fleeing Snatcher-Gar and shrieks of unadulterated rage broke from their taut mouths. Their cries travelled far, shattering windows, causing dogs to bark across London and their owners to shuffle angrily in their beds. The shrieks reached the escapees just before they flew from earshot. "The 'Hunk o' Flesh finalists' are NOT happy," shouted Henry, clinging on to Gob's claw for dear life, his eyes tightly shut.

A minute later, Jack opened his eyes and spotted the British Telecom

Tower, a soaring beanpole of a building rising from the heart of London. "Quick! Land on the top of that," he said, pointing it out. Gob knew he'd burnt all his bridges where The First Evil was concerned and did what his young ward told him. And so it was that the group found themselves on a small, windy patch of concrete some fifty stories above London.

"So?" said Gob, scanning the heavens anxiously, "what be this plan to save me?" Jack ignored the selfish way in which the question had been posed and prayed the 'pitch' he'd been rehearsing in his head would work.

"All right … this is the plan," he began, noticing that Henry and Samantha were as keen to hear it as Gob. "To ensure your survival, we're going to have to close the Earth Gate … with you on *this* side of it."

"I must remain here? What would I do?"

Henry proposed an idea: "With your people skills? A job on London Underground, perhaps?"

"Henry!" said Jack, giving him a stinging look.

"Sorry … the uniform probably wouldn't suit you … Postman Pat blue … I'll shut up now."

"I don't think it's so much a question of what you would do," continued Jack, "as where you would go."

"Exactly! Where would I go?" said Gob, motioning to the city below.

"Have you heard of … the Amazon rainforest?"

"No. Where be this forest?"

"It's in South America," said Samantha, who'd just twigged what Jack was up to.

"That's right," continued Jack. "It's in South America and there are parts of the rainforest that are still completely isolated … cut off from mankind."

"If you went there, you could rule the jungle. You'd be like … like a king among beasts!" said Jack.

"A king you say?"

Jack nodded.

"Among beasts you say?"

All three children nodded.

"Be there rats there?"

"In the rainforest?" said Henry, who didn't have a clue what he was talking about. "Oh, yeah … as many rats as a hungry Snatcher-Gar can eat."

"I like the sound of this place … what's the catch?"

"Catch? There is no catch … more of a mission," said Jack.

"What be this mission?" replied Gob, his tiny green eyes opening wide before narrowing to mere pin pricks.

"It's quite simple really … all you have to do is help us close the Earth

Gate. That way, The First Evil won't be able to send the Snatcher-Guard after you. You'd be safe."

"Close the Gate you say? It cannot be done," he said, shaking his head.

"We know how to close the Gate. But, before we can do it, we need to get into a museum and steal a Winged Shaman that's on display there."

"It really is the only way to save your hide," said Samantha.

Gob sniffed the air nervously. "Where be this museum?"

"It's not far from this very spot," said Jack, crossing his fingers behind his back. The beast looked at Jack. Then Samantha. Then Henry. Its gaze returned to Jack: "Well?" he asked. "Why are we wasting time? Let us be gone!"

At night, from three hundred metres in the air, the museum was trickier to locate than Jack had expected. They circled the area north of Oxford Street several times before Jack spotted the glass dome of the reading room. "There!" he said, pointing towards it.

A security guard, seated at the entrance to this enormous circular room, was scribbling in a notepad. He rolled his eyes and crossed something out. Then he looked up to see three children in the farthest reaches of the dome, floating down towards him unaided – eyes wide, dark robes billowing about them. As he drew breath in readiness to cry for help, a sepia beam left Gob's eyes and placed him in a bug-eyed trance. His notepad tumbled to the floor and he landed on top of it with a meaty thud.

"Neat trick," said Henry, as their feet touched the ground.

"Useful trick, too," said Samantha.

"Perhaps you should consider a career in burglary?" suggested Henry.

"A career in burglary, you say?"

"Henry, would you *please* stop giving him career advice," said Jack. "Now," he continued, "the Shaman is in Gallery 24, just behind there." Jack pointed to the rear of the reading room. "Gob, you go on ahead and use your sleeping mojo on any security between here and there. But that's all. Don't harm anyone. Do you understand?"

"Indeed I do," replied Gob, heading off to deal with the museum staff.

"Do you really think we can trust this creature?" said Samantha.

"Yes. He needs us now, as much as we need him."

They heard a muffled scream followed by the sound of glass smashing. Fearing Gob may have injured someone, or worse, they ran out of the reading room and dove-tailed in the direction of Gallery 24.

Gob was standing in its gigantic doorway. "What have you done?" asked Jack, barging past him into the gallery.

"*Done* you say? As you asked ..." Jack ran over to the two night watchmen who had been patrolling the museum and were now spread eagled on the ground. There was a broken gin bottle lying on the floor beside them. Henry and Samantha caught him up.

"They look okay, considering," said Samantha, bending down for a closer inspection. "He must have dropped the bottle as he fell," she said. "Drinking on the job it seems. Tut, tut."

"They're at slumber … their nightmares be of … ambush," said Gob, sniffing the air above them.

They made their way over to the glass display case containing the Good Shaman. "We'll have to smash it," said Jack, thinking out loud.

"Smash?" said Gob, phasing his clammy hands through the glass. Gob grasped the tiny Shaman between thumb and forefinger and drew it out and up to his face. After a beat, his hands began trembling and steam billowed from where he held the Shaman. Gob shrieked, and the Shaman tumbled from his grasp. Jack reached up and, fanning the fingers of both hands, caught the falling object.

Everyone expected Jack to get 'burnt.' He didn't. "Remember," said Jack, breathlessly, "this Shaman is nothing like the evil one in the cathedral … this one has been forged from the spirit of humanity … from ingredients taken from The Greater Good."

"Really? … and what are the ingredients of The Greater Good?" asked Samantha.

"I don't know, Sam," replied Jack … "but it's some question, don't you think? The ultimate question maybe."

"Don't encourage him," said Henry. "Questions are what brought us to this in the first place."

"Come on, Henry … the ingredients of The Greater Good? They have got to be worth knowing. Haven't they?"

Jack retrieved the Altar Shaman from his pocket and held it side-by-side with its brother. It was the first time they had been together since the endareolfs made them thousands of years before. Henry grabbed Jack's sleeve and tugged … "What?" asked Jack. Henry pointed up at the model of the horse riding demon suspended from the ceiling. "So much has happened … I'd completely forgotten about that thing," muttered Jack.

"What?" said Samantha. "After all you've been through, you're worried about a plastic demon on a pantomime horse?"

"It's not plastic," said Henry. "It's papier-mâché."

"Papier-mâché is it? *Okay*. Now I'm *really* scared."

"It's not the same demon … it's different," said Jack.

"I think you're right, that one's wearing a cape for starters – the one that tried to skewer us had no cape. It didn't, did it, Jack?"

"Can we *please* just get on with switching the Shamans?" said Samantha.

"If that skeleton moves … kill it," Jack said to Gob. Gob and

Samantha glanced at each other with raised eyebrows. Realising the similarity of their expressions, they quickly lowered their eyebrows and looked away. Jack handed Gob the Altar Shaman who placed it on the now vacant hook inside the wall cabinet.

"That was easy enough," said Henry, rubbing his hands.

Above the museum, the Sleepers had been hovering in the same positions for several minutes. They extended their arms and a red mist billowed from their fingertips. The mist snaked down the building's stone facade and searched out the cracks around and under the main entrance. Once inside, the mist made its way across the stone floor of the lobby, before heading left and ascending the museum's main staircase. It reached the first floor and paused – hovering – as if awaiting further instructions. They came, and the mist once again had purpose. It moved off and sped through room after room after room of ancient curios. It was being guided towards something specific: the Egyptian Galleries. These famous galleries contained the largest collection of plundered mummies in Europe. The red mist swirled about the mummy-filled rooms like a creature unsure of which Egyptian noble to inhabit first. Once again, instructions were received from the Sleepers. The mist separated into dozens of strands and made for some forty seven mummies. It found microscopic cracks in their glass containers and wasted no time in engulfing them. Within moments, the wraps about their stomachs heaved into life, and they were breathing for the first time in three millennia. Many scowled at their surroundings, causing the bandages about their faces to loosen and hang free. The realisation of their horrifying fates, the desecration they had suffered, filled them with inescapable grief and rage. Cabinets rattled and shook before erupting in explosions of glass and fury. Two security guards came running into the gallery to investigate the din. They immediately turned on their heels and ran for their lives.

A dozen mummies gave chase. They bounded, leapt and slid after their quarries like homicidal gazelles. The men didn't stand a chance. They were flattened to the ground by vicious blows that rained down upon them from every angle.

In Gallery 24, all and sundry were feeling rather chuffed at a job well done.

"How easy was that?" said Henry.

"I smell more guards approaching," said a sniffing Gob, "I will send them into slumber!" He flapped off towards the central courtyard.

"Wait!" said Jack, realising it was mission accomplished and time to leave. But it was too late. Gob had flown through the room and disappeared.

Silence.

The silence was broken by a faint tapping sound coming from somewhere inside the museum. "Can anybody else hear that?" said Samantha.

"You bet," said Henry. "It's an odd sound and ... isn't it coming this way?"

"I have a *very* bad feeling about this," said Jack. He moved swiftly to the rear door of Gallery 23 and looked up the marble steps, listening to the approaching clamber.

"Let's just run and find Gob," said Samantha, gesturing in the opposite direction.

"I agree," said Henry. "Sounds like we're gonna need him." Just then, a gang of mummies leapt into Jack's view. They were some twenty metres away at the top of the marble stairs.

"RUN!" Jack screamed. Henry and Samantha ran across the hockey pitch size room headed for the main entrance and the covered courtyard beyond. "No!" shouted Jack, "It's too far! They'll spot us. Quick! Down here!" he continued, making for some stairs directly under the winged demon on its horse. They hurried down the white marble stairs. At the bottom, they turned to their right: another flight of stairs led down to the African galleries in the basement. As they bolted down, a ruckus erupted in the room above. To their horror, much of this ruckus now clambered down the stairs behind them. They ran into the darkened gallery at the bottom and turned left. They were in a room full of tall cabinets containing African objects: shields, spears, swords, bows and arrows. The fearsome weapons displayed in the dim glow of the blue security lights only heightened their sense of impending doom.

"This way!" shouted Samantha. She snaked off around a corner and then another to find a dead end: albeit punctuated by a silver lift. Jack ran past her and bashed the lift's call button. The number '1' appeared in green neon. "It's on the ground floor," said Samantha, "it's never going to get down here in time!"

"Come on lift!" shouted Henry.

From the room they'd just navigated, the sound of display cases being ransacked for their weapons rang out: a cacophony of splintering glass and mob howls. The children huddled together by the lift's silver doors, willing them to open.

DING! The doors burst open and they collapsed into a heap on the lift's floor. They turned over to see the maddened mummies charging at them – spears raised high, swords clasped in fury. "This is it ...were finished!" said Henry as the doors slammed shut.

"Mummies?" said Samantha, grabbing at a rail around the edge of the lift and pulling herself to her feet.

"Yeah. Mummies. And they're *seriously* annoyed with us for some reason," said Henry.

"Wherever this lift ends up, we're going to have to run and hope Gob finds us before they do," said Jack, helping Henry to his feet.

The lift stopped and the doors opened. Three anxious heads poked out into the covered courtyard. They were next to the gift shop and not far from the entrance to Gallery 23. "The coast looks clear," said Jack. All three sprinted in the direction of the museum's main entrance. Halfway across the courtyard, Samantha lost her footing on the slippery floor and landed on her side with a thud. The boys skidded to a halt, returned, grabbed an arm each and pulled her to her feet. They turned to see half a dozen mummies standing in a line blocking their exit, all brandishing spears, swords and shields liberated from the African galleries. They glanced behind them and beheld a similar sight.

"We're trapped!" shouted Samantha.

Above the museum, the Sleepers grinned behind their unresponsive features. "*Capture them alive and bring them to us,*" they communicated to the mummies. The mummies surged forward and hoisted the struggling trio above their heads. As they moved towards the museum's front entrance, they were thwarted by a powerful back draft of air. The mummies looked stunned and gazed about for its source. Many of them scowled and attempted to move forward but couldn't. Invisible to all but the children, Gob was hovering on the spot and flapping his immense wings for all he was worth. The mummies continued to struggle against the rushing air, their ancient bodies now bent double, their bandages trailing like tickertape behind them. At once, Gob stopped flapping – the mummies collapsed onto the ground and spilled the children ahead of them. Gob flew forward, swept his three cohorts up in his claws, and ascended through the glass roof of the courtyard into the sky.

Henry looked down: a child mummy clung to his leg – its mouth wide open, its rotten teeth hungry for his flesh. The 'child' began pulling its way up Henry's body: its goal his throat. Henry kicked its face – particles of ancient dust shot out and hung in the air. The mummy shook its head but clung fast. Henry kicked it again and again until it slid free and plunged back to earth; its hate-filled glare sucked into the darkness below. The mummy landed with a THWACK at the feet of the Sleepers. The Sleeper in the centre lifted a leg and stamped it into a pile of dust. At the same moment, the other mummies now smashing their way through the museum's glass doors, collapsed into a lifeless heap. "*The Snatcher Guard are approaching from the north,*" the centre monk informed the other two. They all raised their right arms and pointed in the direction of the fleeing Snatcher-Gar – instantly communicating Gob's location to the three

151

members of The Guard.

"You can let up a bit now, Gob," Jack shouted up to the increasingly manic Snatcher-Gar.

"Let up, you say? Let up! With the Snatcher-Guard on our tail?" he continued, sniffing frantically at the air.

"What?! What are you going to do?" asked Jack.

"It be your intention to take the Good Shaman to Dark Matter?"

"Yes …"

"Then we must return now! It be our only means of finding sanctuary."

"Return now? But how?"

"A storm. It brews across the narrow water in the land of Bonaparte."

"Huh?" said Jack.

"I think he means across the English Channel in France," said Samantha.

"Look!" said Henry, pointing behind them.

"The Guard!" cried Gob. "We must reach lightning and escape into The Dark Matter!"

"Won't they just follow us?"

"They must enter *our* lightning bolt or they will arrive elsewhere."

"But Gob!" yelled Jack. "You aren't carrying our essences! We are flesh and blood!"

"This is not the time to bother Gob with minor details – if we stay, we're doomed." In the distance, they saw a flash of lightning, its reflection bouncing across the choppy waters of the Channel below.

"They're gaining on us!" cried Samantha, looking back at the approaching Snatcher-Guards.

"Of course they be gaining!" shrieked Gob, "they have but swords and hefty egos to carry! I have all of you!" Jack looked up. The three members of the Snatcher-Guard were now poised directly overhead.

"They're preparing to dive bomb us!" he screamed, as a bolt of lightning momentarily blinded him.

When the white blobs finally cleared from Jack's vision, he could see the forests of The Dark Matter extending for miles below him.

THIRTY TWO

Flesh and blood

The children remained silent as Gob descended towards the forest below. He swooped beneath the canopy of trees, weaving gracefully between them, seeking a place to land. He found one and lowered his passengers into a small clearing.

It was early morning. The light from the sun was just beginning to filter through the trees. It invigorated a swarm of butterflies causing them to flutter about in the crisp morning air. "It's so calm here," said Samantha, breaking the silence.

"Armageddon would seem calm after that," said Henry.

"Are you okay?" Samantha asked a forlorn looking Jack.

Jack shrugged and collapsed onto his bottom at the foot of a tree. "We have a serious problem, guys," he said, sounding troubled and shattered.

"We're actually here now, Samantha," said Henry, slumping down next to Jack. An exhausted Samantha joined them. "You mean we're physically here as opposed to just our essence being here … is that really such a problem?" she asked.

"It is if we ever want to return home," said Jack, losing a tussle with a yawn. "Perhaps … perhaps the endareolfs will know of a way out of this mess," he added. They sat in silence trying to think and, before long, gave in to the increasing weight of their eyelids and fell asleep. "Humans, no stamina," muttered Gob, as he sniffed the air. "Huh!" He turned swiftly to see a member of the Snatcher-Guard staring at him from within a clump of thorn bushes. The two Snatcher-Gars eyeballed each other like gunfighters preparing to draw. Moments later, the Guard member collapsed onto his belly with a thud. *Did the power of my gaze do that?* thought Gob.

Gob turned it over and discovered a horrific burn at the base of its neck. "Thought you could catch Gob, did you? Thought you could share Gob's lightning bolt! Fast? You were not fast enough!" he muttered, giving the cadaver a swift kick.

Jack awoke several hours later. He stood up unsteadily and gazed down at his friends asleep at the base of the tree. *This is all my fault …*

they're here because of me. Just then, he heard a metallic noise from behind him in the woods … 'Clink.'

Jack negotiated his way through a thicket and came upon the dead Snatcher-Guard. The creature was now spread-eagled on its back, its silver body armour glistening in the sun's rays. 'Clink!' Jack looked up.

Gob was perched on a thick branch high above him. "He thought he was SO superior," said Gob, removing a large round nut from the branch next to him and throwing it at the dead guardsman – 'Clink!'

"The other two didn't make it through then?" asked Jack.

"Neither did this one – 'CLINK!'

Jack knelt down and withdrew the creature's sword from its scabbard. "I need to find some friends of mine, Gob," said Jack, examining the sword's razor sharp edge.

"You speak of the woodsman and the endareolfs?"

"That's right," replied Jack, plunging the sword into the earth beside the dead Snatcher-Guard. "The endareolfs may be our only hope of returning home once this is all over. How far are we from the Woods of Despair?"

"Not far enough," replied Gob.

"If we could just get back to their tree dwelling … maybe they've left us a clue. They could even be waiting for me to return, using magic to keep themselves hidden."

Gob floated to the ground beside him. "The last I heard, the Woods of Despair were infected with The Guard. It would be suicide to journey there."

Jack withdrew the sword from the ground. "Hold this a second," he said, handing it to Gob. Gob grasped the weapon in both hands and grinned maniacally as he lifted the blade up in front of him.

"I've had an idea," said Jack, kneeling for a closer inspection of the dead Snatcher-Guard's armour. "That sword really suits you," he went on. "I bet all this other gear would look great on you, too."

"Such finery is the preserve of The Guard. It is forbidden for Carriers to wear it."

"You're a free agent now. You can wear whatever you like."

An enormous grin spread across Gob's face and he wasted no time in unfastening the rusty garments he'd been wearing all his life.

"I'll be over here with the others," said Jack. "When you're dressed, come and show us your new look!"

"I shall, child."

"Where's Gob?" asked Samantha, standing and brushing some forest debris off her robe.

"He's over there, changing into the uniform of a Snatcher-

Guardsman."

"Where did he get that?" asked Henry, also standing.

"From one of those guards who were chasing us. The creature made it through the lightning bolt but was fatally injured."

"If Gob could pass for a member of The Guard, that would be useful," said Henry. "He really needs to take a shower though."

Jack lowered his voice: "I'm going to suggest that he uses the disguise to investigate the Woods of Despair ... perhaps he could find some clues as to what happened to Perkin and the endareolfs. We need those guys now like never before."

"Yeah, and it's not like they can send us a text message," said Henry.

Just then, Jack let out a yelp. He pulled his robe over his head and tossed it to the ground. Jack was now standing in his boxer shorts. "This would be a good time to halt the disrobing process," said Henry.

"Don't mind me," said Samantha, smiling awkwardly.

"Something felt like it was burning a hole in my pocket!" said Jack. He gingerly grasped the robe and attempted to shake the fiery object out onto the ground. The Shaman dropped to the forest's floor and glowed a deep red.

"Has it ever done that before?" asked Samantha.

"No never ..." said Jack. All of a sudden, the Shaman projected an image of a crystal ball above it. All three took a step back.

"Hello?" whispered a voice that didn't belong to anyone present.

"Jack? Are you there?"

"It's coming from the ball!" said Samantha, rushing over and crouching beside it.

"Sa*mantha*?" whispered the voice.

"Yes ... but who ... or *what* are you?" she replied, as Margrin's face appeared in the ball.

"Grinmar!" exclaimed Jack, dropping to his knees. "You have no idea how good it is to see you!"

"I am Margrin, child ... and it's good to see you. We feared you'd perished. There's someone here who wishes to speak with you. You must be brief, warrior," said Margrin, glancing to his left. "The spell is not strong and could collapse at any moment."

Perkin's face appeared in the crystal ball alongside Margrin's.

"I knew they'd never find you, Perkin!" said Jack.

"I have kept faith with you too, my young friend. And that faith has been rewarded," said Perkin, smiling warmly.

"Listen," said Jack, "my friends and I ... we're back in the Dark Matter, *physically*. Doesn't that mean that ... that we can never return home?"

155

Margrin said, "You let us worry about that. And be sure to keep faith in our abilities … as we have kept faith in yours. My word! You have been successful in liberating the Good Shaman!"

"Yes … but, how did you know?"

"Because we're contacting you on it."

"Bit of a no-brainer really," said Henry, patting Jack on his bare shoulder.

"Where are you?" asked Jack, reddening.

"Too far away for you to reach us, I fear," replied Margrin.

"Maybe not," said Jack. "We have a new ally … a Snatcher-Gar."

"A Snatcher-*Gar*? Are you sure the vile creature can be trusted?"

"Oh, yes. He's on the run with us now. We would have been captured or worse if not for Gob."

Margrin turned to his right and consulted with his brother in even quieter whispers. He shrugged his shoulders. "All things considered, we are prepared to trust your instincts in this matter … even taking the creature's name into account. Tell the beast to bring you to Firefly Mount." With that, their faces began to fade, and the crystal ball vanished.

"They must've run out of credit," said Henry.

"ON GUARD!" cried Gob from behind them. They turned to see the ecstatic Snatcher-Gar, waving his new sword about indiscriminately. He was dressed in the full silver and gold body armour of the Snatcher-Guard.

"Careful," said Samantha, "you'll do yourself a mischief."

"I would never have believed it possible … am I not MORE magnificent now?"

"It's very fetching," said Samantha.

"Gob, have you heard of Firefly Mount?" Jack asked.

"Indeed," he replied, sounding surprised.

"Can you get us there?"

"I can … it is no more than twelve leagues south of here. But the mountain contains nothing but pesky fireflies."

"It's where our friends are hiding out."

"How can you know such things? Your resourcefulness is unequalled in all the universe!"

"It was elementary, my dear Gob," said Henry, puffing at an imaginary pipe.

Gob, feeling decidedly regal, spread his silver-plated wings and rose majestically into the air. "All those travelling to Firefly Mount, your carriage awaits," he said, opening his claws to resemble an organic funfair ride.

The First Evil awoke in his four-poster bed. On each of its four posts, the Four Horsemen of The Apocalypse bubbled from the wood like a quartet of wooden nightmares. The First Evil sat up and gazed at his reflection in the multitude of blazing sconces around his bedchamber. If it were possible for him to arrange his angry features into a smile, he would have done so. He reached for a red rope hanging by his bed and gave it an almighty tug. A Dark Monk opened the double-doors that led to his throne room: the monk's silhouette bowed and awaited instructions. The First Evil climbed out of bed. He secured his robe with a silver cord about his waist and said, "Have the spies brought to my throne room immediately. And have a cauldron of hungry eels sent up, a cauldron with room enough to add three small humans." The Dark Monk hesitated before bowing more deeply and leaving the room. The First Evil noticed the monk's hesitation but, the idea that something else had gone wrong, that the Sleepers had failed in their mission, was surely inconceivable.

The Dark Monk sent word to the kitchens before hurrying to the cathedral's south transept in the direction of Salcura's private chamber.

When he entered the chamber, he found the Master Prior kneeling beside his bed in meditation. "The First Evil has requested an interview with me?" asked Salcura.

"No, my Lord, he wishes to interview the three spies," continued the Dark Monk, scanning the chamber as though half expecting to find them there.

"I'm just making my peace, before ..." said Salcura, standing up.

The First Evil was pacing up and down in front of his throne. He was looking forward to extracting the information about the endareolfs from the children and eager to fatten his breakfast with them. The doors to his throne room swung open. The First Evil was disappointed by the sight of two Snatcher-Gars carrying his breakfast cauldron. They placed it down on its usual spot before his throne and made a hasty retreat. Moments later, Salcura entered the room with head bowed low and hands clasped behind him. The First Evil watched him approach the cauldron of starving eels and then, without the slightest hesitation, vault over its edge. Screams and gnawing and thrashing about followed, a goodly amount of the Master Prior ending up on the ceiling of the throne room.

After the eels had finished their Master Prior snack, The First Evil sat on his throne and stroked his chin. "I had no idea Salcura was so ... depressed." Then the possible reason for the Master Prior's actions dawned on him. "Bring me the spies," he muttered at the attendant monks. "Bring me the spies! NOW!"

THIRTY THREE

Reunion

"Firefly Mount be atop those mountains," said Gob. The children gazed ahead to a grey-white mountain range, its peak engulfed by dark clouds.

As the mountain drew nearer, Gob climbed steeply, causing all three passengers to shut their eyes and tighten their grip on his claws. They entered the clouds and opened their eyes to discover their vision reduced to the ends of their noses. Even though Jack and Samantha were wedged against each other, for all they could see, they might as well have been alone. *We must get above these clouds soon*, thought Jack. Moments later, the clouds sank beneath them and they were treated to their first views of the mountain's peak. "There it be," said Gob. "Firefly Mount!" They gazed in awe at the mountain's peak that punctured the clouds, leaving them to linger far below. As they moved closer, the reason for the location's unusual name became clear. It was swathed in tiny sparkles that hung, darted and danced about it like an explosion of snowflakes.

"Do ah ... do the fireflies bite?" said Henry.

"Bite you say? No. They are but a harmless annoyance," replied Gob.

"Ever eaten one?" said Henry, licking his lips.

There was no reply.

Gob flew into the swarming mass of fireflies and, while Samantha reached out a hand as though making first contact with an alien species, the boys were relieved that the luminescent, dragonfly-sized creatures kept their distance.

Gob landed on the mountainside. The terrain was littered with boulders, all engulfed within grass which stood waist height. "Well, we're here," said Jack, doing his best to ignore the tiny lights darting all about him.

"Where do you think your friends be?" said Gob, sniffing at the prevailing wind.

"No idea. I suppose we'll just have to try and contact them."

"Using the Shaman?" said Samantha.

"Let's try something more basic to begin with," said Jack. He drew a deep breath and cupped his mouth with his hands: "PERKIN! PER-KIN!"

They listened for a reply.

None came.

And then they heard a neighing that Jack hoped he recognised …*Vargo*?

"Wasn't that a horse?" asked Samantha.

"Not just any horse, I hope," said Jack.

"Vargo?" said Henry.

"There it is again. It's coming from below us," said Jack. He beat a path through the long grass to the edge of the mountain. "Look, down there … a track that leads down the mountain."

"Where?" said Henry, catching up with them.

"There!" shouted Samantha, pointing below them. The boys followed the tip of her finger to see a riderless Vargo dart around a bend.

"Vargo!" cried Jack, waving his arms. "We're up here!"

Vargo reared up on his hind legs and let out a thundering neigh.

"I'm no horse whisperer," said Henry, "but I think that means he wants us to follow him, Lassie style."

"I agree," replied Jack. "Gob, pick us up and follow that horse!" Gob scooped them up and flew towards the galloping horse. Vargo's legs appeared to contain pistons that hurled him over the descending, undulating terrain.

"Look at him go!" said Samantha.

"Yeeees!" cried Henry.

"Go Vargo!" cried Jack.

After several minutes, the horse came to a crashing halt outside a crack in the side of the mountain. He turned towards them and, having reared up on his hind legs, spun about and disappeared inside.

Gob landed just outside the entrance. The children ran over and poked their heads inside. It was pitch black.

"Where's he gone?" mumbled Samantha.

"I can't see a thing," said Henry.

"Vargo!" shouted Jack.

They listened but heard nothing.

Once their eyes had grown accustomed to the dark, they were able to make out flickering lights some way off. "Gob, you wait here," said Jack. "If you see, hear or smell anything suspicious, come and find us," he continued as he walked through the crack and stumbled towards the illuminations. Henry and Samantha followed him in.

The lights seemed to sense their approach and flock in their direction.

"Fireflies," muttered Samantha, as the mini swarm gathered about them. The airborne insects cast much needed light on a narrow path that led deeper inside the mountain.

159

Not long after, Henry's nose started to twitch. "Can anybody else smell that?"

"Yes, someone's cooking stew," said Samantha.

"Oh, thank God!" exclaimed Henry, clasping his hands together in mock prayer.

"It is one of Grinmar's finest stews! And … what kept you?" said a deep yet friendly voice from a ridge above them. They looked above them to see Perkin smiling down.

"Dishy," muttered Samantha, as Perkin leapt down.

Jack rushed forwards and threw his arms around his mentor. "These are my best friends, Henry and Samantha," he said, turning and beaming at them.

"Come," said Perkin. "You have travelled far, and your bellies must be empty. Fear not, for a craftsman, Grinmar makes a fine cook!"

THIRTY FOUR

The Light of True Vision

Grinmar was looming above a pot with a long ladle in his hand.

"Grinmar!" enthused Jack, waving at the endareolf.

"Well done, boy! Well done on all you've achieved," came his whispered reply, a smile (or sorts) perceivable behind his expression of perpetual surprise.

"Where's your brother?" asked Jack.

"Deeper inside the mountain, working on powerful magic – magic that he hopes will get you all home safely," replied Grinmar, looking at Henry and Samantha. "Hello!" said Samantha, trying not to gawp.

"Welcome child," said Grinmar, tipping his head slightly.

"That smells good … what are you making?" asked Henry.

"It's an ancient endareolf delicacy … I'd tell you the ingredients but, then I'd have to add you to them," he said, before breaking into a whispered chuckle. The sound of his quiet mirth was most welcome and brought a smile to the faces of all present.

Margrin loomed from the darkness carrying a small wooden box. He was surrounded by several dozen hand-picked fireflies. "Good to see you … alive and vital, Jack," said Margrin, squinting through the dulled illuminations.

"It's good to be alive, wizard," said Jack.

Margrin bent double and placed the wooden box in a hollow in the wall. Then he whispered excitedly: "May I see it?"

"See what?" asked Jack, who was more interested in the contents of that mysterious little box.

"The Good Shaman."

"Of course," said Jack, producing the tiny Shaman from his pocket.

Margrin approached him reverently and held out his hand. He held the Shaman up amongst the fireflies … "I never thought I'd hold it," he said, tears welling in his saucer-shaped eyes.

"It is the stuff of legend. Truly it is," said Grinmar, putting down his ladle and moving closer to his brother.

"Indeed it is, brother. Made from the ingredients of The Greater

161

Good."

"What *are* they then?" asked Jack in awe.

"What are what, Jack?" said Margrin, sitting on a boulder and polishing the Good Shaman with his sleeve.

"What are the ingredients of the Greater Good of course? I mean … what is the Good Shaman made of?"

"We are uncertain. Legend tells of a great journey our ancestors undertook to acquire the ingredients."

"A journey? Where?" asked Jack, as intrigued by the possible answer as he had ever been about anything.

"All we know is that the ingredients of the Good Shaman could not be found in The Dark Matter," said Grinmar.

"That makes sense," said Samantha, emerging from the shadows and standing beside Jack.

"The Shamans were made thousands of years ago. So much from that time is shrouded in myth and legend," said Grinmar.

"Our ancestors were set a task to build a gateway … and they fulfilled it," said Margrin.

Perkin approached Jack. He placed a hand on his shoulder and said: "I have given your question much thought. I have consulted many oracles in this world and others …"

"And?" said Jack.

"I believe that Good and Evil are made from the same two things: intention and action. When good intentions are followed by good actions, it resonates positive energy into the universe. This energy travels far into the cosmos and is eventually absorbed by The Greater Good. On the other hand, when acts of evil are perpetrated, in thought or deed, it generates negative energy. This energy is absorbed by The Greater Evil. It seems these two opposing energies, positive and negative, are finely balanced, as if perched on measuring scales. When good is championed, it adds to the positive side of the scales: when bad deeds are committed, it adds to the negative side. As I said, these scales are finely balanced, each side relying on the other."

"Are you saying we *need* evil? What possible use can evil be to us?"

"It ensures that we strive, Jack. And in striving to maintain the balance, to overcome evil, we progress; we grow wiser … and stronger."

"To what end?" asked Samantha.

"That I do not know. However, one thing is clear; The First Evil's goal is to tip the scales in favour of the negative and, should we fail in our quest to close the Earth Gate, he will succeed." Perkin leant against the side of the cave and sighed. "All remaining goodness in mankind will be routed. The just wars fought against tyranny and oppression will have been in vain. We cannot allow that to happen."

Jack sat down on a rock beside Margrin. He looked up at Perkin and said, "Are you saying that the Good Shaman is made from … from good *deeds*?"

"Not exactly. I believe it's made from the positive energy that's generated by good deeds … and by empathy, humility, tolerance and courage in the face of adversity."

Jack glanced at Margrin. "So … presumably, your ancestors had to travel to some kind of font … something that held this positive energy from which they made the Good Shaman."

"Yes, Jack … they somehow discovered a way to reach The Greater Good."

Margrin rested the Shaman in his upturned palms and, using the alteration spell, enlarged it to its full size.

"So?" Perkin asked him. "Have you been successful in your magic?"

"I believe so," replied Margrin, gazing at the now owl-sized Shaman on his lap. "Jack, would you fetch the small box I placed in the wall and bring it here."

"Absolutely."

Jack took the box from the hollow in the tunnel's wall and made his way back over to Margrin, all eyes upon him. "Sit down beside me, Jack," continued Margrin. Jack lowered himself onto the boulder beside the wizard. "Open the box," said Margrin. Jack removed the lid. Inside were two tiny, wedge shaped objects that glistened like diamonds.

Samantha leaned over for a closer look. "They're *beautiful* … are they earrings?" she mumbled.

"No child," said Margrin, removing one from the box and slotting it into the Shaman's right eye socket.

"It's a perfect fit," mumbled Jack. Margrin inserted the other into the Shaman's left eye socket. Moments later, a celestial light emanated from the Shaman's eyes. It filled the cavern and made everyone present feel wholly content with their roles in the universe. Margrin uttered the alteration spell and the Shaman shrank to its original size and the light vanished.

"Wow! What was that?" asked a breathless Henry.

"That was the Light of True Vision. When the Good Shaman is returned to its full size on the Priory's altar, The Light will emanate once more and restore the true natures to everyone at The Priory of Chaos."

"Free them from their trances you mean?" said Jack, his voice full of hope.

"Yes, child."

"Do it again, man … show me the light," said Henry, sounding like a spaced-out hippy.

"Your food is ready," said Grinmar, sternly.

"I don't care about the food, man ... show me the light."

"True vision is a powerful elixir. One that must be earned through study and contemplation."

"If you say so," Henry huffed.

Jack took the now shrunken Shaman with the jewelled eyes from Margrin and put it in his pocket. "And ... what about us? I mean, will The Light enable us to return home? Now we're here physically?" asked Jack. There was a considerable pause, during which the children's hearts thumped like marching drums.

"Well? Answer the boy. Will it enable our young friends to return home?" said Perkin.

Margrin grasped the lapels of his shadowy black coat and said, "It will ensure the Earth Gate transports every child at the Priory, flesh or essence, to the place they're *supposed* to be."

"Not only that," continued his brother, "it will also throw a Halo of True Vision around the Earth ... all the adults within it will be freed from the Priory's Spell of Misdirection."

"That is seriously great news," said Jack ... "but what about the kids under the enchantment on Earth?"

"Yeah," said Henry. "Please tell us the local gang will become pillars of the community."

Margrin shook his head. "I am sorry. There is nothing I could do for those children."

Perkin shrugged. "But their evil deeds will no longer be hidden from the eyes of adults. They will now face the consequences of their actions."

"You know what this means guys?" said Jack, looking at Henry and Samantha, "all those kids will just use the Priory's teachings in different ways ..."

Henry shuddered. "That's right. They're gonna get all sneaky and subversive ... take the darkness underground."

"One step at a time," said Perkin. "If we can destroy the Earth Gate, we'll be plugging a dam of evil that would have swamped humanity ... right now, that is our only goal."

THIRTY FIVE

The best laid plans

They enjoyed a hearty meal, the ingredients of which would forever remain a mystery, and sat about the campfire nursing their bloated bellies.

"We've been working on a plan," said Perkin, placing his bowl on the ground. "A plan that will allow you to evacuate as many pupils as possible before the Earth Gate is closed forever."

"The plan is audacious. It will place considerable strain on my brother's powers," said Grinmar.

"I appreciate your concern, dear brother, but the survival of humanity is of greater importance than the exhaustion of one old wizard."

"What does your plan involve?" asked Jack.

"A distraction," said Perkin. "A distraction of such magnitude that it draws not only the Snatcher-Guard but the Dark Monks and even The First Evil away from the Priory – giving you enough time to evacuate as many pupils as you can."

"And then close the Earth Gate before they return," said Margrin.

Perkin drew his sword with a flourish. "Emerge from the shadows, beast!" he said.

Gob edged into view.

"Are you spying on us, loathsome animal?" said Margrin, thrusting out both hands as though ready to cast a spell.

"A loathsome *animal* you say? *Spying* you say? What madness!" said Gob.

"I honestly don't believe he's a spy," said Jack, moving between Gob and Perkin's blade.

"*Lis*ten to the boy," said Gob.

"He rescued us from The Sleepers, mistakenly perhaps, but The First Evil is gunning for him too."

"Are you sure it was a mistake?" said Perkin.

Jack thought for a moment. "Yes ... he has as much to lose as any of us should the Earth Gate stay open."

Perkin returned his sword to its scabbard. "If Jack believes you mean to do right by us, whatever your motives, then so shall we all. Come

165

forward Snatcher-Gar, and join us."

"I'm glad we've cleared that up," said Samantha. "You were about to tell us the plan?"

Grinmar nodded slowly. "You are all aware of the Reader?" he said. "The mystic who has *seemed* a thorn in your sides?"

"Oh yeah," said Henry.

"That chattering creature has been under our control. Although, she does not know it."

"Since the very beginning," added Margrin, brimming with pride. "We chose her with as much care as we chose you Jack Tracy … and you Perkin Beck."

"You chose the Reader?" said Jack.

"Yes. And now the time has come to turn her chattering portents to our advantage for the last time," said Grinmar.

"How?" asked Samantha.

"By opening up the flood gates … and enabling her to learn just about everything."

"Everything?" said Henry, raising an eyebrow.

"Indeed!" said Grinmar, stretching to his full height of 3 metres. "She must be made aware that you took the Altar Shaman and replaced it with a decoy. She must also be made aware that you were successful in liberating the Good Shaman from the museum."

"And, most importantly of all, it's imperative that she lets The First Evil know that we are all hiding in the forest … and intent on using the Good Shaman to destroy the Earth Gate."

"As regards letting the Reader know everything, I think that about covers it," said Jack.

"*Okay*. And how can letting The First Evil know so much possibly help? It sounds like suicide," said Henry, hugging himself.

"It's not what we tell her that's important … but the information which we withhold," said Grinmar.

"And by this, my brother is referring to our location in the forest. You see, The First Evil's paranoia regarding endareolfs will lead him to believe that, now we possess the Good Shaman, we may also possess the means to close the Gate from beyond the Priory's walls, from our forest hideaway. We cannot of course … but it will ensure that he commits his every resource to hunting us down."

"And in what way is that a good thing?" asked Henry, his grip on himself tightening.

"It is an Earth saying I believe … 'while the cats are away the mice will play.'"

"And we're the mice, I take it?" squeaked Henry.

166

"That's right. The mice that plan to close the Earth Gate ... for good," asserted Margrin.

"Well, I think it's a great plan," said Samantha.

"It is not without great risk to you all," said Perkin.

"We've come this far," said Jack, turning to his two friends. "A proposal!" said Jack. "All those in favour of returning to the Priory and seeing this through to its end, raise your right hand and say, I."

"I!" they shouted (even Gob).

They all turned to look at the Snatcher-Gar. Gob scrunched up his ugly face and said: "I do not understand what drives good beings to do what is right ... but that does not mean I cannot admire your foolish determination to fight until the bitter end!"

"Maybe someday you will understand," said Jack.

"Come children. It is time to send all we know to the Reader," said Margrin, walking off into the mountain with his fireflies buzzing about him.

THIRTY SIX

Hollow texts

They followed Margrin and his organic light source deep inside the mountain. It wasn't long before they came upon the wizard's makeshift workshop. It consisted of a dozen crystal beakers alive with bubbling liquid and several ancient looking texts. On the ground, a large triangle had been marked out in the dust. "Now children," began Margrin, "listen to my instructions carefully … and follow them with conviction," he whispered, stroking his long chin. "I'd like you to sit cross-legged at the triangle's three points. Jack, you sit at the triangle's top."

They did as they were told.

"Now children, close your eyes and stare into the darkness. On the count of three, I want Jack to fill his mind with his memories of taking the Altar Shaman. The triangle is imbued with magic that will assist you in ordering your thoughts. Ready? Do it now, Jack … re*member* …" A three-dimensional image of that night in the cathedral appeared in the centre of the triangle above them. Samantha and Henry, who could not resist opening their eyes, gasped at the three-dimensional image of Jack peering over his shoulder at The Guardsman, before taking the Altar Shaman and lowering it into his bucket.

This is great! thought Henry. *All I need now is a bucket of popcorn.* At which point, a bucket of popcorn appeared beside the Shaman on the altar. Margrin glared at Henry, and the bucket faded from the image. Margrin raised his arms to the ceiling, whispered something in an alien tongue, and the image swooped up through the roof like a swallow taking to the sky. "Good boy, Jack. Now," continued Margrin, swallowing hard, clearly weakened by his efforts, "I want you all to cast your minds back to switching the Shamans at the British Museum." The children complied and, within moments, the space just above them was filled with various images of their derring-do at the British Museum: Gob lifting the Good Shaman from its display case; Jack shrinking it; the Altar Shaman being placed on the hook in its place. These images were also sent to the Reader like a holographic text message. "Finally, cast your minds back just a few

168

hours to your arrival here," said Margrin, sinking to his knees, grimacing. The space filled with recollections of Grinmar stirring the pot, and then of Margrin approaching from deeper within the mountain. These images followed the others. "Our work here is done," said Margrin, breathlessly. "The Reader will receive your memories … and our fates rest with her." The children leapt to their feet and supported Margrin who looked close to collapse.

The starved and emaciated Reader lay on the stone floor of her cell. She was asleep and dreaming about goulash when the 'holographic texts' entered her mind. She awoke suddenly and sat up against the damp stone wall. Her eyes moved rapidly from left to right as though she were reading from a printed page. After a few moments, she dragged herself to the cell door and hammered on it. The attendant Monk put down his well-thumbed copy of The Dark Bible and opened the cell door. "I have important news for The First Evil!" she cried. The monk reached down and pulled her to her feet.

The First Evil had convened a meeting of the ten surviving members of the Monk's Council. The two seats either side of him, where Sinosa and Salcura had once sat, were vacant. "It seems inconceivable … but the spies have escaped our clutches yet again," drawled The First Evil, staring into the middle distance.

"Yes, Sire. But the Sleepers' report indicates that the Earth Shaman is still in place at the museum," said Fostado, an ambitious young monk recently promoted to the council.

"But the question remains, what business had the spies at the location of the Earth Shaman?"

"It is uncertain, my Lord, but we can rest assured the Earth Shaman is still where it's supposed to be."

The doors to the throne room flew open and the Reader was marched up to the table. "Your Highness, the Reader claims to have information of interest," said the monk accompanying her.

"Keen to earn your supper, Reader?" said The First Evil.

"What I'm about to tell you should earn my freedom!" she cried in famished desperation.

"I suggest you spit it out before I consume and spit you out."

Through quivering lips she said, "The two Winged Shamans …"

"Well? What of them?"

"They are not what they appear … they have been *switched*."

Fostado leapt to his feet. "The Reader is troubled, my Lord! A lack of food has twisted her mind."

"No!" the Reader cried, "I have seen it … the boy intruder was out there!" she continued, pointing in the direction of the cathedral behind her. "He was cleaning the Altar Shaman ... he had a bucket and a sponge ... within the bucket was a decoy Shaman. The boy used it as a replacement. He *stole* the true Altar Shaman and smuggled it to Earth!"

"Preposterous!" said Fostado.

"It's true! And there's more," said the Reader.

"More?" said The First Evil, standing up.

"The Earth Shaman ... it is now in The Dark Matter."

"Where in The Dark Matter?" asked The First Evil, his eyes widening.

"In the southern forests; they are intent on using it to destroy the Earth Gate!"

"Who is?"

"The children, My Lord ... the children and ... and the endareolfs!"

The First Evil grabbed the edge of the oak table and hurled it across the throne room. He thundered out into the cathedral with the council and Reader in tow. The First Evil marched out onto the stage in the middle of the morning service. Friar Cirrhosis, who had been preaching about the merits of encouraging binge drinking, fell silent as The First Evil crashed onto the stage before the altar. With thousands of curious eyes upon him, The First Evil picked up the decoy Shaman. "Like me, the true Altar Shaman is indestructible. Its precious metals have been combined with the blood that courses through these veins!" he said, alluding to the black veins standing out from his neck and shoulders. "If the Reader speaks the truth, if this Shaman *is* a decoy, then it will be unable to resist my wrath ..." The First Evil began to squeeze, turning *even redder* in the face. Once he'd unleashed three quarters of his strength, his expression became one of rapturous relief. He looked at the expectant Reader as if to say, *Your head is next and it won't be so resilient.* Then it happened. The Shaman bent and folded like weak tin. The First Evil lunged at the Reader. "Say again, where in the forests are the endareolfs?" he snarled, barely able to contain his rage.

"The southern forests!" she gasped.

"Send The Guard to the southern forests!" barked The First Evil. "Send the Carriers! Send the monks! I want every available being in the southern forests searching for the endareolfs. We must destroy them before they can close the Earth Gate. Maybe it has already been destroyed?" The First Evil crashed to his knees. He raised his fists above his head and pounded the floor of the cathedral – tearing out great blocks of stone and hurling them away. A hole appeared, and The First Evil gazed into the swirling mass of the Earth Gate below. "The Gate ... it still functions ... but for how long? Hunt down the endareolfs and exterminate them! Now! Go!"

The endareolfs had snatched a couple of hours of sleep and were making their way slowly towards the mountain's exit with their young allies. "Do you think the Reader has received the visions we sent?" asked Jack.

"Oh yes, I'm sure of it," replied Grinmar.

"How can you be sure?" asked Samantha.

"I sensed a painful loss a short time ago."

"You mean … the Reader's *dead*?" said Samantha.

"No, child … the replacement Shaman has been discovered and destroyed."

"How do you know that?"

"I felt it. The First Evil alone could have crushed it."

"So what now?" asked Jack, as they emerged from the mountain and squinted into the early morning sun.

"The Reader will have led them to believe we are hiding in the southern forests."

"We're not actually *in* the southern forests though … are we?" asked Henry.

Grinmar shook his head. "Firefly Mount is in the north."

Perkin had spent the night outside keeping watch. He approached the group with Vargo in tow. "Is all going to plan?" he asked the brothers.

They nodded.

"My friends," he continued, gathering the three children together with his outstretched arms, "your finest hour is upon you. Jack, you have fulfilled the full weight of expectation placed upon your shoulders and shown the courage of a true warrior."

Jack felt humbled. "Not just me," he said.

"Indeed not," said Perkin, glancing at Henry and Samantha. "Your friends have proven themselves most worthy."

"You know what you must now do?" said Grinmar, leaning down and squeezing Jack's shoulder.

"Yes. We must take the Good Shaman to the altar in the cathedral."

"That's right, Jack," said Margrin. "And then enlarge it using the alteration spell. You only need recite the first two lines … the last two reflect only my love of poetry. When you do, The Light of True Vision will bring the Priory's students to their senses."

"It will then be at your discretion as to how many make it through before you shrink the Shaman … and destroy the Gate for good," said Grinmar.

"Once I've shrunk it and The Light vanishes, how long will I have to use the Gate myself?" asked Jack.

"Good question, Jack," said Henry.

"Seven seconds after you've uttered the spell, the Earth Gate will close forever." Grinmar gazed down at Jack. "Remember, Jack ... once the Shaman has been shrunk and the Light of True Vision is no more, you will have just seven seconds to use the Gate yourself."

"Seven seconds," muttered Jack.

"Not much room for error ... but we have the utmost faith in you," said Margrin.

"You must continue to trust your intuition, Jack," said Perkin. "Even if it seems all hope is lost, it will guide you to the correct path."

Jack nodded.

"Gob!" shouted Perkin, "It is time!"

Gob took to the air and hovered above the three children.

"Will I ever see you again?" Jack asked them all.

"Who can say what the future holds?" replied Perkin.

"The fight against evil goes on then?" said Jack.

"Oh, yes. And it will continue to make us stronger and wiser ... all of us." Perkin smiled and, with that, he signalled to Gob who swept them off their feet and ascended slowly into the sky. Samantha and Henry waved while Jack simply stared at his friends and tried to capture an image in his mind that he hoped would stay with him forever.

THIRTY SEVEN

The final showdown

As Gob carried the children south in the direction of The Priory of Chaos, an enormous shadow was also moving south over the Priory's moats – a shadow cast by thousands of the Snatcher-Guard setting off in the wrong direction. The front line consisted of all ten thousand members of Snatcher-Guard. These elite troops were fitted with harnesses containing seats – in each seat a Dark Monk was tasked with scanning the forests below for human emotions.

The second line consisted of the regular Snatcher-Gars. These scruffy monsters were honoured to be included in a mission of such importance.

The last to depart the Priory was The First Evil, his carriage carried by a V-formation of the Elite Snatcher-Guard. There was one Snatcher-Gar missing from these proceedings (besides Gob), Phlem was watching the crises unfold from his cell window at the base of the citadel. "Gob, you obnoxious fool! What a fuss you have caused," he said, as he gazed at the departing multitudes through iron bars.

An hour later, Gob spotted the silhouette of the citadel on the moonlit horizon. For the last 20 minutes, he'd been dwelling on the bravery and selflessness he'd shown in recent days. It was certainly beyond anything he had been able to muster before he'd been forced to change allegiance to The Greater Good. *Maybe there's something in this 'doing the right thing' nonsense after all? Doing the right thing by Gob, perhaps. Is that not* always *the right thing?*

"Look! There! Isn't that the Priory's spire?" said Samantha, distracting Gob from his burgeoning conscience.

"It is the Priory's spire. The most wicked school in all creation … and soon to be the emptiest!" cried Gob.

As they moved closer, the thing which struck them most was the stillness of the place. It looked deserted and, with the exception of the students and tutors confined to their classrooms, it was. "Gob!" shouted Jack, as they made their final approach towards the cathedral, "We must head *straight* for the altar … take us through the ceiling."

Gob hovered momentarily before phasing slowly through the

173

cathedral's roof. All three children fell silent as they gazed down inside the empty, cavernous space. No one was present. No children. No monks. No cleaners. No guards? "I've seen this movie," said Henry. "It's too quiet. It's a trap!"

"Grinmar *did* say that The First Evil would commit his every resource to searching the forests for us," said Jack.

"And if there is a crack team of Snatcher-Guardsmen hiding in here, what exactly is the plan?" asked Samantha, her heart racing.

"Plan?" said Jack. "I thought we'd play it by ear as usual."

"As plans go, it's not exactly up there with the best of them, is it?" sighed Samantha.

"Okay, we've snuck a peek and the place is obviously crawling with well-hidden enemy combatants ... so what now?" said Henry.

Jack felt for the Good Shaman in his pocket. He drew a deep breath ... "Take us down Gob ... to the altar."

Moments later, they were standing before the altar. They looked about, half expecting The First Evil to jump out from the shadows. The First Evil, for his multitude of sin, was miles away, carried high above the southern forests and awaiting news of a breakthrough from below. To his chagrin, every report had, as yet, yielded nothing.

In the cathedral, Jack placed the Good Shaman on the altar. "I think we're ready," said Jack. "Brace yourselves, guys, all hell may be about to break loose."

"Don't be greedy, Jack," said Henry. "Save some hell for later."

"Just *do it*, Jack. It's payback time," said Samantha, her blue eyes sparkling in anticipation. Jack's lips parted in readiness to utter the alteration spell. Everyone present was surprised, therefore, by the eruption of venomous shrieks from all sides. They looked up to see the Sleepers descending from three directions. "THE SLEEPERS!" screeched Gob, stepping backwards and toppling down the six stairs that led up to the altar. The children were about to run when the Sleepers grabbed and then hoisted them into the air.

"Shouldn't you be *sleeping* or something!" screamed Samantha, as she kicked at the powerful being with her heels.

Meanwhile, hands grasped Henry's neck and began to squeeze. "Jack, do something!" he gargled.

"Shaman without, Shaman within,
Shrink or grow, for con*cealing*!"

With that, the Good Shaman on the altar enlarged and The Light of True Vision filled the cathedral. The Sleepers released the struggling children, clasped their hands to their faces and fell to the ground, writhing in agony.

Jack ran to the hole The First Evil had punched in the stone floor and gazed down into the Earth Gate. The Light of True Vision had blended with it, creating a giant vanilla swirl effect. "Wow!" said Henry, gazing over Jack's shoulder, holding his bruised throat.

The Light of True Vision took flight and shot through the citadel ... seeking out and illuminating its every darkened corner. It quickly reached the thousands of students at their desks, invigorating and waking them from their evil trances. The Light informed them of everything: their abduction, their location and the need to use the Earth Gate before it was sealed for good. The Dark Tutors watched in disbelief as the children leapt from their chairs and clambered towards the classrooms' exits.

Meanwhile, above the southern forests, a messenger-guardsman flew up towards The First Evil's carriage. The messenger landed on the platform around its edge and tapped frantically on the door. A Dark Monk opened it and beckoned him in. The messenger looked ready to collapse under the weight of information he carried. *Looks promising*, thought The First Evil, as the expectant face drew nearer.

"You have them?" he asked. The messenger, struggling to find the words he'd been rehearing all the way there, simply pointed over The First Evil's shoulder to a window in the rear of the carriage. The First Evil turned his head and saw The Light of True Vision illuminating the horizon to the north. "Back," he muttered. "Back! Back! BACK!"

In the cathedral, Gob picked himself up off the ground. "It's too bright!" he exclaimed, "It's making me feel sick. TURN IT DOWN!"

"Sorry, Gob," said Jack, "There's no dimmer switch and even if there was, do you really want to release the Sleepers?" he continued, pointing at the convulsing monsters.

"I see your point."

Much clanking and banging then ensued as Underlings began appearing from everywhere: out of vents, from under pews, several even emerged from the hole The First Evil had torn in the ground. "The king is on his way with the renegades," said an Underling, dressed in the decayed clothing of a Victorian public school boy.

"What about Ken? Where's Ken?" Jack asked him.

"I'm here, gov," came a familiar and breathless voice from behind.

Jack turned and threw his arms around his friend. "You came back, you really came back!" said Ken.

"And so can you – back home to Earth. The Good Shaman has made it safe for us *all* to return now, Ken."

"I can scarcely believe it ..." replied Ken, his eyes filling with wonder.

"It's true. It's safe for you ALL to use the Earth Gate now!" Jack shouted to the excited throng gathered about him. This remarkable news took hold and spread like wildfire amongst the jostling Underlings – it quickly reached the ears of the approaching king.

"Is it true Master Tracy?" said King Edward.

"Yes, your Majesty. The endareolfs said it's safe for everyone to use the Gate now. They said it will get everyone to 'the place they're supposed to be.'"

"Supposed to be?" muttered the king.

Jack looked into Edward's blue eyes and at once knew his thoughts: the overwhelming majority of the Underlings should have been 'at rest' long ago. The king reached out and squeezed Jack's shoulder. Then he glanced about him and shouted, "Follow me! The time has come to leave this cursed place and seek adventures anew!" Edward smiled at Jack, "Thank you, Master Tracy ... for reuniting us with our loved ones at long last." He bowed and turned and hastened towards one of the many exits that led down to the Earth Gate.

Jack, Henry, Samantha and Ken followed the throng down a tight spiral staircase, the steps worn and sloping like pummelled pillows.

At the bottom they were greeted by a scene as euphoric as it was chaotic. Students were pouring from dozens of doors about the Earth Gate. Without hesitation, they ran, leapt and dived into the mass of swirling colour.

The three stunned liberators and Ken moved to the outer rim of the circular space and watched, gob smacked. "It's like someone's removed the plug and all the water is trying to get down the plughole at once," said Henry.

Jack watched the Underlings leaping into the Gate with wild abandon, and wondered what Margrin had meant by the words he now realised had been chosen with such care. Jack turned to Ken, "The endareolfs said the Gate would get you to 'where you're *supposed* to be.'"

"I know gov, you told me already, ain't it great!"

"Ken, what if you're supposed to be ..."

"Dead?" replied Ken. "I'm going to where I'm supposed to be ... I'd wager that's with my family ... whether in this life or the next ... what could be better?"

"Listen! My address is 22 Barton Road, Wimbledon," said Jack. "If ...no, *when* you get back, come straight over. We'll find your sister together. I promise, we'll find her ...we'll find Shelia ... do you understand?"

176

"22 Barton Road, Wimbledon," he repeated, before continuing: "Don't concern yourself with me. You've already done more for me than you can know. Just do what you need to do and get home safe ... please do that."

Jack nodded as Ken backed slowly away from the group. He waved at his three friends and, without hesitation, turned and sprinted towards the Earth Gate.

Meanwhile, back on Earth, Samantha's father padded downstairs in his dressing gown and slippers. It was early morning and his wife had told him to fetch the Sunday paper from outside on the porch. He opened the front door and shuddered as a gust of wind blew up his dressing gown. Then he yawned, stretched his arms and gazed skyward. "What in the name of ...! Am I *dreaming*?" He could see the Halo of True Vision blazing across the sky, its light constant and true. His gaze dropped to Barton Road. The local gang's vandalism was now visible – *GOOD GOD!* He hurried back inside and made for the phone in the kitchen. Along with stunned adults all over the world, he was contacting the police.

An hour later, the last of the children had finally disappeared through the Gate – leaving just three. Gob landed next to them and they made their way over to the edge of the swirling mass. "Well, that seems to be everyone," said Henry.

"This is it then. It's time for you to use the spell and shut this thing forever," said Samantha.

Henry nodded and said, "Then we'll have seven seconds to take our final bows and exit stage down."

Jack shook his head. "I'm not using the spell until you guys are safely through the Gate ... I mean, what if Margrin got his calculations wrong? What if the Gate closes immediately?"

"We're not going anywhere without you Jack," said Samantha, folding her arms.

"Gob," said Jack, motioning towards his two friends. Gob took to the air and picked them up.

"Hey!" cried Samantha, as Gob hovered over the Earth Gate.

"I'll see you in the morning. I ... I love you guys," said Jack beaming.

"Don't take ANY chances, use the spell and jump straight in!" Samantha shouted.

"Straight in!" added Henry.

Gob descended through the Gate, leaving Jack all alone. "We've done it, Perkin. We've really done it!" he muttered, as he gazed at his emptied surroundings. "You've done it all right!" said a screeching voice from behind him. It was Phlem, driven half mad by The Light of True Vision.

He grabbed Jack in his claws and lifted him into the air.

"And now I'm going to do *you*! The First Evil will be so pleased with me!"

"I am pleased!" boomed The First Evil as he came thundering into the departure area. The shock of seeing The First Evil momentarily stunned Phlem and he loosened his grip. Jack, struggling for his life, slipped from the Snatcher-Gar's claws and fell a couple of metres to the ground. Infused with fear and adrenalin, he scampered around the side of the Gate muttering the spell that would shut it for good: "Shaman without, Shaman within, shrink or grow ..." In a flash, The First Evil's thigh muscles, the width of tree trunks and as powerful as a hundred charging bulls, propelled him over the Earth Gate. He landed beside Jack and flung him from the Gate's edge. If not for his suspicion that Jack's death might trigger the Gate's destruction, he would have killed him instantly.

"Silence!" bellowed The First Evil. "You must not complete the spell ... you must spare the Gate!"

Jack had tumbled some ten metres, dazed, confused, his world collapsing. "Open your eyes, *boy*. The universe needs the Gate. Without it, the balance between good and evil will be lost ... and then we shall ALL perish!" Jack stumbled up onto his shaky legs. He faced the red giant and felt like an insect about to be trampled by a stampeding bull. "What do you want, *boy*?" The First Evil, asked. "I can grant riches and power beyond imagination."

"I – I don't want anything you have to offer me," said Jack, taken aback by the courage of his own words.

"We ALL have our price. You only need tell me yours and I shall grant it."

"Price? I don't have a price. My *want* is to fight ... to fight for The Greater Good. You talk of price," he said, his voice fearful yet determined, "but how can anyone put a price on the sacrifice of so many, who, like me, shared the same wish and died for it?" Tears filled Jack's eyes as the realisation of what he must now do crystallised in his mind – he must follow the example of the brave warriors who came before him – and sacrifice himself for The Greater Good. His lips parted in readiness to finish the spell, thus closing the Gate and trapping himself in The Dark Matter, forever. The First Evil looked into Jack's eyes. He knew what the boy was about to do. "Boy!" he cried. "Don't do it. Yours will be a thousand years of pain – a millennium of unending torment!"

"Better me than ... everyone," replied Jack, tears rolling down his deathly pale cheeks. Perkin's words flashed across his mind; *trust your intuition, Jack.* His intuition told him what he must do – the next moment, he heard himself uttering the final words of the spell: "... for con*cealing*."

The destruction of the Earth Gate was set in motion – in seven seconds it would be sealed forever. The First Evil roared and charged at Jack, his great horns levelled at him, his eyes red and raging. Jack instinctively threw himself to one side. The horns snagged on his robe and The First Evil tossed him into the air like a rag doll. Jack lunged through the air in the direction of the closing Earth Gate. Down he crashed ... upon solid rock. The Earth Gate was gone. Jack lay in the centre of the area and grasped at his vanished escape route. He heard The First Evil's cloven hooves thundering towards him. Images of his mother sobbing over his empty grave dug at his very soul. Standing either side of her, Henry and Samantha.

"Look after her, guys," Jack muttered, tears pooling on the stone beneath him. Just then, a Snatcher-Gar phased through the roof above ... it barrelled down towards Jack, clasped him in its great claws, and plunged through the ground ...

The First Evil came to a halt on the now empty spot where Jack had come to rest. He raised his fists towards the heavens and bellowed, "This is not over! I will find you, Jack Tracy. There is no place in the universe you can hide from me! I. Am. EVERYWHERE!"

Gob sped down, down, down. Jack was utterly disorientated, the G-forces now bearing down on him immense. He turned and looked up for a moment ... and then he passed out.

Gob could see the remnants of the Earth Gate now. It fizzed below him like a firework in its dying moments – sparks, crackles, flares and bangs. The Gate was almost within reach of his claws and the unconscious boy within them ... Gob made one last, desperate lunge ...

THIRTY EIGHT

The return to Rotherhithe

Jack opened his eyes and gazed dreamily at his bedroom ceiling. He took a deep breath and didn't blink for fear this welcome sight would be replaced by The First Evil's face.

Sit up, Jack. Sit up! He grasped his duvet and heaved himself upright. "Did ... did we do it?" he muttered. *Yes ... I think so. I closed the Earth Gate ... but ... how did I get back?*

His final terrifying minutes in The Dark Matter flooded his mind, causing a chill, a wince and a shudder. *I was lying on the floor of the Earth Gate ... I had a vision of my mother standing over my grave ... The First Evil was charging towards me ... and then ...?* His mind was a blank after that and, for one fraught moment, he thought the whole thing may have been an enormous nightmare. Then he spotted something glinting at the foot of his bed ... *a sword.* Jack leaned forward, took hold of its hilt and pulled it towards himself. He was confused, his head cluttered and aching. Then he remembered ... *Isn't this the sword that ... that I took from that dead Snatcher-Gar? The sword I gave to Gob.* "Gob!" The moment of clarity before he'd passed out came back to him: Gob's face, full of determination and focused on something beneath them. *The Earth Gate? It was Gob. He came back for me. Gob saved my life! ... And left me the sword he cherished ...*

Jack's mobile phone, which had remained on his bedside table throughout, suddenly indicated he'd received a text message. The message read: "Respond!" It was from Henry. Jack quickly typed his reply, "All's well!" and pressed 'send.'

He climbed out of bed and looked over at Samantha's window. At first, he could see nothing but the back of her curtains. Then they twitched and Samantha's smiling face appeared. They gave each other the thumbs up, and then Samantha pointed to Jack's side of the street. Jack craned his head and saw a group of adults, some standing with arms folded, others gesticulating wildly as they surveyed the damage done to their homes and cars. "The Halo of True Vision ... it must have worked ... they can *see* now ... they can see everything!"

Jack collapsed onto his bed and punched at the air in jubilation. Then he thought, *there's still one person missing – Ken!*

In 1941, a Snatcher-Gar had abducted Ken from Kings Cross station, some seven miles from Barton Road. A longish journey, it would take him a couple of hours to reach Wimbledon on foot.

Jack watched the minutes pass.

At 8am, he pulled back the curtains and looked down the street for any sign of the boy to whom he owed so much – nothing but irate neighbours and a stressed-out policeman busy taking their statements.

At 9.00am, Jack was still propped up against his window sill, the sword resting against the wall beside him. He had barely budged. At last, he saw a figure approaching. He craned his head to get a better view and felt a surge of disappointment as an old man, with thinning grey hair and a stoop, doddered up Barton Road. He was wearing a dingy grey mac that looked as though it had been liberated from a skip.

When the man reached Jack's house, he paused and appeared to be trying to read the number on his front door. He leaned over the garden gate and squinted at it. *He must be lost*, thought Jack. Then the man looked straight up at him, his lips parted, and he mouthed, "Jack."

Jack looked into the man's tired grey eyes. *Do I know you? You look familiar ...* "Ken?" murmured Jack. *Ken!*

With heart in mouth, Jack made his way downstairs as quickly and as quietly as his legs would carry him. He skirted across to the front door, removed the chain and turned the key that was always in the lock. The door opened. The old man stretched out his arms as if greeting a long lost relative.

"It's me Jack, it's Ken," he said.

Jack stepped forward and, without uttering a word, threw his arms around the frail figure. "I'm so sorry," he said ... "I had no idea ..."

"It's fine, gov," came a familiar yet gruffer voice. "This *is* who I'm supposed to be ..."

Samantha came rushing across the street. She recognised the old man immediately. "Ken?"

"Yes, it's me," he replied, hugging her.

"What's this? A reunion? Why no invite?" said Henry, turning into Jack's front path. "And, who invited the old ... *Ken*? ...You were supposed to come straight over, not wait a hundred years."

"Cheeky whipper-snapper! I'm ninety one."

Shortly thereafter, they all set off for the bus that would take them to Rotherhithe and the home Ken had not seen since 1941. The bus rolled through neighbourhoods filled with adults coming to terms with the destruction. Their children huddled in groups close by, hungrily observing the grown-ups who could see everything now. The brutal gangs that had ruled the streets for months were nowhere to be seen. As Jack had suspected, they were laying low, regrouping, adapting to the new environment in which they found themselves. For several minutes, the four friends travelled together in silence.

Jack broke the silence. He told his friends about his showdown with The First Evil. During this re-telling of events, Henry's ruddy cheeks turned decidedly pale and Samantha remained close to tears. They realised they'd come to within a whisker of losing him. "Who'd have thought it?" said Samantha. "Gob turned out to be a real hero. He saved us too, Jack … delivered us to our beds."

"That's right," said Henry. "Otherwise, we'd have re-materialised half a kilometre up over the English Channel."

"It just goes to show. There's hope for everyone," said Jack.

"Where do you think Gob is now?"

"The rainforest, presumably," said Samantha.

"Befriending the rat population," said Henry. "So, what's it like getting on for a hundred?" he continued, raising an eyebrow at Ken.

"Oh, it's not *so* different from being eleven. Only, the air feels like … thick treacle, making it a right struggle to get about. My back hurts … my nose won't stop runnin'. Apart from that … this is it!" said Ken, as the bus pulled up at a stop on Jamaica Road. "The area's changed a lot all right. Hitler's bombs saw to that. But I'd recognise that old church and the turning beside it any day. It's my home!" Ken stood up and hastened as quickly as his weary legs would carry him to the exit of the bus.

They walked with him past the old church and down a short path that led to a row of terraced Victorian houses.

"That's it. That was my house," said Ken, pointing to a well-kept property with an apple tree in full blossom in the front garden.

"Look," said Jack. "There's someone in the kitchen."

"It looks like an old lady … making her breakfast," muttered Samantha.

Ken peered through the window … and held fast to the garden fence. The others quickly propped him up. "It's *her* … it's Sheila!" he gasped.

"Your sister?" asked Jack.

Ken turned to Jack and gripped his arms. "Thank you!" he said, tears filling his eyes. "I never imagined … not in a million years that I'd ever …"

"There's no need to thank me," said Jack. "You've done far more for me … for *all* of us." Ken nodded and hugged his friends one last time. Then he walked slowly up the garden path. The children backed away and watched from across the street. Ken stood at the door, his finger poised on the bell. He turned and looked at them. "Go on!" they all mouthed. Ken pressed the bell.

The door opened. At first, the old woman looked confused. Ken must have said something, for the next moment she was wiping tears from her eyes and hugging Ken for all she was worth. The pensioners stepped inside. Ken looked back at his departing friends one last time ... and then closed the door.

"What do you think he's going to tell her?" said Henry. "How's he going to explain where he's been for the last eighty years?"

"I expect he'll just tell her the truth," said Jack, as a rumble of thunder rolled in the distance. "... Did ... did anyone else hear that," he asked.

The End

To be continued in '*Jack Tracy and the Quest for the Greater Good*' Thank you for reading!

If you enjoyed this book you might also enjoy the following books by the same author:

The Scratchling Trinity

The Lost Diary of Snow White Trilogy

The Fabled Journal of Beauty

Diary of a Wizard Kid 1 & 2

I Am Pan: The Fabled Journal of Peter Pan

The opening pages of The Scratchling Trinity follow here ...

One
Max Hastings

London, England, 2016

Max Hastings was leaning low over the handlebars of his bike, and pedalling like he'd flipped out. The distance from his school to his home was two and a half kilometres, and Max *had* to smash his personal best time. The reason was written on a scroll of parchment, held closed by a black ribbon and jutting from his blazer pocket like a piston powering him towards a new school-to-home record. He sped up his drive, leapt off his bicycle and sprinted, arms flailing, towards the front door. Once through it, he darted into the living room, unclipped the strap on his bicycle helmet, and cast the helmet onto the couch. Max was twelve years old, of average build if a little on the chunky side, with a shock of white-blond hair that grew every which way except the way Max would have liked. Max drew the scroll from his pocket, gunslinger style, straightened his back, and announced his extraordinary news to his parents: 'I've finally *won* something!'

Mr Hastings looked at Max over the top of his newspaper. 'There must be some mistake,' he said.

'That's what I thought when Miss Hale announced the name of the re-cip-ient.'

Mrs Hastings, who was holding Max's one-year-old sister Maxine, put the baby down in her walker. 'Congratulations, Max! So what have you won?'

Max gazed at the rolled-up parchment in his hand. 'It's a grand prize, Mum. They picked *my name* out of a hat during the last assembly of term.'

'You've broken your duck, then?' said his astonished father. 'If memory serves me correctly, you've never won anything in your life. Not even when you went through that annoying competitions phase.'

'I know, Dad. I was there.'

'So *what* have you won, exactly?' asked Mrs Hastings.

'No idea.'

'Well, then, I suggest you untie that ribbon and find out.'

Max glanced from the parchment to his mother and back again. Mrs Hastings placed her hands on her hips. 'Whatever is the matter with you?'

'It's just so …'

'So what?' said his father.

'Official-looking.'

'Which must bode well for the prize,' said Mr Hastings, putting down his newspaper. 'Give it here, son. I'll open it.'

Max shook his head. 'I'll do it.' He untied the ribbon and unfurled the parchment. His lips moved slowly as he read it, and his brow furrowed.

'Well?' pressed his mother.

His father leaned forwards in his armchair. 'What are you the recipient *of*?'

'Of a life-time membership ...' murmured Max.

'A life-time membership of *what*?' said his mother testily.

Max read the words slowly. 'The Ancient Order of Wall Scratchings.'

'Of *what*?' said Mr Hastings.

'Of *wall* scratchings,' repeated his mother helpfully.

'But what does that even mean?' mumbled Max, his eyes glued to the parchment for some clue.

'Oh, for pity's sake, give it to me,' said his mother, sliding it from his hand.

Mrs Hastings scanned the parchment. 'Oh, my goodness. Max has been invited to a private viewing of their wall scratchings tomorrow, at Mansion House!'

Mr Hastings cleared his throat. 'What? The place where the Lord Mayor of London lives?'

'Yes!'

'There must be some mistake,' asserted Mr Hastings.

Mrs Hastings shook her head. 'No mistake. The Ancient Order of Wall Scratchings, Mansion House, City of London, London.'

Max sighed. 'Trust me to win a grand *booby* prize. Tomorrow's *Saturday,* not to mention the first day of the Christmas holidays. I'm not going.'

'Not going?' echoed Mrs Hastings.

'Why would I? Since when was I interested in *wall scratchings*? I don't even know what they are!'

'They're scratchings on walls, presumably,' said Mr Hastings, happy to apply his keen insight to the problem at hand.

'Well, whatever they are,' said Mrs Hastings, glancing at the parchment in her hand, 'it says here that they have the world's largest collection of them.'

'Not helping, Mum,' said Max. He went to the dining table and opened his laptop, muttering absently to himself as he typed *the ancient order of wall scratchings* into the search engine. He sat back in his seat and breathed a sigh of relief. 'Just as I thought. There's no such place. It doesn't even exist! ... What are you doing?' Max asked his mother.

'There's a phone number on here. I'm calling them.'

'But—' said Max.

'But nothing. I intend to get to the bottom of these ... these *scratchings*.' She tapped her foot impatiently as the phone rang at the other end of the line.

A woman with a cut-glass English accent answered. 'Thank you for calling the Ancient Order of Wall Scratchings. How may I help you?'

'My name is Mrs Hastings, and my son Max has just won a free membership to your organisation.'

'Hearty congratulations!' said the woman.

'Be that as it may, there's no mention of you on the internet. No mention whatsoever.'

The woman drew a deep breath. 'Ours is an ancient organisation, Mrs Hastings. As such we frown upon all modern conventions.'

'Alright. But your address appears to be the very same as the Lord Mayor of London's.'

'That's right.'

'And the Lord Mayor?'

'What about him?'

'He's happy to share his residence with your organisation?'

'The Ancient Order of Wall Scratchings has been located at this spot for over a thousand years, Mrs Hastings. Since the year 1065, to be exact. The first Lord Mayor didn't move in until some seven hundred years later, in 1752.'

'*And?*'

'And since then we've had no complaints from any Lord Mayor in office.'

A man's voice came on the line. 'Max is going to benefit greatly from his membership, Mrs Hastings,' he asserted.

'*Max is going to benefit greatly from his membership,*' repeated Mrs Hastings, as though in a trance.

'And he'll meet a great many important people.'

'*And he'll meet a great many important people,*' echoed Mrs Hastings.

'People,' the voice went on, 'who will be able to help him in his chosen career.'

'He wants to test video games for a living,' murmured Mrs Hastings.

'*Help him in his chosen career,*' said the man, raising his voice.

'*Help him in his chosen career,*' repeated Mrs Hastings obediently.

'Tell Max he's welcome to bring a friend tomorrow. Goodbye.'

'Goodbye!' said Mrs Hastings, putting down the phone. She turned to Max. 'You're welcome to take a friend tomorrow,' she said, grinning terrifically from ear to ear.

Max scratched absently at his left cheekbone, just below his eye, where there was a birthmark that looked as though someone had signed their initials in black ink. 'O-kay. Are you alright, Mum?'

'Never better,' she replied. Mrs Hastings's smile then did the seemingly impossible and grew wider still. Max had never realised his mother had so many teeth.

Two
Eric Kettle

Yorkshire, England, December 1st, 1840

Inside a carriage drawn by two horses, a frail boy sat shivering beside a giant of a man. The man was expressionless and granite-faced, and indeed any onlooker might have thought him cut from granite. The only clue to his being flesh-and-blood was the smile that curled his lips whenever the carriage hit a pothole and the boy yelped. The man took up most of a bench designed for three adults, squashing his young companion against the carriage door like an item of worthless baggage. The boy's name was Eric Kettle, and Eric looked so fragile that he might break in two every time the carriage lurched over a bump in the road – of which there were a great many, and many more potholes besides. Despite these hardships, Eric's saucer-like brown eyes gazed with extraordinary hope from a face gaunt with hunger.

It was gone midnight when the carriage came to a halt at its destination: the St Bart's School for Boys. The school was a crumbling mansion that rose from the Yorkshire countryside like a vampire's abandoned lair. The carriage door was opened by the driver, who was hidden by an entire closet's worth of coats, scarves and gloves. The brute heaved himself out of his seat. 'Fall in behind, sir,' he grumbled at his young ward. Eric followed as quickly as his shivering legs would allow. He hugged himself for warmth, and stumbled towards the promise of heat beyond the door that now opened for them. Once through the door, Eric wondered if it hadn't actually been warmer outside.

They'd been admitted by a pale and hungry-looking boy swaddled in a threadbare coat several sizes too large. He was carrying a paraffin lamp, and, without uttering a single word, he illuminated their path across a cavernous entrance hall and up a sweeping staircase. Two flights up, he lit the way down a long corridor before finally stopping outside a door, on which a gold plaque read: *Headmaster. Augustus Mann.* Augustus took a key from his pocket and unlocked the door. He turned to the boy carrying the lamp, now hastily lighting a candle by its flame, and snatched the lamp from his grasp. The boy scurried off on bow legs, and Eric watched the candle light until it disappeared from sight at the end of a corridor. 'Fall in, sir!' came the gruff voice of Augustus Mann, from inside the study.

The headmaster placed the lamp on a desk piled high with books, and pointed to a spot on the wooden floor before the desk marked with an X in chalk. 'Stand there, arms at your sides, chin held high. That's it. And stop your shivering.'

'I'll try, sir, but it's just so ...'

'Say the word *cold,* and as God is my witness, I'll thrash you where you stand. Perhaps you think that I should light a fire for you? Waste good wood? Is that what you think?'

'No, sir.'

'Speak up when I address you!'

'No, sir!'

'No what?'

'No, I don't think you should waste good wood on me, sir.'

'Spoilt! That's what you've been. Spoilt to the core.'

Eric shook his head. 'They work us very hard at the orphanage, sir.'

The headmaster sat down and opened a folder on his desk. 'It says here that your father went off to seek his fortune the day after you were born. Wherever he went, he must have liked it there.'

Eric smiled. 'Do you think so? Why do you say so, sir?'

'Liked it more than he liked *you,* anyway.' Eric's smile vanished as the headmaster grunted and went on, 'I see your mother went looking for him soon after, and whether or not she found him, nobody knows. Never seen nor heard from again. But whatever she *did* find, she must have preferred it to you.' The headmaster observed Eric through narrowed eyes. 'What is it about you that so vexes others, *boy*?'

Eric's gaze dropped to the ground. 'I'm sure I don't know, sir.'

'After so many years in an orphanage, I dare say you thought your ship had come in, with your name chosen from a hat to receive a scholarship to attend a fine Yorkshire school of good repute. Thought you'd get yourself a proper education, eh? Those abominable do-gooders, passing their laws that say the likes of *me* must look with charitable eyes upon the likes of *you*. The paltry compensation I will receive for your keep will barely cover my costs.'

'I'm very sorry, sir.'

'You will be. The fact is, you are worth more to me *dead* than you are alive – a fact that doesn't bode at all well for you,' said the headmaster, rising from his chair and turning to face a collection of canes hanging on the wall. He stroked his grey moustache thoughtfully, smiled, and then reached for one.

'Please,' implored Eric. 'I don't know why my parents left me. I did nothing wrong. I was just a baby, and that's the God's truth, sir.'

The headmaster turned and swiped the cane back and forth to gauge its suitability. 'I would strongly advise you not to take the Lord's name in vain. Not in this establishment, *sir*, or God help me …'

As Augustus Mann made his way around his desk towards him, Eric closed his eyes and willed himself back at the orphanage. It didn't work, although the heavy blow that struck his face might almost have launched him back there. Eric's legs gave way beneath him, and he collapsed to the ground, groaning and clutching a cheek that felt savaged by a thousand bee stings. Augustus Mann loomed over him, cane in hand. 'Down at the first lash? Pathetic! That is what you are, pathetic. Is it any wonder your parents left you?' The headmaster yawned, ambled back around his desk, placed the cane back on its hook and walked towards the door. 'You can spend the night there on the floor, like the dog you undoubtedly are. Although I can assure you that your life expectancy is considerably shorter than a dog's. A truth I intend to take *considerable* comfort from,' he yawned. Augustus Mann stepped through the door, closing it and locking it behind him.

Eric dragged himself into a corner, where he huddled miserably for warmth, trying to remember a legend he'd heard some years before at the orphanage: *If a child of kind heart and noble mind is ever in mortal danger, all he needs do is scratch a message of help into a stone wall, and help will find him.* Eric fumbled down his side for one of the safety pins that kept his clothes from falling apart, and with it he scratched the following words in tiny letters into the wall: *If ever a boy was in mortal danger, it's me. Please, if anyone's there, help me!*

Thank you for reading! If you enjoyed this sample, The Scratchling Trinity is available from Amazon.

71725804R00113

Made in the USA
Middletown, DE
28 April 2018